Dear Reader,

Some of the greatest love stories are about people who overcome seemingly insurmountable odds in order to be together. In fiction, as in real life, tragedy and ecstasy are often flip sides of the same coin. In *Lone Wolf's Lady*, Luke and Deanna were young, star-crossed lovers, with all the odds against them. As a couple of kids, with the deck stacked against them, they allowed circumstances and other people to tear them apart. Later as adults, each with a tremendous amount of emotional baggage, they're given a second chance. But in order to find true love again, Deanna must gain the strength to stand by Luke no matter what, a quality she lacked as a teenage girl; and Luke must learn one of life's most difficult lessons—how to forgive.

If you like your heroes macho tough and lone-wolf brooding, then you'll love Luke McClendon. I believe you'll enjoy seeing two wounded souls find redemption—and a passionate, enduring love, so long denied them.

All the best,

Beverly Barton

GREATEST TEXAS LOVE STORIES OF ALL TIME

★ GREATEST TEXAS LOVE STORIES
OF ALL TIME

LONE WOLF'S LADY
Beverly Barton

He's a Cowboy!

Silhouette Books

Published by Silhouette Books
America's Publisher of Contemporary Romance

SILHOUETTE BOOKS

ISBN 0-373-65222-4

LONE WOLF'S LADY

Visit Silhouette at www.eHarlequin.com

Printed in U.S.A.

BEVERLY BARTON

has been in love with romance since her grandfather gave her an illustrated book of *Beauty and the Beast*. An avid reader since childhood, Beverly wrote her first book at the age of nine. After marriage to her own "hero" and the births of her daughter and son, Beverly chose to be a full-time homemaker, aka wife, mother, friend and volunteer. The author of over thirty-five books, Beverly is a member of Romance Writers of America and helped found the Heart of Dixie chapter in Alabama. She has won numerous awards and has made the Waldenbooks and *USA TODAY* bestseller lists.

To Barbara Harrison, with whom I spent endless hours on the telephone during the conception stage of this book. Thanks, my friend, for all your valuable input.

And to Molly Bull, whose knowledge of Texas, the Hill Country and ranching helped me immeasurably in the writing of this book. You were a godsend for me. Thanks a million.

Prologue

"The state calls Deanna Atchley to the stand," the district attorney said.

Every muscle in Luke McClendon's body tightened. A quiet murmur spread throughout the courtroom as the witness rose from her seat. Luke turned his head a fraction, just enough to catch a glimpse of Deanna as she walked past him. God, she looked like she'd been drugged. Her big sapphire-blue eyes were dazed and lifeless, and she moved as if hundred-pound weights were attached to her ankles.

Woody Bowers, the high-priced, good-old-boy lawyer from Austin, whom Luke's father had hired to defend him, had told him that Deanna would be the prosecution's star witness. He hadn't wanted to believe she'd do it, but here she was swearing an oath to tell the truth, in a soft, slurred voice that didn't even sound like the girl who had sworn she'd love him forever and "then some."

The only way she could help the state's case was if she lied. And even now, after months of having to face the cold hard facts—Deanna had neither cleared him of the crime nor made any effort to see him since the night of her father's death—Luke held on to the hope that Deanna could never lie about what had happened.

Luke stared intently at her while she answered the district attorney's routine questions about her relationship to the deceased and her whereabouts on the night of his murder.

"I know this is very difficult for you, Miss Atchley," District Attorney Lamar said sympathetically. "But we need to know what happened the night of April twenty-eighth. The night your father, Rayburn Atchley, was brutally stabbed to death with a pitchfork."

Phyllis Atchley, Deanna's mother, moaned loudly. All heads turned to glance at the grieving widow. A rumble of mixed voices reverberated in the room, and the whispered words "hot-headed bastard" and "good-for-nothing breed" spread like wildfire from one bigoted tongue to another. Internally Luke cringed, but outwardly he showed no sign of having heard the ugly epithets. He'd heard them all his life, before his arrival in Stone Creek when he was fifteen, before his father had legally recognized him, and for the five years since he'd become a part of the McClendon clan. No one outside his family had accepted him—no one but Deanna.

"Miss Atchley, were you with Luke McClendon the night of April twenty-eighth?" the district attorney asked.

"Yes." Deanna choked on her reply, then cleared her throat. "Yes, I was with Luke."

"Your father had forbidden you to ever see Luke McClendon again, had he not?"

"Yes." Deanna sat stiffly in the chair, her spine and shoulders straight, her entire body rigid.

"In fact, only eight days before his death, your father had horsewhipped Luke McClendon and warned him to stay away from you, but Luke wouldn't leave you alone, would he?"

Luke glared at Deanna, his heart stopping for a split second as he waited for her to look at him. But she looked in the opposite direction, toward her mother.

"It wasn't…I mean, Luke and I…" Deanna rubbed her hands together repeatedly.

"You didn't invite Luke McClendon to the Circle A that night, did you? He came uninvited, with revenge on his mind, with every intention of confronting your father and taking you away."

"Objection," Woody Bowers said in his deep Texas baritone. "The district attorney is leading the witness, your honor."

"Sustained," the judge said. "Mr. Lamar, ask your question, and save the rest for your summation."

"Yes, your honor." Lamar sauntered leisurely toward the witness stand, stopping only inches away from Deanna. "You didn't invite Luke McClendon to the Circle A the night of April twenty-eighth, did you?"

"No, I—I didn't invite him." Entwining her fingers, Deanna laid her hands in her lap.

"Where were you when Mr. McClendon arrived?"

"I was at the stables. I'd been out for a ride and had just returned." Clutching the fabric of her linen skirt just above her right knee, Deanna nervously twisted the material.

"Tell us, in your own words, Miss Atchley, what happened when Luke found you at the stables."

"I told him he shouldn't be there, that if Daddy caught us, he'd…" Spreading her hands out over her knees, she leaned her head down and stared at her skirt. "Luke asked me to run away with him. But I couldn't." She snapped her head up and looked pleadingly at Lamar. "I was afraid—"

"While you were trying to explain to Luke Mc-Clendon that you wouldn't run away with him, your father found the two of you together, didn't he?"

"Yes."

"What happened then?"

"Daddy told Luke…he said he'd warned him that if he ever came near me again, he'd kill him." Deanna lifted her trembling hands from her knees and held them, palms open, in a pleading gesture, toward the district attorney. "Daddy was so angry. And I—I was scared. Daddy had his whip—the whip he had used… He came toward Luke. I screamed for Luke to run. But he didn't."

"What *did* Luke McClendon do?" Lamar asked.

"He grabbed a pitchfork that was leaning against the stable wall and he…he—" Deanna's trembling voice lowered to a whisper. "Luke told Daddy that if he tried to use that whip on him again he would—" Tears trickled down Deanna's pale face. Her chest rose and fell with her labored breaths.

"Miss Atchley, please go on. Tell us what Luke said to your father."

"Luke said he would—would kill him."

A powerful uproar erupted in the courtroom. Loud voices demanding justice. Phyllis Atchley's hysterical scream. Baxter McClendon's booming voice declaring his son innocent.

Drumming his gavel repeatedly, the judge called for order.

Keeping his gaze riveted to Deanna, Luke ignored the unruly clamor around him.

Raising his voice to be heard over the slowly fading rumble of voices, the D.A. said, "And that's exactly what happened, wasn't it, Miss Atchley? Luke McClendon stabbed your father with the pitchfork."

Deanna's shoulders trembled; her head shook involuntarily. She stared at the district attorney with huge, sad eyes. "I—I don't know. I can't remember what happened, after...after Luke pointed the pitchfork at Daddy."

"I understand, Miss Atchley. Dr. Penson has testified that you're suffering from a form of temporary amnesia due to the trauma of seeing your father brutally murdered. But what you do remember is of great importance to us." Lamar turned dramatically toward the jurors and pointed his long, lean index finger at Luke. "The last thing you remember is Luke McClendon, with a pitchfork in his hands, moving toward your father and threatening to kill him, isn't that right?"

Deanna's teeth chattered. Her body quivered. She gulped in tiny, shivering breaths. "Luke didn't..." She glanced at her mother. "Yes, yes, yes! The last thing I saw was Luke holding the pitchfork." Deanna's loud moaning sobs echoed throughout the courtroom. She looked at Luke then, her lips parting as a final cry rose from deep within her. "Luke..."

Deanna Atchley slid out of the chair and onto the floor in a dead faint.

Luke McClendon sat ramrod straight, his teeth clenched, his big hands balled into tight fists. He didn't move while others hovered around Deanna. Luke sat stone-faced and silent as D.A. Lamar lifted Deanna in his arms and carried her from the room.

Baxter McClendon rose from his seat directly behind his son and placed a meaty hand on Woody Bowers's shoulder. "The girl's testimony hurt Luke's case, didn't it?"

"She was the only witness to the crime," Woody said. "And her testimony, along with her mother's and the Circle A foreman's doesn't leave much room for doubt. Things don't look good, Baxter. The best we can hope for is to bargain for a lesser charge."

"Manslaughter?" Baxter asked.

"With luck, he could be out of prison in five years."

Luke heard the conversation and knew he didn't have a snowball's chance in hell of beating this rap. It didn't matter that he was innocent, that he'd tossed the pitchfork into the ground at Rayburn Atchley's feet and then walked away. He had hoped Deanna would leave with him that night, but she'd refused. He didn't know what had happened after he left, didn't know who had killed Deanna's father. But whoever the real murderer was, he or she was going to get off scot-free.

The people of Stone Creek had their killer—Baxter McClendon's quarter-breed bastard son. The boy who'd been in and out of trouble with the law since he was twelve. The man who had dared to love a girl whose feet he wasn't fit to kiss. He had reached for the stars, had hoped for the impossible—that he was worthy of being loved. He should have known better.

Deanna Atchley had shown him what he already knew. She had simply reinforced a lesson he'd been taught long ago. He wasn't worth a damn and he never would be. He didn't deserve to be loved. Not now. Not ever.

The woman he loved had betrayed him. She had taken her family's side against him. Now, Luke knew for sure that he didn't matter, that what happened to him was unimportant. He wasn't worth saving. The only thing that did matter to him, the only thing that *was* important to him was the child Deanna Atchley was carrying. His child. The baby she had told him she loved and wanted. What would happen to his child now?

Chapter 1

She was going home. Home to Texas, on the southern edge of the Hill Country, where she'd been born and raised. Home to face the demons from her past—the demons that had recently reappeared in her dreams, forcing her to accept the inevitable. No matter how many years or miles she put between herself and Luke McClendon, she could never be free of the pain and agony of what had happened until she remembered the truth. The truth could set her free, at long last. But what could the truth do for Luke, after all this time? No one could give him back the years he'd lost in prison or the value of an innocent verdict.

Facing Luke again, after fifteen years, would be difficult. But she could do it. She had to do it. Her therapist had helped her realize that Luke was the key to remembering her past. She had to face him, accept her guilt and seek his forgiveness. She was no longer a spoiled, pampered teenage girl, dominated by her family, scared to stand up against them. She was a woman now, an independent woman who had fought long and hard to overcome the weaknesses that had almost destroyed her.

A great deal had changed in Texas in fifteen years and yet the closer she got to Stone Creek the more things seemed the same. There was something ageless and eternal about the Hill Country, about these green hills and rolling fields, the clear, clean streams and the bounty of wildflowers.

She wasn't far from home; only a few miles separated her from the past she dreaded facing. From her mother, with whom she spoke on the telephone only a few times a year. From her brother and sister-in-law. And a twelve-year-old niece she'd never seen. She needed time, just an hour or two, to prepare herself for the moment she thought would never come—seeing her family again.

She had called her mother two days ago, only hours before she left her home in Jackson, but she hadn't mentioned the reason she was returning to Stone Creek. Her mother had seemed genuinely pleased, in her quiet, reserved way. And Deanna had breathed a sigh of relief that, apparently, she would be received with open arms.

Taking the long way home, she circled the Willow City Loop, exiting off onto a back road that led southward to Luma County. Traffic was sparse, only an occasional vehicle and one tractor blocking her way for several miles. Spring in the Hill Country, even the southernmost edge, was picturesque, a nature painting unequaled by any view in the world. Rolling pastureland and wild canyons. Mesquite growing along the road and in the hills. Bluebonnets covering the land with a purple haze. Other wildflowers of red and white and yellow spreading over the landscape like a multi-colored rainbow.

When Deanna entered the iron gates leading up the long road to the main house on the Circle A, her heartbeat accelerated and her palms dampened with sweat. Despite the years of separation, these people were her family. *They love me,* she told herself. *I have nothing to fear from them.*

Then why are you so afraid? a tiny voice inside her head taunted. *Is it because you know someone other than Luke McClendon killed your father, someone on the Circle A, possibly someone in your family?*

Yes, she was afraid. Afraid to face the truth. But she was even more afraid to go on living with the nightmares and the frightening memory flashes she couldn't control. During the five years she had spent at Millones, the expensive, private sanitarium in California, where her mother had committed her a week after Luke's trial, she'd been plagued by horrifying dreams and recurring, fragmented memory flashes. But once she'd recovered from the nervous breakdown and gone back out into the world, the dreams and flashbacks had ended—until six months ago.

Deanna had witnessed a bloody car wreck shortly before Thanksgiving. A young mother had driven out in front of an eighteen-wheeler and she and both of her children had been killed. Deanna had witnessed the accident, had been the first on the scene, had called 911. But she had watched helplessly as the car burst into flames.

That horrible accident had shaken her hard-won mental stability. Shortly afterward, she'd begun having the nightmares again—seeing Luke and her father arguing, seeing Luke with the pitchfork, seeing her father's bloody body lying on the ground. And some-times the dreams would be about the trial. She couldn't really remember much about the trial, but in the dreams, she could see Luke's glaring green eyes look-ing at her with hatred.

Months of recent therapy had convinced her that she had to face Luke—after all these years of trying to escape from a truth too painful to remember. Through hypnosis, Dr. Kirkland had discovered that in Deanna's subconscious mind, her memory loss was interwoven with Luke McClendon—her love for him, her guilt over betraying him, her desperate need for his forgive-ness. She was convinced that without him, she wouldn't be able to unearth the truth buried deep within her.

Deanna pulled her white Mustang up in front of the house, opened the door and stepped out onto the drive. The two-story brick house, built by her grandfather in a style reminiscent of his wife's family home in Ken-tucky, hadn't changed at all. Big, sprawling and im-maculately maintained, the structure dominated the land around it. She had loved this old house, had loved the Circle A, had been happy as her parents' spoiled little girl, but all that had changed drastically when her father found out she was in love with Luke Mc-Clendon.

She hadn't been happy ever again. She had learned to accept life for what it was, had taught herself to be content, but true happiness had eluded her.

The front door swung open and Phyllis Atchley, her perfectly coiffured blond head held regally high, stepped onto the porch and smiled at her daughter. Deanna's heart skipped a beat. A part of her wanted to run to Phyllis and absorb the pleasure of being held in her mother's arms once again. It had been such a long time—not since her mother had hugged her and said goodbye the day Deanna had left Millones ten years ago.

"Deanna, darling." Phyllis rushed down the steps and out to the drive, opening her arms in a welcoming invitation. "It's so wonderful to see you."

Her mother had aged, but she was still a very attractive woman. Tall, slender and forever fashionably dressed. The moment Phyllis wrapped her arms around her, Deanna froze. The touch she had longed for was strained and devoid of any real affection. As quickly as she had taken her daughter into her embrace, Phyllis released her, stepped back and inspected her from head to toe.

"You look well, Deanna," Phyllis said. "Maturity suits you, darling. You take after me. Don't you think I've aged well?"

"You're as beautiful as ever, Mother." Despite their love for each other, there had always been a sense of rivalry between Phyllis and Deanna. More on Phyllis's part; Deanna had simply picked up on her mother's envious vibes. She knew her mother had resented the strong resemblance between them. Except for her brown hair, Deanna was a younger version of her gorgeous mother.

Phyllis took Deanna's hand. "Come inside. Junior and Benita are eager to see you. And Lauren. She's such a sweet child."

"How is Junior?" Deanna asked as she followed her mother up the front steps.

Phyllis paused momentarily on the porch. "Your brother is making the best of his situation. There really isn't anything else he can do. The doctors have said he'll never walk again.'' A lone tear trickled down Phyllis's rosy cheek. "Four years in that wheelchair!"

"It's hard to believe that a good horseman like Junior could have a riding accident that would leave him paralyzed." Deanna remembered her older brother as a big, robust man, a great deal like their father had been.

"Eddie shot that horse the very day it happened. Junior didn't want Durango killed, but Eddie said it was what Rayburn would have done." Phyllis squeezed Deanna's hand. "I don't know what we would have done all these years without Eddie. He's been totally devoted to us and to the Circle A."

Smiling weakly, Deanna nodded. Eddie Nunley, the rough, wiry ranch foreman, had been at the Circle A as long as Deanna could remember. Eddie had taught her how to ride her first pony. Growing up, he'd been like a second father to her. But all that had changed the night he and Junior and her father had trapped Luke and horsewhipped him nearly to death. She had never truly forgiven them for what they'd done that night.

"Eddie's looking forward to seeing you." Phyllis led Deanna into the foyer. "He'll be here for dinner this evening."

Deanna stopped and looked around inside the house. Unchanged. Still elegant. Perhaps too elegant. But Phyllis's tastes had always been expensive and rather ostentatious. Being the widow of a millionaire whose wealth had afforded him the luxury of playing at being a rancher gave Phyllis the means to live the life of a queen.

A dark-eyed child, dressed in jeans and plaid shirt, stood just inside the living room doorway. She stared at Deanna. Deanna smiled and the girl returned her smile.

"Lauren, come meet your Aunt Deanna." Phyllis motioned to the child.

"Is Deanna here?" a booming male voice asked.

"Yes, she's here," Phyllis replied. "Our girl has finally come home."

Junior Atchley, maneuvering his motorized wheelchair, zoomed past his daughter and out into the foyer. "Good God, gal, it's good to see you. Come here and give me a hug!" Junior lifted his big, muscular arms.

Deanna walked over, bent down on one knee and put her arms around her brother. He encompassed her in a bear hug, then released her, but before she could stand, he ruffled her hair. She giggled. The brotherly action created a warmth inside Deanna she hadn't felt in years.

"Stand up and let me have a look," Junior said. "Been ten years since we last saw you. That's a damn long time."

"Too long," Benita Atchley said as she came up behind her husband's wheelchair and placed her hands on his shoulders. "We have missed you, Deanna, and we are all very glad you've come home for a visit."

As she lifted herself off her knee, Deanna glanced up at her sister-in-law, the woman who had once been a young Mexican housemaid. Although Benita had to be at least thirty-five now, she still maintained most of the dark, fiery beauty that had captured Junior's heart as well as his libido. The woman now possessed a polish that had been lacking in the girl. Phyllis's doing, no doubt, Deanna thought.

"Come here, Lauren, and meet your Aunt Deanna." Junior slipped his arm around his daughter's waist.

"Well, what do you think of my little girl? She's as pretty as her mama, isn't she?"

"Hello, Lauren." Deanna offered her hand to her niece, who shyly accepted it in introduction. "You are every bit as pretty as Benita."

"And as smart as her papa," Benita added. "She is much like my Junior."

"Well, why don't we all go into the living room for a nice little chat," Phyllis suggested. "I'll ring for Carlotta and have her bring us—"

"If you don't mind, Mother, I'd really like to rest a while before dinner," Deanna said. "I'm a bit tired after the drive. I left Dallas fairly early this morning."

"Oh, my. Yes, of course. How unthinking of me." Phyllis glanced at the staircase. "I had your old room prepared for you. I'll get one of the boys to bring in your luggage. Would you like for me to go up with you and help you settle in?"

"No. I—I'd just like to be alone for a little while."

"If you'd prefer, I can put you in another room." Phyllis cut her eyes toward Junior. "I wasn't sure, so I—"

"My old room is just fine, Mother. And please, you don't have to tiptoe around me, afraid something you say or do might set me off. I've been quite sane ever since I left Millones ten years ago."

"Oh, darling, I didn't mean to—"

"Mother wasn't implying that she thinks you're still unstable," Junior said. "It's just that we don't want anything to ruin your first visit home. We want you to enjoy being with us and have a good time while you're here."

"Your mother and I have planned a party for Saturday night to welcome you home," Benita added, a hopeful smile on her face. "We have invited half the county. It will be the biggest and best barbecue the Circle A has ever had."

Oh, dear God, surely they hadn't! But Deanna knew that they had. They were pretending that nothing was wrong, that nothing bad had ever happened. They were giving her the prodigal daughter's welcome, killing the fatted calf and inviting the neighbors in for the barbecue!

"I didn't come back to Stone Creek, to the Circle A, to enjoy myself. And I don't expect to have a good time while I'm here."

"But, darling..." Phyllis whined.

"I should have told y'all when I called, but...I've been having nightmares and flashes of memory," she said. "The same nightmares I had when I first went to Millones. And the memory flashes are stronger and more vivid than they ever were."

"Hell, Deanna, don't you think you ought to be back under a doctor's care. Mother can call Doc Penson and have him—"

"I don't want Dr. Penson or any other doctor," Deanna said. "I'm not unstable or mentally incompetent. I can handle these dreams and flashbacks. In fact, I want to have them. I need to have them."

"What are you trying to tell us?" Phyllis asked.

"I've come home in the hopes that these dreams and flashbacks will help me fit all the pieces together. I want to remember what happened the night Daddy died. And I want to be able to remember everything that happened after that...the trial...my first few months at Millones...and—and my baby."

Silence hung in the air like an invisible vulture, waiting to pounce and devour. Deanna's gaze traveled from her mother's pale face and gaping mouth to her brother's tense jaw and sad eyes to her sister-in-law's flushed cheeks.

"I didn't realize until recently that I've been running away from a truth I couldn't bear to remember. I thought I'd made peace with the past, that I'd moved on and made a new life for myself. But I can never have a new life—a real life—until I come to terms with the past."

Deanna took several steps up the stairs, then turned her head a fraction and looked down at her family. "I don't remember what happened the night Daddy died, but there's one thing I do know. Instinctively. In my heart of hearts. Luke McClendon didn't kill my father. So that means someone else did. And that someone let an innocent man spend five years in prison."

Without another word, Deanna walked up the stairs, down the hall and away from the whispered murmurs. She'd shocked and upset her family. She could have waited to tell them the real reason she'd come home. But in the long run, it wouldn't have mattered. Whenever she told them, their reaction would have been the same. They didn't want Luke McClendon's name cleared of a crime he hadn't committed. After all these years, they still hated him.

Deanna opened the door to her old room, took a deep breath and walked inside. Late afternoon sunlight danced across the hardwood floors and illuminated the frilly, flowery teenage girl's room with a muted pink glow. She sat down on the antique painted metal bed that had belonged to her grandmother.

She was home, in her old room, on her bed. She should feel warm and safe and content. But she didn't.

Here, in the bosom of her family, she felt alone and uneasy.

Was she strong enough to stay and face the demons? Face Luke McClendon? Would he give her a second chance to help prove his innocence? Or did he still hate her too much to ever trust her again?

Kizzie McClendon stared at the invitation in her hand as if it were a deadly spider. She wished she could smash it, destroy it, keep it from doing harm to anyone. She could burn it, she supposed, or rip it into a hundred pieces and throw it into the trash. But the destruction of the handwritten note wouldn't change the facts. Deanna Atchley had returned to Stone Creek.

Why now, after all these years? Couldn't she have just stayed away and left well enough alone? It had taken Luke years after his release from prison to begin putting the past behind him. And only recently had she seen a glimpse of the young man who had, fifteen years ago, just begun to believe he had a place here at Montrose, as a part of the McClendon family. But Rayburn Atchley's murder had ended the progress she and Baxter had made with the boy. Ended it, perhaps, forever.

Even now, as a man of thirty-five, who ruled Montrose with the same easy authority Baxter had, Luke kept himself separate from the family, from her and his brothers. Her stepson lived his life, now more than ever, as a loner, isolated within himself, allowing no one—not even his family—to penetrate the defensive barrier that kept him at arm's length from the rest of the world.

Deanna Atchley had done this to him. He had given her his young love, his blind trust and she had used it to destroy him. She had taken the witness stand against him and doomed him to prison. Not just the five years in the penitentiary, but a lifetime imprisoned within himself. Unable to reach out to others. Unable to love or trust.

How had the woman had the nerve to send the McClendon family this damn invitation to her homecoming barbecue? One of the Circle A ranch hands had hand-delivered the thing only minutes ago. If she'd known what it was, she would have thrown it back in the man's face.

Clutching the cream-colored stationery in her hand, Kizzie paced the floor in the den. The invitation wasn't the problem, even the Atchleys' grand celebration wasn't the problem. The problem was that Deanna Atchley was back and Kizzie had no idea how Luke would react once he found out. Much as she wanted to keep the truth from him, she knew she couldn't. And this news should come from her, not one of the hands, who had, by now, probably heard about Deanna's return. The whole county was no doubt buzzing with the gossip that Phyllis Atchley's crazy daughter had come back from wherever she'd been hiding these past fifteen years.

Nobody knew what had happened to the girl after Luke's trial. She'd simply vanished off the face of the earth. Kizzie wondered what had really happened to the child Deanna had been carrying. Luke's child. He never mentioned the baby, just as he never mentioned Deanna. But Kizzie knew that a man with Luke's past, born illegitimate, not knowing his father until he was fifteen, would agonize over the fate of his own son or daughter.

There was no point putting it off. She'd saddle up

Minerva and go find Luke. But she'd rather face an angry bull than tell Luke that Deanna had returned to Stone Creek.

Luke watched the sun lying on the western horizon like a fat orange ball. Tendrils of ripe pink and purple and gold spanned the length of the sky, mingling with the clear blue that spread upward to the heavens. He readjusted his hips in the saddle and breathed in the sweet evening air. Looking out over the vast acreage that comprised Montrose, he felt the same sense of contentment that he always did when he remembered that this ranch was his home as well as his responsibility, and his pleasure to oversee for the whole McClendon clan.

When Kizzie had come to him, after his father's death five years ago, and told him that she and her sons, Tyler and Grant, had decided they wanted him to take over the reins of Montrose, he'd been dumbfounded. He couldn't believe that they wanted him—Baxter's bastard son—to be in charge of the ranch. But neither of Baxter's other sons loved the ranch the way Luke did and neither wanted to step into their father's shoes and run the whole operation.

Montrose had become Luke's life—he ate, slept, breathed and lived for the ranch. It was all he had. All he'd ever have.

Montrose was enough. It was all he needed.

Luke caught a glimpse of Kizzie heading up the dirt path that led from the northern range into the hills where he'd paused to enjoy the view. What was his stepmother doing out here at this time of the evening? She didn't usually disturb him unless there was a problem.

He waited until she was almost at the top of the hill,

then waved and called out to her. "What are you doing out here? Thought you'd be helping Alva get things ready for supper. Tyler's still coming over tonight, isn't he?"

"As far as I know, your brother's still coming. Unless he has some sort of emergency. Ever since he got himself elected sheriff, we see less and less of him."

"You didn't answer my question," Luke said. "What are—"

"I've got something to tell you and it couldn't wait." Kizzie reined in Minerva, bringing the mare up beside the big, dun quarter horse that Luke had raised from a colt.

Luke searched his stepmother's dark eyes and a sudden uneasiness hit him square in the gut. Kizzie wasn't the type to get unduly concerned about things. She was the most levelheaded woman he'd ever known.

"What's wrong? Has something happened? Have you heard from Tess?"

"No." Kizzie's voice was edged with pain. "I haven't heard anything from your sister. As much as I wish that girl would write or call, I'm afraid that's not what I rode out here to tell you."

"Then what is it?"

Luke dismounted, then reached up and helped his stepmother to the ground. Side by side, they walked, leading their horses behind them.

"There's no easy way to say this…and no use beating around the bush." Kizzie took a deep breath. "Deanna Atchley's come home. She's at the Circle A, and they're giving a big welcome-home party for her tomorrow night."

Luke didn't flinch, but his jaw tightened as he narrowed his eyes and looked down at the ground. "How do you know?"

Kizzie scrambled in the side pocket of her slacks and pulled out a crumpled piece of paper. When she held it out to Luke, he stared at it, but didn't touch it. "It's a personal invitation from Deanna herself. One of the Circle A ranch hands delivered it to the door about twenty minutes ago."

Luke pulled the cream-colored stationery from Kizzie's hand and quickly scanned its contents. He immediately recognized Deanna's bold feminine handwriting. A hard knot formed in the pit of his stomach. She had written him love letters when she was seventeen—letters in which she poured out her heart to him, promising him her love forever. Forever and "then some" had been her favorite declaration.

Luke crushed the invitation in his fist. The blood thundered through his body as his heartbeat accelerated. Damn her! Damn her! What was she doing back in Stone Creek? Why hadn't she stayed away? He had finally put his life back together and was finding contentment and a sense of purpose in running Montrose. He didn't want or need any reminders of his deep insecurities, of a past he could never change and a sense of unworthiness that he could never overcome.

"Of course, none of us will go to the barbecue," Kizzie said, her hand hovering near Luke's shoulder.

He knew she wanted to touch him, offer him some motherly comfort, but he also knew that she wouldn't force her maternal attentions on him. He admired and respected Kizzie. Not many women would have so readily accepted their husband's illegitimate son and welcomed him into the family. But Kizzie had. The woman was made of strong stuff and possessed a heart as big as Texas.

"I think you should go to the barbecue," Luke said.

"Why on earth would I go to a barbecue at the Atchleys'? I haven't had any use for them since…" Kizzie shook her head, then glanced up at Luke.

"We need to find out why she's come home after fifteen years." Luke bent over and picked up a handful of pebbles. "Something's brought her back to Stone Creek. Her return might not have anything to do with us. Then again, maybe it does. With the Atchleys, it pays to know."

"You want me to go to the barbecue alone?"

"You could ask Tyler to go with you."

"But you aren't going, are you?"

The knot in Luke's stomach tightened painfully. The very thought of seeing Deanna again ate away at his insides like acid melting through metal. When she'd taken the stand against him at his trial, he'd told himself he never wanted to see her again. And in his mind, he had meant it. Even in his heart he believed that he hated her. But in his subconscious, in his dreams, he was never free of her. Just when he thought he'd vanquished her from his memories, she would return to haunt his dreams, like a spirit who refused to leave this earth.

"No, I'm not going," Luke said. "But I wish you'd ride over there tomorrow night and find out what's going on."

"She won't be the same girl, you know," Kizzie told him. "She'll be a woman now. She's nearly thirty-three. Could be she's married and has a…"

"And has a couple of kids," Luke finished for her. "What do you want to bet she hasn't got my kid." He threw the pebbles, one at a time, into the thicket. Flushed from the bushes, birds flew into the air.

"Oh, Luke…son." Kizzie did touch him then. Her work-roughened hand clasped his wrist.

He clenched his teeth so tightly that a sharp pain ran up his neck and into his head. "I've wondered all these years whether or not she really got rid of my child or…or if she had my baby, and if she did, what she did with it. I know she wouldn't have kept it. If she didn't get rid of it, I hope she made sure the kid went to a good home."

"I'll go to the party," Kizzie told him. "And I'll find out why Deanna has come back to Stone Creek. But don't you worry, son, she won't ever hurt you again. Even if I have to run her out of this county myself." Kizzie squeezed Luke's wrist, then released him and mounted her horse. "Don't you stay out here all night brooding. Do you hear me? Come on home for supper with me and Tyler."

Kizzie headed the mare down the hill while Luke stood alone and watched her descent. He was damn lucky to have someone care about him as much as Kizzie did. He didn't deserve her love. Until recent years, he hadn't done anything to warrant her kindness. But no matter what he'd done or how many messes he'd gotten himself into, she'd stood by him, just as his father had. And he'd been grateful. He just didn't know how to express his gratitude in words, so he tried to do it with his actions—by running Montrose the way Baxter had, with strength and caring and dedication. He owed his father that much. And he owed Kizzie even more.

Luke mounted Cherokee and rode higher into the hills, farther and farther away from the ranch house and closer and closer to the remains of a shack hidden deep in the woods. The shack had been an old log cabin that had been built by Baxter's great-grandfather when he'd first claimed this land as his own. Now it was nothing but charred remnants of a burned building.

When Luke reached the cabin site, he reined in Cherokee, but didn't dismount. He sat there in the saddle and looked at the crumbling gray chimney of his ancestor's home and remembered the nights he had brought Deanna Atchley here. The nights they had lain in each other's arms. The nights they had made passionate love. Fifteen years ago. Another lifetime. He had never loved anyone so much. Had never trusted anyone so much.

But he should have known all along that what he had thought was so perfect, a love so pure and true, was nothing but a lie. He'd never been worthy of Deanna Atchley, never deserved to have a girl like that truly love him. He'd been a fool to think that she would stand against her family and defend him.

He had loved and trusted the wrong woman, and she had proved to him how totally worthless he was. His stupidity had cost him far more than five years of his life—years spent in hell. He had lost not only those years, but the hope of ever being worthy of love.

And he had lost the only child he would ever have.

Chapter 2

Deanna had forgotten how elaborate barbecues at the Circle A could be. Her mother was the consummate hostess, making everyone feel welcome. Phyllis, who had come into her marriage to Rayburn Atchley with a sizable inheritance of her own, never skimped on important things. Things like parties and clothes and vacations in Europe and the Caribbean. Phyllis lived for the adoration and envy of her peers. Looking back, Deanna realized how devastating her relationship with Luke had been to her mother, and how her involvement the night of her father's murder had been a death knell to Phyllis's social standing. There had been a time when she'd thought her mother was perfect. She'd learned the hard way how false her mother's paragon facade really was.

Deanna stood inside the den, looking out the double French doors at the crowd swarming around on the huge rock patio and beyond, covering the ground like insects. Searching the crowd for any sign of Luke McClendon, she cursed herself for a fool. He won't come, she told herself. Why did you think sending him and his family a personal invitation would make any difference? She was certain that the McClendons and the Atchleys hadn't spoken in the past fifteen years. Not since Luke had been arrested for her father's murder.

Deanna nervously smoothed her hands over her hips, adjusting the drape of her royal blue silk slacks. The last thing she wanted to do was go outside and face all these people—her mother's and brother's friends. People who would remember the fragile, helpless, desperate girl she had been. The girl who'd had a mental breakdown and disappeared from Stone Creek for fifteen years. She wasn't concerned that anyone would be rude to her face, but she could imagine the snide remarks that would be made behind her back. Texans were pioneer stock, tough, independent and fiercely proud. People in these parts didn't approve of weaknesses of any kind, least of all mental instability. And she wasn't going to degrade herself and try to explain that she'd been completely *sane* for over ten years and living a productive life in Jackson, Mississippi. She didn't owe anyone an explanation. No one except Luke McClendon.

Benita scurried through a horde of laughing guests, making a beeline straight for Deanna. Grabbing her sister-in-law's arm, Benita pulled her aside, all the while smiling like an idiot as her gaze danced over the crowd, checking their reaction.

"Mother has been wondering where you were," Benita whispered. "She was worried about you. Tonight is very important to her. You don't want to disappoint her, do you?''

"Disappoint Phyllis?" Deanna's lips curved into a mocking smile. "Heaven forbid."

"Please, do not embarrass your mother." Benita glared at Deanna, a frown marring her forehead. "She is so pleased that you are well and that you've finally come home. She does love you very much, you know."

Did Benita truly believe what she'd just said or was she simply repeating Phyllis's words. After all these years, was Benita still so insecure about her position in the Atchley family that she felt it necessary to kowtow to Phyllis, to bow and scrape to her?

"I promise that I won't say or do anything to embarrass Mother." Deanna eased her arm out of Benita's tight grip. "I'll mix and mingle and put on my very best phony smile. That should please her, shouldn't it?"

"You still blame her, don't you?" Benita's dark eyes held a glint of disbelief. "After all she did to protect you, you still—"

"Deanna, honey, how wonderful to see you." A tall, rawboned brunette, a few years older than Deanna, threw open her arms as she approached. "God almighty, you look wonderful. Prettier than when we were girls."

"Patsy Ruth Waters!" Deanna gasped when the robust woman grabbed her in a bear hug. Patsy Ruth was one of those big, athletic women who could outride, outrope and outdrink most men. Phyllis never quite approved of her as a friend for Deanna, but since Patsy Ruth's father was a multimillionaire, and a state senator to boot, she had tolerated the girls' friendship.

"It's Patsy Ruth Dawkins, now, honey." Releasing

her hold on Deanna, Patsy Ruth stepped back a couple of feet and shook her head. "Still got a to-die-for body and that mane of honey-brown hair! And just look at me, after twelve years of marriage and three kids, I look every day of my thirty-five years. And then some." Her strong laughter filled the evening air like a roll of welcome thunder promising rain after a long dry spell.

"You haven't changed a bit and you know it," Deanna told her old friend. "Marriage and motherhood must agree with you."

"Lordy, it sure does. I want you to meet that man of mine. Glenn's around here somewhere. Probably over at the feed trough. That man likes to eat as much as I do." Patsy Ruth grasped Deanna's hand and dragged her over to a couple of unoccupied chairs at one of the picnic tables dotted around the yard. "What about you, honey? Are you married? Any kids? Where have you been these past fifteen years? And why didn't you keep in touch?"

"Whew, take it easy on the questions." Deanna said, sitting down at a table with her old friend.

"I'm just anxious to catch up with you. So, where are you living now?" Patsy Ruth asked.

"Jackson, Mississippi," Deanna said. "I'm a teacher at a private school for children with emotional and mental problems that make learning in a regular classroom difficult. And I'm not married."

"Mercy me, I never imagined you as a school-teacher. You were always so involved in all the social activities, a cheerleader and homecoming queen and…Well, I guess you didn't turn into a replica of Phyllis, did you?"

"No, I'm nothing like my mother. After my nervous

breakdown, I changed a great deal. My priorities are different than they would have been if…if I hadn't…'' She wanted to tell her old friend about the years at Millones, yet she hesitated, uncertain even of Patsy Ruth's reaction to the truth.

"Say no more. Not here. We'll do lunch real soon and have us a heart-to-heart. For this evening, let's just concentrate on the present. I'll tell you all about Glenn and the kids and you tell me about your job and your life in Jackson. Any special man in your life?"

"There hasn't been anyone special in my life since…not since Luke." Deanna lowered her voice. Even now, just the mention of Luke's name created a deep sadness inside her.

"Well, speak of the devil. Sort of anyway." As her gaze traveled across the crowd, Patsy Ruth let out a long, low whistle.

Deanna scanned the milling guests, searching for Luke. Her heart was suddenly beating faster, thundering in her ears like war drums. "Where?"

"Oh, honey, it isn't Luke himself," Patsy Ruth said. "It's Kizzie and Tyler. Never thought I'd live to see the day a McClendon would set foot on the Circle A again."

The moment Deanna caught sight of Luke's stepmother and stepbrother, her heart soared. Maybe Luke had come with them. Maybe she'd get a chance to talk to him—tonight! She stared, uncaring that others might notice, watching the McClendons walk proudly through the horde of astonished people gaping at them.

"Patsy Ruth, will you excuse me, please." Deanna rose slowly from the chair. "I really need to speak to Kizzie."

"You go right ahead, honey. I think I understand."

Deanna wove her way through the guests, many stopping her to say hello and welcome her back to Stone Creek, a few others smiling weakly at her as she passed them. Not deterred by anyone or anything, she zeroed in on Kizzie McClendon. She would have recognized Luke's stepmother anywhere, so little had the Montrose matriarch changed. Still tall and slender, with a whipcord-lean strength in her body, Kizzie towered over most of the other women. Her short, curly, steel-gray hair framed her plain face. A face that belied the inner beauty of the woman's magnificent spirit. Deanna had always liked Kizzie and appreciated her kindness to Luke.

In her peripheral vision, Deanna caught a glimpse of her mother heading toward the McClendons. Moving quickly, Deanna spanned the distance between her and Luke's family, reaching them before Phyllis could detach herself from a talkative guest.

"Mrs. McClendon." Deanna's voice quivered ever so slightly. "I'm so glad you accepted my invitation." She glanced up at Tyler, who'd been only a kid of fifteen the last time she'd seen him. Now he was a tall, attractive man, with his mother's dark, piercing eyes. "Thank y'all for coming tonight. I—I don't suppose—"

"Luke didn't come," Tyler said. "You really didn't expect him to, did you?"

"No, I suppose not," Deanna replied. "But I had hoped he might."

"I had no intention of coming," Kizzie admitted. "But Luke asked me to find out why you're back in Stone Creek, after all this time."

Clutching her hands together in front of her, Deanna looked pleadingly into Kizzie's keen eyes, eyes that seemed to see through her, past all falsehoods and directly to the deeply buried truth.

"I had to come back," Deanna said. "You see I've been—"

"Mrs. McClendon?" Phyllis Atchley stood stiffly at her unwanted guest's side, her nose tilted haughtily in the air. She glanced at Tyler. "Sheriff. I must say I never expected to see y'all here tonight."

"The McClendons are my guests, Mother," Deanna said. "I invited them."

"Then of course, they're welcome." Phyllis's cheeks flushed as she obviously fought to compose herself. "This is Deanna's welcome-home party and she certainly has the right to invite whomever she wishes."

Phyllis glanced around as if searching for someone. Following her mother's line of vision, Deanna saw her brother glaring at the McClendons. Eddie Nunley's big hand rested on Junior's shoulder, as if he was physically restraining him, keeping him from barreling his wheelchair across the patio and out into the yard. Junior had hated Luke McClendon almost as much as her father had. Her brother had been present, along with Eddie, the night her father had horsewhipped Luke within an inch of his life. Junior might not have participated in the brutal beating, but he hadn't done anything to stop their father. Neither had Eddie. A part of her still blamed both men for the parts they had played in the destruction of her life. But the person she blamed most of all was herself. She'd been the one who had destroyed her life and Luke's life, too.

"If Luke hadn't asked me to come here tonight, no power on earth would have made me set foot on the Circle A," Kizzie said, glaring at Phyllis. "I came here to find out what Deanna's doing back in Stone Creek."

"She's come home to visit her family," Phyllis said quickly. "What other reason could she possibly have? Besides—" Phyllis lowered her voice to a whisper, apparently aware that all eyes were on their little four-some "—my daughter's return to Stone Creek has nothing to do with your family. Her visit here is none of your business."

"Is that true?" Kizzie focused her dark gaze on Deanna.

"I want Luke to know why I've returned," Deanna said. "But I don't want the message relayed to him by a third party. I want to tell him myself."

Kizzie's eyebrows lifted, her facial features tightening. "Then your return's got something to do with Luke."

"No, it most definitely doesn't!" Phyllis snapped, then glanced around at all the curious, staring faces and smiled at them in an obvious effort to pretend nothing was wrong.

"I can speak for myself, Mother." Deanna reached over and laid her hand on Kizzie's arm. "Where is Luke tonight?"

"Deanna, you wouldn't—" Phyllis said.

"He's home tonight, probably eating supper in the kitchen with Alva." Kizzie laid her hand over Deanna's and squeezed tightly. "Don't you hurt my boy again."

Every nerve in Deanna's body screamed as Kizzie and Tyler walked away. She wanted to beg Kizzie to believe that she had never intentionally hurt Luke, that she, too, had paid a high price for her immature and selfish behavior.

The moment the McClendons were out of earshot, Phyllis grabbed her daughter's arm.

"You are not going over to Montrose tonight to see Luke McClendon," Phyllis's words hissed out from between tightly clenched teeth.

"Yes, Mother, I am." Deanna jerked away from Phyllis. "Luke has a right to know that I'm having memory flashes about the night Daddy was killed. If my memory returns completely, then we can clear Luke's name and discover the identity of Daddy's real murderer."

"But Luke is the real murderer." Phyllis balled her ring-adorned fingers into her palms.

"No, Mother, he isn't. Even though I don't remember what really happened, I know in my very soul that Luke didn't kill Daddy."

Deanna turned and walked away, leaving her mother speechless. But Phyllis quickly caught up with Deanna just as she entered the house through the French doors.

"Don't do this," Phyllis said. "Don't dredge up all those horrible memories. Don't put me through all that agony. Not again."

"Agony, mother? If you want to talk about agony, let's discuss what agony it must have been for Luke those five years he spent in prison. Or perhaps you want to have a mother-daughter chat about my years at Millones. Would you like me to tell all your friends that I spent over four years locked away in a private sanitarium for people with mental problems?"

"Go ahead then. Go see Luke McClendon. But I warn you. The man hates you as much as he hates the rest of us. To him, you're nothing more than an Atchley. Don't forget that you testified against him and helped put him in prison."

"No, Mother, I haven't forgotten what I did or why I did it." Deanna squared her shoulders and met her mother's determined glare head-on. "You can't intimidate me any longer. I'm not afraid of you or what you can do to me. You played your trump card fifteen years ago."

Fleeing from her mother, Deanna raced out of the den and up the back stairs to her bedroom. She picked up her purse off the dressing table, pulled out her key chain and hurried back downstairs. If Luke McClendon wouldn't come to her, she would go to him. And somehow, she'd find a way to make him listen to what she had to say.

Deanna sat inside her car looking at the weathered limestone McClendon ranch house, with its huge arched openings leading to the front porch. Sprawled out to encompass over six thousand square feet, the entire house was encircled by a rock patio, with niches cut out for shrubbery, small trees and springtime flowers. Creamy light shone from most of the front windows, like beacons to guide lost souls to safety. There was a warmth, a welcoming feel about this old structure that had been added on to over the years since it had been built by Luke's great-grandfather, in the early part of the century. Despite the complexity of the McClendon household's individual relationships, Deanna had always thought they held the secret to what a real family should be. When Kizzie and Baxter had married, each had brought a son into the relationship and then together they'd had Tess. And ten years later, Luke had shown up on their doorstep. But instead of destroying the McClendon marriage and family, Luke's appearance had seemed to strengthen it.

To this day, Deanna admired Luke's stepmother, a woman who had opened her home and her heart to her husband's illegitimate son. But Luke never had allowed himself to fully accept the love his new family offered. He hadn't actually told her that he didn't feel worthy of being a McClendon, but Deanna had suspected the truth. Only after they had fallen madly in love had Luke seemed to begin believing he had a right to his place at Montrose, his place in the world and most of all, his place in her life.

Had she destroyed that budding belief in his self-worth, just as she had destroyed the rest of Luke's life? He had trusted her, put his faith in her, counted on her love and loyalty. And she had betrayed him. She had taken her family's side against him.

Gathering all the courage she possessed, Deanna opened the car door and stepped outside, her knees weak and her hands moist with perspiration. She could do this. She had to; she had no other choice. Only Luke could help her unearth the mysteries of the past—the secrets buried deep within her subconscious mind.

Hurrying, out of fear that she might turn and run, Deanna rushed through the archway and up to the double front doors. Lifting her hand to grasp the heavy pewter knocker, she sucked in a deep, calming breath.

Then the sound of booted footsteps approaching made her heart flutter madly. She wiped her moist palms along her hips and upper thighs, then braced herself for whatever happened.

The left front door swung open. Deanna gasped. Luke McClendon stood just inside the doorway. Tall, rugged, his big shoulders almost touching the door frames on each side, he stared at her. He was more handsome than he'd been as a boy of twenty. Bigger, broader, more muscular. He still had the same ink-black hair, the same hypnotic green eyes, the same strong, chiseled features, but there was a hardness to his face, a wariness in his eyes that had intensified since the last time she remembered seeing him.

The bottom dropped out of her stomach. Her nerves zinged like exposed electrical wires touching. And her femininity came to life, awakening from a long, celibate sleep. Dear God, nothing had changed. After all this time, the very sight of him still stirred to life every feminine longing within her. It had always been that way, since the first moment she'd set eyes on Luke. She'd been sixteen and he hadn't paid much attention to her. But she'd known then that he was destined to be her first lover.

''I'd heard you were back.'' His deep voice held an edge of contempt that he didn't try to disguise. ''What the hell are you doing here?''

''When you didn't come to the barbecue, I knew the only way I'd get to see you was to come here to Montrose.'' She stared him directly in the eye, not allowing his hard, angry glare to intimidate her.

She wanted to reach out and touch him, run her fingers over his deeply tanned face, caress the bulge of muscles straining beneath his cotton work shirt. The longing for this one man—the longing she'd been unable to deny when she was seventeen—was as strong as ever.

''Did you honestly think I'd show up at an Atchley barbecue?'' Luke glowered at her, his body tensed, his jaw clenched. ''Especially knowing you'd be there.''

''No, I suppose I didn't. But I had hoped...'' She flinched when she noticed the way he gripped his hands into tight fists. ''You sent Kizzie to find out why I was back in Stone Creek. I thought it best not to send you a message, but to come here and face you.''

"I'm surprised you had the guts." His lips twitched in a mockery of a grin. "You were never big in the courage department, were you, Deanna?"

The sound of her name on his lips, the word dripping with acrid loathing, wounded her deeply. Wounded not only her heart but her soul. Luke McClendon truly hated her. Maybe he had a right to feel the way he did about her, but she couldn't let his hostility deter her from her mission.

"And you were never big in the compassion and understanding department!" She had spoken more sharply than she'd intended, but if she knew anything about the past, it was that Luke had not been blameless in the destruction of their lives. He had expected more from her than she'd been able to give him. And he hadn't even tried to understand that she was only seventeen and scared to stand up to her parents.

"What was there to understand?"

Luke started to close the door in her face, but she moved quickly, inserting herself in the narrow opening of the partially open door. "I didn't come back to Stone Creek for a friendly family visit. I came home because..." She hesitated momentarily, waiting—hoping—Luke's expression would soften just a fraction. But it didn't. "I came home because I've been having dreams and flashbacks about the night Daddy died."

"You're still sticking to your story that you can't remember what happened that night?" With his big hand gripping the edge of the door, Luke snorted.

"I have very little memory of anything that happened after..." She lowered her head, unable to look directly at Luke. "After you picked up the pitchfork that night. I don't even remember much about the trial or—"

"You don't remember the trial?" he asked, disbelief plain on his face. "Do you expect me to believe you?"

"Believe me or not," she said. "It's the truth. I did not see who killed my father. I remember only bits and pieces of the trial, only bits and pieces of what happened before the trial and afterward. I know that I testified against you. Mother told me some of what happened and later I—I talked to Mr. Lamar and he told me everything."

After her release from Millones, she had called the former district attorney and asked him to share as much information as he could about the trial, about her part in it and about Luke's sentencing. For four years after the trial, she had forced any thought of Luke or her family from her mind, but in the last year she was at the sanitarium, she'd had a breakthrough that enabled her to begin the healing process, and when she left Millones, she began to rebuild her life, but only after she learned as much of the truth as others knew. Once she found out Luke was in prison, that he'd been convicted of manslaughter and that her testimony had helped put him there, she'd known she couldn't return to Stone Creek. There had been no hope of renewing her relationship with the one man she loved.

"I've come back to try to discover the truth about that night." Lifting her hand, she let it hover over his where it held the door. "I want to remember. I want to remember everything. I've come home to find out who really killed my father and I want your help."

Luke gripped the door with white-knuckled strength, wanting to shove Deanna Atchley outside—out of his sight. He didn't want to see her, didn't want to listen to her voice. But at the same time, another part of him wanted to grab her, pull her into his arms and devour her with the raging passion ripping him apart inside.

From the minute Kizzie had told him Deanna was back in Stone Creek, he'd known this moment was inevitable. When he'd heard the knock at the door a few minutes ago, he had known it was her.

He hated this woman—this incredibly beautiful woman, whose blue eyes were boring into his soul, pleading with him to believe her. And yet on some level, he still cared about her, still wanted her, still needed her. God forgive him, after all these years, he was still vulnerable to the way Deanna made him feel. She had possessed a power over him no one else ever had. But he was no longer some outcast kid who didn't belong. A boy not good enough for Rayburn Atchley's precious little girl. He was a McClendon. Hell, he was the McClendon. Montrose was his in a way it never could belong to Grant or Tyler or Tess. Unlike Baxter's other children, Luke had the land and the ranching business in his blood, the way it had been in his father's and grandfather's.

Who are you kidding? he asked himself. You may be a powerful man in these parts, and you may not be the insecure boy you were back then, but you're still Baxter's quarter-breed bastard. Nothing can ever change that fact.

But he could control his feelings for Deanna. He was a man who had learned to protect himself from every outside influence. When he'd been released from prison ten years ago, he had promised himself that no one would ever hurt him again. He certainly wasn't going to let the woman who had betrayed him come back into his life and rip out his guts a second time. No matter how much his body longed for hers, no matter how strong the desire, he wouldn't allow Deanna the upper hand. Whatever happened now, he would be the one in charge.

He glared at her hand hovering over his. He realized she wanted to touch him. The thought sent shock waves through his tense body. It had always been that way between them. Heat so intense that it nearly burned them alive whenever they touched. After fifteen years, there shouldn't be any fire left, only cold ashes. But there it was as blazing hot as ever. The passion neither of them had been able to resist. The need that drove them both beyond reason.

"What makes you think I'd help you?" he asked, his gaze riveted to her hand, only inches above his.

"Because I know you didn't kill Daddy. I've always known it. In my heart. And now, maybe I can help you, the way I wasn't able to help you before. If only I can remember…" She laid her hand on top of his and for one brief moment, the electrical charge zipped through her body, robbing her of her breath.

Luke's jade eyes darkened to a black forest green. He jerked his hand away, unable to bear her touch. "What good will it do if you remember anything? You can't change what happened. Your father's dead. And I gave five years of my life for a crime I didn't commit. Babe, you're fifteen years too late."

Deanna felt as if he'd slapped her. But she didn't blame him for the way he felt. Maybe he was right. Maybe she was too late. But was it ever too late for the truth?

"Look, I'm here to stay until I find out what really happened that night," Deanna told him. "I haven't had nightmares about Daddy's death since—" she had been about to say since she'd left Millones, but she wasn't

ready to tell Luke about *her* five years behind bars
"—in years. But they've come back and they are more
vivid than ever before. And I'm experiencing memory
flashbacks about that night and about the trial and... I
realize that knowing the truth won't change the past,
won't give you back the years you lost in prison, but
this is something I have to do. Please, Luke, will you
help me?"

"I don't know," he admitted. "If you could remember what happened, who killed your father, then you
could clear my name. My family's name."

"I'm sorry." Deanna's voice was a mere whisper.
"I'm sorry that I wasn't able to help you when you
needed me the most."

"Yeah, I'm sorry, too. Sorry you weren't *able* to
help me. I knew you couldn't possibly love me. I told
myself I was living a lie to think I was worthy of a
girl like you, but you almost convinced me that what
we had was real."

"It was real!"

"No, babe, it was nothing but flash and no sub-
stance." Luke took a step toward her and grinned
wickedly when she instinctively backed away from
him. "When it came to the point of no return, you
didn't have the guts to stand with me against your family. All that love you professed for me was just lust.
You wanted to walk on the wild side with a real bad
boy. All you ever wanted from me was this!"

He shoved her up against the front door, swinging it
and her against the wall. She gasped when he pressed
his aroused body into her and blatantly ground his sex
intimately against her. He grabbed the back of her
head. She struggled, but soon discovered how truly

weak she was compared to his superior strength. She ceased fighting him and boldly gazed into his eyes.

"Isn't this why you really came here tonight?" he asked. "You want to hop in the sack for old times' sake?"

"Don't do this, Luke. Please." Oh, sweet mercy, how her body yearned for his. But she didn't want him this way. Not filled with anger and hatred. Once, long ago, he had taken her with love and passion. His wildness tempered with gentleness. Once he had loved her as she had loved him. But now he hated her. And she was afraid of him. Of the power he possessed to break her heart.

Luke leaned over as if he were going to kiss her, his lips almost touching hers. "If you're lying to me this time, I'll make you sorry you ever knew my name." Spearing his fingers through her hair, he jerked back her head. "Do you understand? If I agree to help you and then find out you're not being honest with me, I'll—"

"I promise that I'm not lying. All I want is to find out the truth about the night Daddy was killed."

He released her with the same abruptness with which he'd manhandled her. "Go home. Leave me alone. I need to think."

"Then you'll consider helping me?"

"I said I need to think about it. Come back tomorrow and I'll let you know."

"Thank you, Luke."

"Don't thank me, babe. I'm not the boy you remember, the boy who would have walked over live coals for you. I'm a man without a heart and without much of a conscience. Five years in Huntsville will do that to a man. Spending time with me won't be any fun for you, I promise you that.''

''I—I'll come back tomorrow and we can talk.'' She backed away, out onto the rock porch.

''If your mama finds out you've been sniffing around me, she might not let you out of the house tomorrow.'' Luke's broad, mocking smile revealed a row of perfect white teeth.

''I'm not the same spoiled, scared girl I was fifteen years ago. My mother doesn't control me now. No one tells me what I can do and who I can see. I'm my own woman.''

''Are you?''

''Yes.''

''Guess we'll find out.''

She nodded. ''I'll see you tomorrow.''

He didn't reply, just stood in the open doorway, the light from inside the house silhouetting his big body. Deanna backed slowly away from him, then when she reached the patio, she turned and walked away. She had to force herself not to run. When she got in her Mustang, she glanced back at the house. Luke still stood there, big and rugged and powerful, his very presence challenging her. Daring her. Promising her both heaven and hell if she returned to him.

Chapter 3

"Deanna, please, darling, don't do this," Phyllis nervously wrung her hands. "You can't change the past. All you can do is cause trouble for everyone involved. If you bring Luke McClendon into your insane search for another killer, there is no telling what will happen."

"Insane search, Mother?" Deanna shifted the strap on her navy leather bag so that it rested higher on her shoulder. "Just because I spent nearly five years in a private mental hospital doesn't mean that everything I do is insane."

Phyllis followed her daughter out of the living room and into the foyer, reaching out pleadingly when Deanna opened the front door. "I'm sorry, darling. I didn't mean to imply that you're not entirely well now. It's just that I cannot bear to see you or anyone else hurt by this foolish crusade of yours."

Pausing on her way out, Deanna turned to her

mother. "If Luke McClendon is innocent—and I believe he is—then doesn't this family owe it to him to find out who really killed Daddy?"

A pink flush spread up Phyllis's neck and over her face. "We don't owe that man anything! He destroyed this family! Ripped us apart and didn't give a damn!"

"Would it matter if I told you that I'm doing this for myself as much, if not more, than for Luke? I need to know the truth. I can't go on this way, not knowing. How can I live a normal life with these nightmares and memory flashes tormenting me?"

Phyllis took a hesitant step toward Deanna, who turned quickly and rushed outside and down the front steps. Eddie Nunley stood beside her Mustang. The moment she emerged from the house, he eased his hip off the fender and removed his Stetson.

"Morning, Deanna," he said.

She glanced back at the house, where Phyllis hovered in the doorway, watching them. So, now it was Eddie's turn to try to talk sense to her. Junior and Phyllis had both tried and failed to dissuade her from reopening the door to the past, so they'd brought in the big guns. When she and Junior were kids, Eddie had been more of a father to them than Rayburn Atchley ever had. He had certainly paid more attention to them, and they'd often turned to him for support and advice. But Deanna's feelings for Eddie had changed after the night he'd stood by and let her father beat Luke nearly to death.

"I'm in a hurry, Eddie." She dashed around him and grasped the driver's-side door handle.

"Too big a hurry to give me a couple of minutes of your time, DeDe?"

Deanna knew he'd used his old pet name for her

hoping it would bring back memories from her childhood, days spent in idyllic bliss as a spoiled little girl whose every wish was fulfilled. If her parents had neglected her in any way, they had made up for leaving her alone with the hired help by lavishing money on her, and on Junior as well. And often, Eddie had been the one who had filled in for a father too busy to be bothered with his kids.

Deanna pulled her hand away from the car door, took a deep breath and turned to face Eddie. He hadn't changed much in fifteen years. Still tall and lean, with weathered, freckled skin, a less than handsome face marred by acne scars, and a crop of thick, rusty-gray hair that years ago had been carrot red.

"Let me save us both some time," Deanna said. "I know why you want to talk to me, and I can assure you that nothing you say is going to change my mind. I'm going to do whatever it takes to find out what really happened the night Daddy was killed."

"And Luke McClendon is going to help you? You're heading over to Montrose right now, aren't you?" Eddie slapped his Stetson against his thigh. "Gal, don't you have any idea what a can of worms you're opening up by doing this? Your mama don't need all that sorrow dragged up again. And Junior's in no shape to deal with—"

"Why are y'all so afraid of the truth, Eddie? Tell me that? If Luke killed Daddy and if that's what I'm going to find out or what I'm going to remember, why is my family so opposed to me, once and for all, putting the past to rest?"

"Ain't nobody opposed to your putting the past to rest," Eddie said. "But you ain't doing that, DeDe. You're digging it up instead of laying it to rest."

Reaching out, he placed his big, bony hand on her shoulder. "I wish you wasn't having them nightmares. I'd hoped you'd never have no more problems, once you left that place your mama found out in California. I'd hoped you'd never relive that pain."

"But I am having the nightmares again. And memory flashes. I'm remembering things about the trial. And about that night. And about…about my baby."

"God almighty!" Eddie tightened his hold on her shoulder, then pulled her into his arms and hugged her. "I sure hoped you'd never have to remember anything about the baby."

She wrapped her arms around Eddie, as she'd done more than once in the past, when she'd needed parental comfort and he'd been the only one she could turn to, the only one who'd been there for her.

"It's all right." She patted his back, then eased out of his embrace. "Even though Mother told me what happened, I want to remember. You can't protect me anymore. I'm not a child. And I'm not so emotionally fragile that I can't deal with the truth. The whole truth."

"What if when you find out the truth, you have to make a choice between the truth and hurting someone you love? What will you do then?"

"Do you know the truth, Eddie? Have you known all these years and kept it to yourself?" Deanna searched his face for a sign of emotion that might reveal his thoughts, but he just stared at her with faded gray eyes.

"All I know is that what you're doing is bound to wind up hurting everyone involved, including you." Eddie placed his Stetson back on his head. "Luke McClendon will hurt you, if you give him the chance.

He's an angry son of a bitch. They say those years in prison turned him mean. He's a real loner, more than he was when he was a kid. Don't have no friends and ain't never had nothing to do with no decent woman. They say he's like a wild animal, roaming the hills and the range, staying outside many nights, out in the woods. Don't have no use for another living soul, except maybe Kizzie and her young 'uns.''

"If you'd been convicted of a murder you didn't commit and sent to prison for five years—when you were only twenty years old—what do you think it would have done to you, Eddie?" Deanna asked him, her gaze locking with his.

Eddie didn't reply; he shook his head and snorted.

"I know what it's like to be locked up for years and years, kept caged like an animal," Deanna said. "Only my cage was a lot nicer than Luke's. And while I had to fight to regain my sanity, Luke had to fight to stay alive.''

"Damn, don't you know all I'm trying to do is save you some heartache? If you give him the chance that man is gonna rip out your heart and feed it to the buzzards.''

"Maybe. Maybe not," Deanna said. "I have no power over Luke's actions, just over my own. And I'm tired of living with all these lies, tired of trying to pretend that it doesn't matter that I can't remember the most devastating night of my life or the months afterward.''

"Then do it on your own, DeDe. Don't go to Luke McClendon for help.''

"I'm sorry, Eddie, but I need Luke. And if he's willing to offer his help, then I'm going to accept.''

Deanna opened the car door, slid inside and started

the engine. As she raced out of the driveway, she glanced in her rearview mirror and saw her mother and Eddie on the front porch, both of them solemnly watching her departure.

"You want to talk about it?" Kizzie lifted the glass pot from the coffeemaker and tilted it over her mug.

"Talk about what?" Luke bit into one of Alva's buttermilk biscuits.

Kizzie poured the coffee, picked up her earthenware mug and walked over to the kitchen table. "Deanna Atchley."

"There's nothing to talk about." Luke speared a sausage link with his fork.

"She came over here to see you last night, didn't she?" Kizzie sat down across the table from Luke and placed her mug beside the breakfast plate already waiting for her.

"Yeah, she came by." Luke attacked the scrambled eggs, filling his mouth. He concentrated on eating, hoping he could avoid his stepmother's questions. Sometimes he wished he was the sort of man who could open up and cry on his mama's shoulder. But he wasn't. He didn't cry on anybody's shoulder, didn't share his feelings or his hopes and fears.

"What'd she want?" Kizzie took a sip of black coffee.

"She says she wants me to help her find out what really happened the night her father was killed," Luke said. "She claims she's having nightmares and memory flashes about that night and the weeks afterward."

"Then she knows you didn't kill Rayburn, doesn't she?"

"She says she's always known I didn't do it." Luke

shoved his plate away from him, scooted back his chair and stood.

I've always known. In my heart. He heard Deanna's words taunting him, promising him things he could never have, giving him hope, making him feel again. Hell, he was a fool if he believed her. Deanna Atchley didn't have a heart. She had proved that to him, hadn't she? When she took her family's side against his, she had shown him exactly how little he meant to her.

"Is she still claiming she doesn't remember what happened that night?" Cradling her mug in both hands, Kizzie glanced up at Luke.

"Yep. She's sticking to her story. Same one she told in court, fifteen years ago. Only now, she wants me to help her find out the truth." Luke chuckled, the sound tinged with the deep hurt that was always with him.

"Are you going to do it?"

"Told her I'd think about it."

"And have you?"

"Yeah."

He'd been able to think of little else since Deanna left last night. Tossing and turning as thoughts of her plagued him, he'd finally gotten out of bed around one this morning and taken a walk. He did that fairly often when he was restless, and he was restless a lot. People talked about him. He'd heard that they said he was like a wild animal, spending so much time alone up in the hills, sometimes riding over the whole of Montrose—all eighteen thousand acres—without going home to bathe or eat or sleep. Ever since his release from prison, he had needed to feel that he was free to roam, to go where he pleased, when he pleased.

He hadn't gone far this morning. Just ridden a few miles up into the hills, where he'd waited for dawn to break. Often, his love for Montrose and his sense of obligation to Kizzie and his stepsiblings was all that kept him sane. The land belonged to him in a way it didn't belong to the others, and just as surely, he belonged to the land.

"What are you going to do?" Kizzie asked. "About Deanna?"

"She's coming by today," he said. "If she shows up before lunchtime, tell her to wait. I'm driving into town to place some orders with Fred Swain and then I'm going to stop by Old Man Cooley's and see if he's decided to part with Hercules. I made him a damn good offer two weeks ago and haven't heard a word from him. He's about ready to sell that bull. He just needs a little prodding."

"You want me to entertain Deanna Atchley until you get home?"

"Nope. I just want her to wait. No need for you to stay with her. Put her in the living room or the den and go on about your business."

"Ah." Kizzie grinned.

"Ah, what?"

"Just ah."

"Don't go jumping to any conclusion. Just ask Deanna to wait." He should have known better than to try to fool Kizzie. She was too shrewd and knew him too well. But she was wise enough to leave it be, just as she'd always let him be whenever he needed to be alone.

"You haven't made up your mind whether or not you're going to help her, have you?"

"I've about decided."

Kizzie set down her mug, stood, and followed him

out onto the back porch. "Luke, if you decide to help her, be careful. I don't want to see you get hurt again."

He removed his black Stetson from the hook near the back door, stepped off the porch and called back over his shoulder to Kizzie. "Don't worry. Deanna Atchley doesn't mean a thing to me. If anybody gets hurt this time, it'll be her."

Luke heard Kizzie's gasp as he walked away. She'd worry about him, just like she worried about the others. Sometimes, he thought she worried about him more. His stepmother was a mother hen, not only to her own two, but to him and his half brother, Grant—Baxter McClendon's legitimate son.

Luke got into his truck and revved up the engine, listening with satisfaction to the sound of the motor running. Although he could afford the most expensive sports car or a new Jeep or the best truck money could buy, he preferred his eight-year-old GM truck. The old four-wheel drive had been well used, but never abused. He took care of his vehicle the way he took care of the ranch. With a tender loving consideration that he'd never shown any human being.

He flipped on the radio as he drove along the road. The latest Garth Brooks hit blasted, loud and throbbing, but not loud enough to drown out his thoughts. Maybe while he was in town, he should stop by and see Corrine Watkins. She had told him to stop by any time. Could be that he needed a willing woman before he went home and faced Deanna Atchley. If some other woman had satisfied him, maybe he would be able to control his response this time when he saw Deanna. Then again, maybe Deanna would pleasure him as the price for gaining his help.

Luke grinned at the thought. He liked the idea of

Deanna coming to him, offering herself in exchange for his assistance. Could be her returning home with a mission would finally free him from her—from the hatred, the need for revenge and even the fragments of desire still trapped in his body. What would she say, he wondered, if he offered to help her only if they became lovers again? If she agreed to his demand, she wouldn't be the one in charge. Not this time. He wasn't fool enough to think himself in love with her the way he had when he was twenty, or to believe she loved him. He had long since realized that a man like him wasn't meant to ever have real love. And he didn't care. Not anymore. Sex was good enough without love. Especially sex with Deanna. He wondered how many lovers she'd had in the past fifteen years. How experienced was she now? The first time he'd taken her, she'd been a virgin, and he'd been stupid enough to think her giving her innocence to him had actually meant something.

What Deanna had lacked in experience, she'd made up for in passion. What would it be like to make love with her now that her experience probably matched her passion? If he followed through with his plan, he'd find out soon enough.

"Luke's gone into town," Kizzie said as she welcomed Deanna into her home. "He asked that you wait for him. He'll be back by lunch."

"Oh. Perhaps I should come back then." Deanna hovered in the giant foyer, her nerves jittery from the thought of seeing Luke again.

"No, he said specifically for you to wait for him." Kizzie motioned toward the living room. "I can't wait with you. I've got things to do. You know a working ranch the size of Montrose doesn't run itself.''

Deanna glanced around, taking a better look at the interior of the house than she had last night. The stairs and overhanging landing had been constructed of hand-hewn logs taken from the original log home built on the property in the nineteenth century. The floors in the foyer and living room were stone and the walls had been painted a soft white. She'd never been inside the McClendon house until last night. Not once in the year she and Luke had been together had they ever set foot inside either of their families' homes. They'd sneaked around, meeting here, there, anywhere. And then, when they had become lovers, Luke had taken her to the small cabin up in the hills. A cozy hideaway for two young lovers. The happiest moments of her life had been spent in that cabin, lying naked in Luke's arms.

A searing pain pierced her heart. A memory of the last time she and Luke had been together as lovers. Remembering the pleasure and the joy was sheer agony now.

''Are you all right?'' Kizzie asked. ''You've gone pale all of a sudden.''

''Yes, I'm fine,'' Deanna said. ''Please, just show me where to wait and you can go on with whatever you need to do.''

''All right. Come on in here in the living room.''

Deanna followed Luke's stepmother into the enormous room. The outside end wall was solid stone and surrounded a large fireplace. Barn and buggy lanterns decorated the naturally aged wooden mantel, and a large deer's head hung centered on the wall. On the opposite wall, a portrait of Baxter McClendon dominated the space above the seventeenth-century Charles II oak chest.

"That's Luke's father," Kizzie said, as Deanna's gaze was drawn to a life-size portrait of the big, robust cowboy, who'd been painted in his jeans, work shirt and Stetson. "He was about the age Luke is now when I had that done."

"Mr. McClendon was a handsome man. I—I see some of Luke in him." Deanna walked the length of the room and stood in front of the portrait. "It's his eyes. Luke's eyes are that same mossy green."

"Yes, Luke has Baxter's eyes," Kizzie agreed. "And he got his size from his father, too."

"And the hint of a dimple in his chin." Deanna remembered how Luke would shudder whenever she ran the tip of her tongue up and down that shallow cleft.

"Won't you sit down, Deanna?"

Kizzie nodded to the arrangement of furniture in front of the fireplace. Two overstuffed gray leather sofas faced each other, separated by an English silver chest used as a coffee table. Deanna chose the maroon corduroy recliner that completed the U-shape and directly faced the fireplace.

Kizzie sat down on the edge of the sofa to the right. "I'm fixing to talk plain to you, girl. I wasn't sure whether to say my piece or keep my mouth shut, but... Well, I've decided to say what needs to be said."

Deanna placed her hands in her lap, then shifted her body just enough to be able to look directly at Luke's stepmother. "What do you think needs to be said, Mrs. McClendon?"

"If Luke agrees to help you, it'll mean trouble for you as well as for him." Kizzie took a quick, deep breath, relaxed her shoulders and leaned forward toward Deanna. "Luke's not the boy you remember. He's hard and cold. More even than when he first came to us when he was fifteen. He'd just started to feel like a member of our family when your daddy found out about you two. He was just beginning to trust people when you betrayed him in the worst way possible. That boy loved you beyond all reason. He was so sure you'd defend him, that you'd testify to his innocence."

"I know what I did," Deanna admitted. "I don't remember much about the trial, but Mother told me about it and so did Mr. Lamar. The honest truth is that I don't remember much of anything from the night Daddy was killed up until weeks after Luke's trial. And I haven't recalled anything in all these years, until recently. Nightmares are plaguing me several times a week now. And—and the memory flashes I'm having frighten me."

"I'd like to believe you," Kizzie said. "For Luke's sake, I hope you're telling him the truth. 'Cause, if you aren't, Luke will make you rue the day you came back to Stone Creek. My stepson wants revenge against you. Are you willing to risk his wrath in order to get his help? Just how big a price are you willing to pay to unearth the truth about who really killed your daddy?"

"You think Luke intends to punish me?"

Deanna had wondered if Luke still hated her and last night had left no doubt in her mind that he did. He wanted revenge—against her and her family—and who could blame him, after what they'd done to him? If there was a price to pay for Luke's help, she'd pay it willingly. And if she had to be the recipient of his revenge in order to discover the truth and regain her memory, then, so be it.

"I think your betrayal and those five years Luke spent in Huntsville destroyed a part of my boy that had just begun to grow, a part of him that allowed him to love and trust and feel like he was as good as anybody else."

"Hasn't there been anyone in Luke's life—anyone special?"

"I'll be blunt." Kizzie glanced toward the empty fireplace, as if she weren't quite comfortable looking directly at Deanna when she spoke. "Luke hasn't been a monk. There have been a few women, but…well, there was no relationship of any kind with these women. You understand. A man has needs. But there's no love in Luke to give anyone. He's as alone as a man can be. And that kind of loneliness does things to a person."

"Mrs. McClendon, I need to know the truth about the night Daddy died and I believe Luke is the key to unlocking that truth and restoring my memory." Deanna said.

When Kizzie stared hard at Deanna, a look of doubt in her dark eyes, Deanna shivered involuntarily. It was as if Luke's stepmother was sizing her up, trying to decide whether she was speaking the truth.

Kizzie slapped her hands on her thighs, then stood quickly. "Well, I've said more than enough. So whatever happens, remember that I warned you."

As Kizzie walked away, Deanna shot up out of the recliner. "Mrs. McClendon!"

Kizzie paused, but didn't turn around.

"I did love Luke. And I never meant to hurt him."

As she sucked in a deep breath, Kizzie's broad shoulders lifted, then stiffened. Turning slowly, she aimed her gaze squarely at Deanna's face. "You might have thought you loved him, but you were far too spoiled, too pampered to love anybody but yourself. You were a weak, foolish girl, Deanna Atchley. I just pray to God, you're wiser and stronger now.''

Deanna stood there, her mouth opened on a silent cry of denial, as Kizzie left the room, not once glancing back to check on her guest's reaction. A sick, swimming feeling hit Deanna in the pit of her stomach. She wanted to scream at Kizzie, to deny the woman's accusations, to swear fervently that she had loved Luke— loved him with all her heart. But the words died inside her, the denial as weak and foolish as she had once been.

She had been spoiled, terribly spoiled. Pampered by her parents, by her big brother, by Eddie and the servants, she had been denied nothing money could buy. She *had* been foolish and selfish and very weak. But she had loved Luke as much as her young heart had been capable of loving. Yet, when the showdown came, she hadn't had the strength to take Luke's side against her family.

She had paid a high price for that family loyalty— and she was still paying.

Luke hung his Stetson on the hat rack, came in through the back door and dusted off his feet on the daisy-print doormat. He had stalled as long as he could. It was nearly one-thirty, way past his usual lunchtime. But he hadn't wanted to come home and face Deanna.

He'd been sure she'd wait for him. He just wondered how long she'd been here and if she was fit to be tied about his tardiness. The Deanna he'd known had been impatient and restless, wanting what she wanted immediately. He had known that Deanna like the back of his hand—her personality, her heart and every inch of her sexy body. He knew she was a spoiled brat, but he'd been so wild about her that he hadn't cared. Not until it was too late.

But Luke didn't know this Deanna, the woman waiting for him. Who was she? Where had she been and what had she been doing for the past fifteen years?

Does it really matter? he asked himself. She could have turned herself into a copy of Mother Teresa and it wouldn't change the way he felt about her. And it sure as hell wouldn't change what she'd done to him.

He hoped she'd been waiting for him a long time. Hoped that she had squirmed, wondering when he'd come home—or if he'd come home. It would serve her right if he told her he had no intention of helping her in any way. But if he did that, she wouldn't be vulnerable to him. She wouldn't owe him. And what he wanted from Deanna he could get only if she felt obligated to pay the price for his cooperation. And his price was going to be steep. He wanted Deanna Atchley to come running whenever he snapped his fingers. He wanted her to know what it felt like to be used and then tossed aside.

Hell, he wanted revenge. Plain and simple. Revenge against Deanna and the whole damn Atchley family.

Alva gave him a condemning look as he entered the kitchen. "Did you wipe your feet?" she asked.

"Yes, ma'am, I did." Luke lifted one boot and then the other showing her the condition of the soles.

"Mrs. McClendon's been running in here every ten minutes asking if you had come home, yet," Alva said. "She and Miss Atchley waited until one o'clock, then they ate their lunch. I kept yours warm in the oven."

"Where is Kizzie?" Luke asked. So, his stepmother

had invited his guest for lunch. He hadn't considered the possibility that Kizzie would be that cordial to Deanna. But then Kizzie was a good woman, with a kind heart.

"She and Miss Atchley are having dessert out on the side porch." Alva wiped her fleshy hands on her big, flowered apron. "Do you want me to bring your lunch out there so you can join them?"

"Yeah, sure," Luke said. "I'll go wash up. Tell Kizzie I'm home and I'll be outside in a few minutes."

Luke gave the housekeeper a halfhearted smile, then walked out of the kitchen and down the hall to the rest room. While he washed his hands, he took a quick look at himself in the mirror. Maybe he should have shaved this morning. And maybe he should have gotten a haircut while he was in town. After all, he hadn't had any dealings with a real lady in fifteen years, and Deanna might object to his scruffy appearance. The women of his acquaintance didn't object to a two-days' growth of beard or shaggy hair or the smell of sweat. When he and Deanna had been lovers, he had jumped through hoops for her, trying to be the man she wanted. God, what a young fool he'd been.

Luke grinned at his reflection. "This time around, she'll have to take me just the way I am…and like it."

By the time he walked out onto the side porch, just off the dining room, Alva had laid a place for him at the wooden table. The minute he emerged from the house, Deanna turned and watched him, her gaze both apprehensive and curious.

"I was about to call Tyler and have him check the hospital and the jail," Kizzie said. "What took you so long?"

"I had a lot to do," Luke said, totally ignoring

Deanna, yet seeing her in his peripheral vision. Sitting down, he drew his chair up to the table and lifted his fork. "This looks delicious. I'm mighty hungry."

"Did you have any luck talking Old Man Cooley into parting with Hercules?" Kizzie asked.

Filling his mouth with roast beef and creamed potatoes, he chewed slowly, still not acknowledging Deanna's presence. "I think I'm wearing Cooley down. Today, he named a price. More than anybody in their right mind would pay, even for a prize bull like ole Hercules, but it's the first time Cooley's talked money."

"Well, you could have called to let us know how late you were going to be." Kizzie nodded toward their silent guest. "Deanna's been here since ten o'clock this morning."

He glanced in her direction then and a part of him rejoiced at the sad, solemn look on her beautiful face. And another part of him saw only that beauty. Not the delicate, unblemished beauty of a girl, but the vibrant, powerful beauty of a woman.

Luke gripped the silver fork in his hand so hard that he almost bent it. Realizing what he'd done, he laid the fork beside his plate and glared at Deanna.

"Sorry you had to wait so long," he said unconvincingly. "I didn't know whether you'd even show up today."

Deanna slid her chair back and stood. Glowering at Luke, she snorted mockingly. "You're not sorry you kept me waiting. And you knew without a doubt that I'd show up here today. I came here last night to ask for your help because I truly believe we can unearth the truth together. If you don't want to help me, I can't make you. And if you gained any pleasure out of making me sit around here for hours waiting for you, then I'm glad. But you should know this, Luke McClendon—with or without your help, I'm not leaving Stone Creek until I remember what happened the night my father was killed.''

Deanna rushed into the house, leaving Luke and Kizzie alone on the porch.

"I suppose I'd better go see her out," Luke said.

"You're going to help her, aren't you?" Kizzie let out a long sigh.

"If she's willing to pay my price." Luke stood and followed Deanna inside, not once daring to glance back at his stepmother. He knew Kizzie wasn't pleased with his decision and would have plenty to say on the subject later. But right now, he had to catch up with Deanna.

He called to her just as she was heading out the front door. "Deanna. Wait!"

She whirled around, fire in her eyes. "Why should I wait? I've been waiting for nearly four hours!"

"If you and I are going to work together, you'll have to get used to taking whatever I dish out. If I agree to help you, then I'll call the shots. Do you understand?"

Deanna stared at him, her eyes wide with a combination of fear and hope. "Are you going to help me?"

"For a price." Luke took several steps toward her, backing her against the foyer wall.

With his big body leaning into her, she looked up into Luke's cold eyes and trembled. "What's your price?"

"First, I want answers to a few questions. Then once we've got that out of the way, I'll consider helping you. I might even see if I can enlist Tyler's help. Unofficially, of course.''

"That's all you want, the answers to a few questions?"

She was trembling in apprehension. He liked that. She was afraid of him. And she had every right to be.

"No, that's not all I want," he said. "Once we start spending time together, I'll expect you to be available whenever I need you."

She stared at him questioningly, as if she wasn't quite sure of his meaning.

He grinned. "Let me rephrase that. I'll expect you to be ready, willing and able whenever I need a woman."

Deanna's cheeks flushed. Her mouth opened into a crooked oval. "You—you expect me to—to be your… You aren't talking about being lovers again, are you, Luke? You want me to be your whore!"

"Yeah, something like that." He could tell by the look in her eyes and the way she'd knotted her hands into tight little fists that she wanted to slap his face. He almost wished she would.

"You really do hate me, don't you?"

He pressed into her, crushing her breasts against his chest, pushing his arousal against her mound. Lowering his head to her ear, he whispered, "Yeah, babe. I really do hate you."

And then he took her mouth in a raw, savage kiss that stole her breath and robbed her of coherent thought. While his lips ravaged hers and his body trapped her against the wall, he didn't touch her with his hands.

He didn't dare touch her. If he did, he wasn't sure whether he would caress her or strangle her. Desire blended with anger and hatred, creating a burning rage inside him, a rage that he barely controlled as he deepened the kiss, thrusting his tongue inside her warm, wet mouth.

Although she trembled in his arms, she didn't fight him and made no protest of any kind. She allowed him to do as he wanted. And when he was on the verge of touching her, of ripping open her silk blouse and seeking her breasts, she responded to him. Her tongue slid against his, hesitantly at first, then more boldly. Luke's insides quivered and his sex hardened painfully. He wanted her. Here. Now. Up against the wall. Fast and furious.

Or better yet, on her knees, in front of him, pleasuring him the way an experienced woman could. Ending the kiss, Luke grasped her by the back of her neck and pulled her away from him.

"Now's not the time and this isn't the place for what I want," he said. "You think over my proposition and let me know what you decide. If you want to make a deal for my help, then meet me tonight at the Stone Creek Motel. Nine o'clock."

For a split second, when he saw the stricken look on her face, he regretted being so ruthless with her. But then he remembered just who this woman was and what she'd done to him.

He stepped back from her and allowed her space to maneuver. When she straightened her hair, smoothed out the wrinkles in her blouse and then wiped her mouth with the back of her hand, Luke waited.

She turned, opened the door and walked outside. He followed her, pausing in the doorway. "I'll be waiting for you tonight."

She didn't respond, didn't look back at him as she ran to her car, got inside and drove away. A trail of dust rose in the air behind the little white Mustang as it rounded a bend in the road and disappeared.

Luke watched her go, thinking that now he'd either get what he wanted from Deanna Atchley or he'd never have to see her again.

Chapter 4

Luke had never before brought a woman to the Stone Creek Motel. The place was too public to suit his usual need for privacy. The small, neat motel was situated right on the main street that ran through the town. The single-story units, laid out in a U-shape, were used mainly by out-of-town visitors. But the Stone Creek Motel was perfect for his tryst with Deanna. Anyone passing by—going in or out of town—would see Luke's old truck and Deanna Atchley's white Mustang. By morning, the whole county would know the two had spent the night together. The Atchleys would be outraged and Deanna would be disgraced. And that's exactly what he wanted. He wanted Deanna and her family to get a little taste the hurt and humiliation the McClendons had gone through fifteen years ago. His very soul cried out for revenge.

Tonight Deanna would make the down payment on her debt to him. He figured that by the time she ad-

mitted that she'd always known who really killed Rayburn Atchley, he'd be able to mark Deanna's account
"paid in full." By then, he'd be finished with her. He
could close the door on the past forever!

Luke checked his watch. Eight-fifty. He wasn't going to keep her waiting for this meeting. As much as
he had dreaded seeing her today, he looked forward
just as much to having her come to him tonight.

He supposed there was a possibility she wouldn't
show up, but his gut instincts told him that Deanna
would do whatever he asked of her, if she really wanted
his help that desperately. If she didn't show up, he'd
know the whole thing had been a ruse, her plea for
help just another of her lies. But if she put in an appearance, as he felt she would, then he'd have reason
to believe her. And although discovering the identity
of Rayburn Atchley's real killer after all these years
wouldn't change the past, it would clear his name. His
family's name. McClendon. A name that had been hon-
ored in Texas for generations. A name that his manslaughter conviction had tarnished.

Luke opened and closed the door, making sure he'd
left it unlocked. When she knocked on the door, he'd
wouldn't walk over and open it for her. He'd just call
out for her to come in. And he'd be there, sprawled
out across the bed, waiting.

He'd been thinking about it all afternoon and evening. About how she'd look and what she'd say. And
what he'd make her do. She'd protest at first, but if
this Deanna was anything like the wild girl who'd been
his lover, then she'd warm up lightning quick. The very
thought of what years of experience had surely taught
her made Luke's body tighten with anticipation and his

sex harden with desire. He'd been aroused since he'd walked into room 12.

He unbuttoned his shirt, took it off and tossed it on the brown tweed chair in the corner, then he unbuckled his belt, removed it and laid it on top of his shirt. Sitting down on the edge of the bed, he inspected the room. Typical small-town motel. A king-size bed, flanked by nightstands that held two large, ugly lamps. A nineteen-inch TV sat in the middle of a cheap wooden dresser.

After removing his boots and socks, he strolled into the bathroom and checked out the shower stall. It was big enough for two.

Unwanted memories rushed in on him, forcing him to recall another time when he and Deanna had bathed together. In the cabin. After the first time they'd made love. He had lifted her in his arms and carried her into the bathroom. She hadn't been the least bit self-conscious about her nudity and he'd loved that about her—her lack of shyness or false modesty. They had made love again, standing in the old claw-foot tub, while the rickety showerhead attached to the wall spewed lukewarm water over their hot, sweaty bodies.

Love mixed with hate and created a boiling anger inside him. He couldn't let the sweet memories—moments of love that had turned out to be false—affect his actions tonight. Luke slammed his fist against the tiled bathroom wall.

Damn her! Damn her for making him care about her! Damn her for making promises she'd never intended to keep. And damn her most of all for betraying him!

He had given up hope of ever getting the chance to pay her back for what she'd done to him, what her family had done to his. But she had returned to Stone

Creek and come straight to him. And tonight she would offer herself up—a sacrifice to his needs, a pleasurable retribution for her many sins against him.

Deanna stood outside room 12, asking herself what she was doing there. But she knew. She was here because of Luke McClendon. Because he had named his price—her dignity and her pride—and she was willing to pay it. She was willing to sacrifice anything to learn the truth and to finally set things right. She had betrayed not only Luke with her weakness, with her inability to stand up against her family, but she had betrayed herself. She had allowed her mother to coerce her into doing something she knew was wrong—taking the stand against Luke. Even though what she'd said under oath had been the truth, as far as the truth went, her testimony had been crucial in Luke's conviction.

She couldn't blame him for hating her, couldn't fault him for not being able to forgive her. God knew, there had been years that she had hated herself. The first four years she'd spent at Millones. And even now, although she had forgiven herself, she could never forget the damage she'd caused. Irrevocable damage to the man she had loved. And despite what Luke believed, she *had* loved him. Loved him with the same mindless passion with which he'd loved her.

Deanna's hand trembled as she lifted it to knock on the door. She knocked once, twice. No response. Luke was in there. His truck was parked right in front of the room and the clerk, who had inspected her thoroughly from head to toe, had told her Mr. McClendon had checked into room 12. The clerk hadn't smirked or made any unmannerly comments, but she'd recognized that look in his eyes. The censuring appraisal that had made her feel cheap and ashamed. The way he'd surveyed her body had spoken volumes, each silent word calling her a tramp.

And maybe that's just what she was. A tramp. A whore. Selling herself to Luke. Dear Lord, she hated him for doing this to her. Always with Luke the loving had been beautiful and true and right. Oh, so right! But he had made it perfectly clear that he wasn't the same boy who'd taken her to heaven with his wild, abandoned lovemaking. He no longer loved her, no longer worshiped at her feet.

With her stomach tied in knots and her heartbeat racing rapidly, Deanna knocked again. Louder. More forcefully.

"Yeah, come on in. The door's unlocked," Luke said.

Deanna sucked in a deep breath. He isn't even going to come to the door! she thought. She let out the breath and sighed. If she had any sense at all, she'd run like hell. If she opened that door and walked into room 12, there would be no turning back. Not for her. And not for Luke. But she needed him. Her heart and her instincts told her that he was the key to regaining her memory.

And Luke needed her. He didn't realize how much he needed her and would probably deny it vehemently. But she knew, even if he didn't, that without forgiving her for what she'd done to him, Luke could never heal. And that was the real reason she was here tonight, standing outside a motel room, garnering the courage to go inside and play Luke's game.

Deanna turned the doorknob hesitantly, and let the door swing slowly open, well aware that what awaited her might be damnation. Her own and Luke's. She

stood just outside the room and looked in. Luke was
resting on the bed, barefooted and bare-chested, with
his back braced against the headboard. The very sight
of him took her breath away. She had loved a boy of
twenty, who had made love to her with a wild gentle
passion. But this was a man. Hard as steel. Big and
broad and powerfully rugged. And blatantly aroused.
The look in his smoldering green eyes held no gentleness, only hot, ruthless lust.

"Come on in." He stretched his muscular arms over
his head, expanding the width of his broad chest.

Deanna stepped over the threshold and closed the
door, then turned to face him. He stared at her lazily,
running his gaze down the length of her body, from
neck to ankles and back up, lingering at her breasts.

"Lock the door," he told her.

She obeyed his command.

He glanced over at the digital bedside clock. "It's
five after nine. You're late."

"I knocked on the door at precisely nine o'clock,"
she said. "But you didn't answer."

His wicked grin wreaked havoc on her nerves. Did
he have any idea what just the sight of him did to her?
No, of course not. He had no idea how she really felt
about him. And she didn't dare let him know. If she
did, he was sure to use her own feelings against her.
And Luke already had an arsenal of weapons at his
disposal. The knowledge that she still cared deeply for
him would be the deadliest weapon of all.

"I wasn't sure you'd show up." He placed his
cupped hands together behind his head.

"You're lying," she said. "You knew I'd come to
you, just as you asked me to do."

"You really are desperate for me to believe that you

want to find out what happened the night your father was killed, aren't you?''

"Desperate enough to do whatever you ask because my gut instincts tell me that you're the one person who can help me.'' She laid her purse on the chest to the right of the door.

Luke swung his legs off the side of the bed and placed his big, rough hands down on his knees. "Why now, Deanna? Why not five years ago or ten years ago? Why after all this time is finding out the truth so damn important to you?''

She held her head high and looked him right in the eye. "The truth has always been important to me. It's just that I couldn't—''

"Not always. It wasn't very important to you fifteen years ago.'' Luke rose from the edge of the bed. His eyes bored into Deanna as he walked toward her.

"That's not true. I told the truth.'' Deanna instinctively backed away from him. "I didn't lie on the stand at your trial. I've read the transcripts and what I said was all that I remembered at the time. I swear to you, Luke, I don't remember what happened after you picked up that pitchfork and walked toward Daddy.''

Stopping dead still, Luke grinned, but the look in his eyes was cold and menacing. "Why the hell should I believe you?''

"I can't make you believe me any more than I can make you stop hating me. You'll believe whatever you want to, but if you give yourself a chance to get to know me—the woman I am now—you just might learn to trust me again and believe what I tell you.''

Luke laughed, the sound deep and dark and sinister. He spanned the distance between them, laughing harder when Deanna backed up against the door. Never in the past had she been afraid of him, but now she was—very afraid. Not that he would physically harm her, but that the hatred smoldering inside of him would unleash his desire for revenge and he would rip her to shreds emotionally.

"I don't want to get to know you again, except in the biblical sense." Spreading his hands out against the door, on each side of her head, he leaned toward her. "And you still haven't answered my question. Why all of a sudden do you have this great need to find out the truth?"

He was too close, his big body almost touching her. His chest only inches from her breasts. His lips a hairsbreadth from hers. She couldn't think straight with him hovering over her, ready to devour her.

"I—I told you that the nightmares and memory flashes I had after the trial have come back. And they're stronger than they were before." She locked gazes with him and willed herself not to be the first one to break the contact. "I've tried to put the past behind me and build a new life, but...I couldn't return to Stone Creek, knowing that it was partly my fault that you'd been sent to prison and that—"

"Partly your fault?" Luke lowered his head enough so that their breaths mingled when he spoke. "You were the only eyewitness. The only person who could testify that I picked up that pitchfork."

"I'm sorry. I'm so very sorry." She had wanted to say that to him for fifteen years. If she thought it would do any good, she'd get down on her knees and beg him to forgive her. But she could tell by the hard look in his eyes that nothing she said would change the way he felt.

"Not as sorry as you're going to be." He whispered the threat into her ear, then nipped her earlobe.

She gasped, more from the shock of his unexpected bite than from his warning. "I can't change the past. But if you'll help me, maybe I can clear your name and..." She started to say *earn your forgiveness,* but decided that it was too soon to hope for a miracle.

"You fulfill your part of our bargain, and I'll fulfill mine." He licked a moist line from her earlobe, down her neck and over to the top of her chest, exposed by the V neckline of her silk blouse.

Deanna shuddered as warm, sensual sensations invaded her feminine core and spread slowly through her body. If only Luke were touching her because he loved her and desired her, not out of lust and a vengeful need to humiliate her.

"As long as you make yourself available whenever I want you, then I'll work with you and give you all the help I can."

He kissed her, his mouth hard and hot and brutal. She tried not to respond, not to accept his ravaging, but her body betrayed her, giving in to Luke's plundering insistence. It had been such a long time since she'd felt the stirring of desire, since she'd truly felt like a woman. Not in fifteen years. Not since the last time Luke had kissed her.

With a will of their own, her arms lifted to his shoulders, then draped themselves around his neck. Prompted by her actions, he plunged his tongue inside her mouth, then lowered his hands from the door and eased them down her shoulders and over her arms. When she pressed herself against him, he growled, deep in his throat, and cupped her hips in his hands, bringing her mound up against his throbbing sex. She

clung to him as her mind warned her that she was playing a deadly game. But her body wasn't listening. She
had denied herself any physical relationships, putting
all her energies into recuperating from her mental
breakdown. She had dated several different men over
the past ten years, but she had been too uncertain of
herself to risk having a meaningful relationship with
anyone.

And here she was jumping headlong into a fiery cou-
pling that was based only on lust and revenge and desperate need. Could she really go through with this—
give herself to Luke, knowing the reason he wanted
her?

Sliding her hands over his shoulders and down his
chest, she tried to push him away and gain some sem-
blance of reason. Growling, Luke held her hips tightly,
welding their lower bodies together.

"You—you said that before we..." Deanna gasped
for air as Luke rubbed himself against her. "You said
that first you wanted me to answer some questions.
What—what questions?"

"The questions can wait until later." Holding her in
place with one hand, he reached between them and
ripped her blouse apart. Tiny pearl buttons popped off
and fell to the floor, bouncing softly on the worn tan
carpet.

Deanna gasped. "Luke, please..."

"Please what?" he asked. "Please stop or please
don't stop?"

"It shouldn't be like this," she told him. "Don't you
remember how it used to be? What it was like for us?
Please, don't destroy those beautiful memories by—"

He grabbed her shoulders and shook her. "Beautiful
memories! I don't have any beautiful memories. Just

memories of a girl who used me, lied to me and betrayed me.''

She reached out for him, her hand trembling as it hovered near his face. ''No, don't say that. I didn't use you and I never lied to you. Never!''

''But you can't deny that you betrayed me, can you?''

''No,'' she replied, her voice a throaty whisper. ''I can't.''

Tightening his hold on her shoulders, his fingers biting into her flesh through the silky material of her blouse, Luke glared at her. ''Either you're willing to do this or you aren't. It's your decision. You're free to walk out that door anytime you want to.''

''If I leave, we won't have a bargain will we? You won't help me?''

''That's right. I won't. This is your decision to make. But make it right now.''

The sane, sensible part of her told her to leave, but her heart and her body told her to stay. Whatever happened, however degrading and painful it was having Luke take her this way, she wasn't willing to risk losing the last chance for redemption. Her own and Luke's.

''I'm staying.''

He released her immediately, then backed away from her. ''Take off your blouse and slacks and let me look at you.''

He wasn't going to make this easy for her. No, he would want his pound of flesh. She always had known Luke had an angry, wild side to him, but with her that wild anger had always been tempered with gentleness and love. Tonight there was only the anger and the wildness. And the lust he could not disguise.

Luke turned on the radio, switching stations until he found a country and rock 'n' roll station. The tune was something from the sixties, with an upbeat rhythm and the thundering beat of drums. He dragged the chair out of the corner, placed it at the foot of the bed and sat down, waiting for Deanna's performance.

When he'd turned his back to her briefly, she had caught a glimpse of the faded scars that striped his back—scars left by her father's whip. She desperately wanted to rush over and touch those scars, to caress that marred flesh, to place her lips on the healed wounds. But Luke would not want her pity. Now even less than he had wanted it fifteen years ago.

Deanna took a deep, steadying breath and slipped her ripped blouse from her shoulders, then slowly eased it down her arms and off. Quivering, she dropped the red silk to the floor. She wouldn't—couldn't—look at Luke.

While the music added background to Deanna's pathetic striptease, Luke crossed his arms over his chest and reared back in the chair. She unbuttoned and unzipped her slacks. Hooking her thumbs inside the waistband, she eased the white cotton pants over her hips and let them fall to her ankles. After kicking the slacks and white sandals aside, she lifted her head and tossed her hair over her shoulders and onto her back.

Luke let out a long, low whistle and then applauded. Deanna shivered. Humiliation rose inside her, mingling with sorrow and anger. The emotions lodged in her throat as tears gathered in the corners of her eyes. Dammit, she would not cry. She had cried for years. There weren't many tears left in her. And she sure as hell wasn't going to waste them feeling sorry for herself.

"Come here," he said, motioning to her with his index finger.

Deanna moved toward him, hesitantly, but with her chin lifted and her eyes focused directly on his face. When she was within a foot of where he sat, she paused.

"Is this where you want me?" she asked.

He rose from the chair. She looked up at him. He placed his hands on her shoulders and pressed down, urging her to her knees. She knelt before him, the top of her head reaching his waist and her mouth only inches from his zipper.

"Take off my jeans for me," he told her.

Her hand shook so badly that she couldn't take hold of the zipper tab. Luke grabbed her hand, steadying it, then pinched her fingers over the zipper tab and helped her ease it all the way down. His sex bulged inside his cotton briefs.

Deanna pulled his jeans off his hips and down his legs. He lifted one foot and then the other, assisting her. She tossed the jeans to one side, then started to rise from the floor. Luke cupped the top of her head, shoving her back down to her knees.

"Now the briefs."

"Luke, I—" She gazed up into his face and knew then that there would be no pardon for her sins. Not tonight. He would show her no mercy.

While she tried to control the trembling in her hands, she also tried to quiet the roar of her raging hormones that were overriding any common sense she had left. She removed his briefs, then closed her eyes to blot out the sight of his magnificent naked body. He always had been beautiful, but now that he was a mature man, he was more than beautiful. He was gloriously, breath-takingly male. Big, hard, powerful. And fully aroused.

Luke took her face in his hands. "Open your eyes, Deanna."

She obeyed, but instead of feasting her eyes on his sex, she looked away at the wall. Luke took her face in his hands, forcing her to confront his masculinity.

"You know what I want." He pressed her forward until her mouth touched him intimately.

"Luke, I—I can't. I've never… We never—"

"No, babe, we never did get around to this, did we? You were too young and skittish back then. But you're not a girl anymore, you're an experienced woman. I'm sure you've used your mouth to give more than one man pleasure."

"I haven't. Not ever."

She could tell by the look on his face that he didn't believe her. If he didn't believe her about this, there was no way he'd ever believe that there hadn't been another man in her life—only him. He had been her one and only lover.

"Well, if that's so, then it's time you learned."

Luke showed her no pity as he taught her how to pleasure him. She found herself aroused by what she was doing to him, by the deep, rugged moans he made as her lips and tongue tantalized every inch of him. Her breasts throbbed and peaked. Her feminine core moistened as it clenched and unclenched in preparation.

Just as he was on the verge of climaxing, Luke eased her head away and dragged her to her feet. Deanna was breathless, her heart thumping wildly. She stared at him for one split second and knew he had lost control and was beyond reason.

"Take off your bra and panties! Now!"

She hurried to obey his command, her fingers fumbling at the task. When he grew impatient with her lack of speed, he unsnapped her bra and tossed it across the room, then jerked her panties down and off, throwing them to the floor.

Luke flung Deanna down across the bed on her stomach, with her feet dangling off the side. Before she could turn over, he came up behind her and lifted her onto her knees. She heard a ripping sound and knew he was removing a condom from its wrapper. She closed her eyes and waited. He lowered himself onto her, taking her from behind, thrusting into her to the hilt. She cried out from the unexpected pleasure and the sharp stab of pain. He rode her hard, pumping into her as he sought and found his release.

As fulfillment claimed him, his body pulsing with release, he moaned deeply. Deanna waited still and unmoving, throbbing with need, knowing that Luke had no intention of satisfying her. This had been sex for him, not lovemaking. When he rose from the bed and walked into the bathroom, she turned over and grasped the edge of the quilted spread. Pulling it up around her, to cover her nakedness, she cried inside, tears of pain and shame. But the silent, internal tears were not only for herself, but for Luke. Was there nothing left of the kind, considerate lover he'd once been? Had she done this to him—turned him into an insensitive, uncaring brute?

She eased over to the edge of the bed, stood and walked across the room, dragging the spread behind her. She found her panties and slipped into them, then searched for her other clothes. She put on her bra and drew her slacks up her legs and over her hips. But she couldn't find her blouse. It had to be here somewhere.

Luke emerged from the bathroom, freshly washed and totally naked. Completely unselfconscious, he gathered up his clothes and dressed, ignoring Deanna. After he pulled on his boots, he headed for the door, then paused momentarily.

"I'm going out for a bit," he said. "You wait here. I'll be back."

"But I thought—"

"Don't think. Just wait for me. I'm not through with you yet."

With that said, he opened the door and left, leaving the door partially open behind him. Deanna scurried across the room and slammed the door shut. Damn him!

He wasn't through with her yet? His words rang in her ears, a mocking litany that degraded her almost as much as what he'd done to her. She had thought she could take whatever Luke dished out, but she was having second thoughts. She'd had no idea he could be so cruel, so heartless. There hadn't been a flicker of remorse in his eyes when he'd looked at her just before he left. And he expected her to wait around for more of the same?

She found her blouse at the edge of the dresser. Lifting it in her hand, she inspected it and found only one button remained attached. The others were scattered on the floor, and two of the buttonholes had been ripped through to the edge. Luke had been ruthless with her blouse and even more ruthless with her. But he hadn't hurt her physically, only emotionally. And Deanna knew, better than most, the damage emotional cruelty could do.

She put on her blouse, drew it together under her breasts and tied the ends into a knot, then she picked up her purse and started to open the door. Luke didn't want to help her. He'd never had any intention of working with her to unearth the truth. He had planned this all along—scaring her off with his cruelty. He'd known the old Deanna would turn tail and run. She wouldn't stick around and see their evil bargain through to the end. No, the old Deanna had been soft and weak and fragile.

Her hand hovered over the doorknob. She grasped it, then released it quickly as if it were burning hot. If she left now, Luke's plan would have worked and she would have lost everything. Her pride. Her hopes. Her chance to set things right at long last.

Deanna released the doorknob. She wasn't the old Deanna. She was stronger, braver and determined to win this fight. There was little chance that Luke would ever love her again, but if she could redeem herself and clear his name, he might forgive her. His forgiveness would have to be enough. His love was more than she dared hope for—now or ever. He had just shown her the depth of his hatred for her. And yet... No, she didn't dare think about the longing she thought she'd seen in his eyes, a look he had quickly concealed. But that longing had been so powerful that it equaled the longing in her own heart.

Deanna turned off the radio, then lay across the bed, cradling her head on a folded pillow. If only she could cry. If only she could rant and rave against heaven for allowing her life to become a wasteland of regrets. But all she could do was wait. Wait for Luke. And think about what it had once been like for the two of them. Even if Luke never could love her again, maybe he would learn to like her and respect her enough to allow their moments together to be lovemaking and not sex.

He'd said he expected her to be available whenever he wanted her. That could mean weeks, even months of being Luke's lover. Surely, sooner or later, he would realize that she wasn't the same girl who had betrayed him. If Luke gave her a second chance, she wouldn't disappoint him.

There alone in the motel room, with the air-conditioning humming and the traffic rumbling by outside, Deanna swore that this time she would find the courage to stand by Luke—no matter what.

Luke tossed the cold six-pack in the front seat of his truck, slid behind the wheel and started the engine. He sat there for a few minutes, allowing the motor to idle. The neon sign that read Yancey's Quick Stop flickered on and off and somewhere in the distance a dog howled. He hadn't known why he'd run out on Deanna, he only knew he had to escape that room—fast. Once he'd pulled into Yancey's he realized a drink was what he needed. Maybe a few cold beers would dull his senses and help him forget what he'd done to Deanna.

He had told her to wait at the motel for him, but he knew when he got back, she'd be gone. Even when he'd been taking her, with little consideration for her feelings and none for her needs, he had been torn between the intense pleasure of sex and self-hatred for taking all his anger and pain out on Deanna. For fifteen years, he had wished that he could wreak vengeance on her, make her know the agony, the humiliation, the pain he had suffered when she had betrayed him with her testimony and had sent him straight to Huntsville. Despite the way he felt about her family, his hatred of them hadn't equaled his hatred of her. He had focused all the anger on Deanna because she had been the one he'd loved, the one he'd trusted, the one who had promised to love him forever, "and then some."

Luke exited the parking lot. No need to return to the motel, he decided. Deanna would be long gone and he'd probably never see her again. A nagging ache began in the pit of his belly and the thought that tonight might have been the last time he'd ever see her flashed through his mind.

Damn! What difference did it make? He didn't want her in his life—now or ever. So what if his last memory of her was of her humiliation at his hands. Wasn't that what he wanted, what he'd longed for all these years?

Luke drove past the motel, then slammed on his brakes. Deanna's white Mustang was still parked in front of room 12. She hadn't left! He pulled his truck off the side of the road, turned around and headed back to the motel. He parked his truck beside her car, then got out and walked over to the door. Balancing the six-pack in one hand, he fumbled in his jeans for the key. He unlocked the door and eased it open. The room was dark except for the light shining in from the bathroom. Fully dressed, Deanna lay sideways across the bed.

"Deanna?" he said her name softly as he entered the room.

She didn't respond. He walked quietly across the room, stopping beside the bed. Leaning over, he realized she'd fallen asleep. As he studied her, he noticed that even though she was no longer a girl, she was still slender. But her body had ripened into a woman's. Full-breasted, long-legged and with a waist tiny enough for him to span with both hands, she was as beautiful, if not more beautiful, than she'd been at seventeen.

And she hadn't cut that mane of honey-brown hair. It lay across her back and fell over on her shoulder. He had always loved her hair. Loved touching it. Loved running his fingers through it. Loved the way it had fallen on his chest when she'd sat astride him when they'd made love.

Luke reached out and lifted a strand of her hair. Leaning over her, he brought the silky tendril to his nose and smelled the sweet scent of Deanna.

What the hell was she still doing here? When he'd told her to wait, he hadn't thought she'd actually stay. He'd been so sure that he'd run her off, that he'd scared her away. God in heaven, was it possible that she'd been telling him the truth? Did she really not remember what had happened the night her father died? Was she really having memory flashes? Did she truly want to find her father's killer?

He had dozens of questions to ask her, but none half as important as the one unknown that had plagued him all these years. What had she done with his child? But even if she gave him an answer, could he believe her? Was he fool enough to ever trust this woman again?

Luke sat down on the side of the bed and placed his hand on her hip. She squirmed, nuzzling her body closer, her breasts brushing the side of his thigh. His sex twitched with awareness. He wanted her again. Now. But sex could wait. First he wanted the answer to his question.

He could wake her, but decided not to. Instead he eased her body around in the bed and crawled in beside her, pulling her up against him. Snuggling closer, she threw her arm across his chest and rested her head on his shoulder. Luke cursed under his breath.

He'd let her get a little rest before he roused her.

When she woke, the first thing he'd do was ask her about his baby, and then, if she still wanted to go through with their bargain, he would help her. He'd do just about anything that might restore her memory so that she could clear his name. And in return, she would come to him, here at the motel, whenever he wanted her. And heaven help him, he knew that would be every damn night!

Chapter 5

Deanna awoke with a start, uncertain where she was. The room was semidark and the bed unfamiliar. Suddenly she realized that she wasn't alone—there was a man beside her. Luke.

She was lying in his arms and he was sound asleep. When had he returned to the motel and why hadn't he wakened her? All she remembered was resting on the bed. She'd had no intention of falling asleep.

Deanna eased out of Luke's arms and scooted to the edge of the bed, then got up and went to the bathroom. She caught a glimpse of herself in the mirror and cringed. Her hair was a mess, her makeup faded and her clothes terribly wrinkled. She used the bathroom, washed her hands and went back into the bedroom.

"What time is it?" Luke asked.

Deanna gasped, not realizing that he had awakened, then glanced over at the bed. His head still rested on the pillow, but his eyes were wide open.

She looked at the digital clock. "Four-ten," she said. "It seems we've slept most of the night."

"Yeah, it seems we have." He sat up, turned sideways and rested on the side of the bed. "I sure could use a cup of coffee." He glanced up at Deanna, who stood just outside the bathroom door. "We need to talk. Come on over and sit down." He patted a spot on the bed at his side.

Deanna forced herself to move, to accept his invitation. She sat beside him, but put a good three feet between them. "All right. Let's talk." She folded her hands, placed them in her lap and gazed at the miniblinds covering the one large window in the room.

"I'll do what I can to help you find out the truth about your father's murder," Luke said. "But after all these years, it won't be easy to uncover any new information. If we'd done this years ago—"

"We couldn't! Or rather, I couldn't. But looking back isn't going to help us now. We'll have to deal with the situation as it is today. I truly believe that spending time with you, our working together, will help me remember the past."

"And even after last night, you're willing to continue meeting me here at the motel whenever I want you? That's your part of our bargain."

What did he want her to say, she wondered? Did he want her to acknowledge her humiliation at his hands? Did he want her to admit that despite the degrading way he had treated her, she understood why he'd done it and that she was willing to take more of the same?

But that was the problem—she wasn't willing. Perhaps she had owed him that one act of revenge, but once was enough.

"I'm willing to have sex with you, Luke," Deanna

said, her gaze still riveted to the miniblinds. "But I won't ever let you use me again the way you did last night."

Luke shot up off the bed. Standing with his back to Deanna, he tensed, his broad shoulders rigid and his head thrust high. "If you're expecting me to apologize for what I did—"

"I'm not." She wanted an apology, wished with all her heart that he was capable of giving her one, but she didn't expect one. Not now. Maybe never. "I'd prefer to forget that last night ever happened."

He spun around, his eyes flashing with anger as he glared at her. "You always prefer to forget unpleasant things, don't you, Deanna? Is that how you still deal with life—just forget the bad stuff ever happened?"

She jerked her head up and stared at him, anger rising within her. "No, that's not how I deal with my problems." She spoke slowly, enunciating every word carefully, as she tried to stem the desire to slap Luke's face. "If it was, I wouldn't have come back to Stone Creek. I wouldn't have come to you begging for your help, if I didn't want to remember. You chose to twist my words to suit your own meaning."

"It's not going to be easy spending time together," he said, the glint in his eyes dimming as the anger subsided. "If you don't think you can deal with the way I feel about you, then there's no point in our proceeding. We can call it quits now."

Deanna tilted her chin upward, took a deep breath and stood. "It seems I have no choice but to accept whatever you dish out, but know this, Luke Mc-Clendon, I give as good as I get. The question isn't can I deal with your hatred, but can you deal with the truth about me...about us...about our past?"

"I already know the truth! I've lived with it for fifteen years." He reached out and grabbed her, pulling her roughly up against him. "But I want to hear you say it. I want you to tell me what you did with my child!"

Deanna trembled, every muscle in her body shook, every nerve quivered. *My child.* Oh, God, didn't he know what had happened? "You don't know?" she asked.

"I know what your mother told my father." Luke searched Deanna's eyes for the truth. What he saw was a fine mist of tears—tears that she was obviously trying to control.

"What did she tell him?" Deanna's voice quavered.

"She wouldn't tell him anything at first," Luke said. "Not until he threatened to hire a private investigator to find you and the child. My father knew how concerned I was about the baby."

Not about me, Deanna thought. He hadn't cared what happened to me, whether I lived or died. But he'd been concerned about our child. A lone tear escaped from her right eye and trickled down her cheek.

Luke stared at the teardrop as it descended her face and neck. Tightening his hold on her shoulders, he fought the urge to wipe away that tear.

"Your mother took great delight in telling my father that you had aborted my baby."

Deanna gasped. Dear God, no! Surely her mother hadn't been that cruel. But Deanna knew Phyllis's penchant for annihilating her enemies. And she had seen Luke as the deadliest enemy of all.

Deanna tried to lift her hand, but Luke's tight grip on her shoulders immobilized her arms. She saw the pain on his face and could imagine the agony in his heart—an agony that he had suffered all these years, not knowing the truth about their child.

When she didn't speak, just stared at him, tears gathering in her eyes, he shook her soundly. "Dammit, tell me! Did you abort my baby? Or did you give him up for adoption? I need to know! I have to know…" His voice trailed off to a choked whisper.

"I didn't have an abortion, but—but Mother threatened me with the possibility that she would have the doctor get rid of…she said that if I didn't testify at the trial, if I didn't—" With her lungs aching, Deanna gasped for air.

Luke grabbed Deanna's face in both hands. She swayed against him. "Are you saying that Phyllis forced you to—"

"No! She only threatened. I would have done anything to protect our baby. And I never would have given him away. But I couldn't save him. Oh, Luke, I wanted your baby more than anything on earth, but I lost him."

"What do you mean you lost him?"

"I had a miscarriage a few weeks after your trial." She looked pleadingly into his eyes, wanting and needing his understanding. "I don't remember very much about it, but I checked the records and spoke to the doctor and nurses. I went into premature labor and miscarried when I wasn't quite five months pregnant. The baby—our baby—was a boy."

Tears racked Deanna's body. They overflowed her eyes and covered her face. They clogged her throat and threatened her breathing. They ran over Luke's big hands as he held her face.

Luke's jaw clenched. A vein in his neck pulsed. His child had been a boy. His son. And he had died before he'd had a chance to live. Agony greater than any Luke had known gutted him, leaving him open and bleeding inside. And when he stared into Deanna's misty blue eyes, he saw the same agony, the same internal anguish.

I wanted your baby more than anything on earth, but I lost him. All these years he had desperately needed to believe that Phyllis Atchley had lied to his father—that Deanna hadn't aborted their child—but a part of him had believed the lie. And it *had* been a lie. He knew that, at least about this one thing, Deanna was telling him the truth. She had wanted his child and she still mourned their baby's loss.

"Why did you want my child?" The words were a tortured plea, ripped from Luke's soul.

Gulping for air, Deanna cried out. Luke jerked her into his embrace. She wrapped her arms around him and held on for dear life. His big hands rested tensely on her shoulders, as he struggled against the need to comfort her. Yet his pride forced him to remain unmoving while Deanna sobbed.

"You honestly don't know?" She spoke so faintly, inaudibly. "I wanted your baby because I loved you."

Her heartfelt confession hit Luke square in the gut, like the blow of a sledgehammer. Damn her for saying she had loved him! For fifteen years he'd been convinced that she'd lied to him about her feelings. Damn her now, for giving him hope that what they'd had was real!

He couldn't allow her sorrow or her declaration of past love to confuse the issue. Maybe she hadn't aborted his child or given the child up for adoption, but that didn't change the fact that her testimony had sent him to prison for five years—five years in hell!

Mother threatened me with the possibility that she would have the doctor get rid... She said if I didn't testify at the trial...

He could hear those words ringing inside his head, over and over again, like a wicked litany. Don't believe her. She could be lying. She would tell you anything in order to gain your help. She betrayed you once; she'll do it again, if you let her.

God, how he wanted to believe her. How he wanted to comfort and caress her, to lift her into his arms and carry her over to the bed and make slow, sweet love to her—to ease their mutual suffering. He could feel her pain inside him, mingling with his, intensifying the agony and yet at the same time diminishing it because it was shared.

He wanted to tell her how sorry he was that she had lost their child, but he couldn't speak, couldn't respond to her needs. He wanted to, but he couldn't. He didn't dare show her any weakness. She was the only person on earth to whom he'd ever surrendered himself, opening up and becoming vulnerable. She had nearly destroyed him once, but never again. Deanna was responsible in part for the hard man he had become, so she would have to deal with that man.

Luke released her and stepped back, putting some distance between them. Deanna stumbled without Luke's support, but quickly caught herself and stood straight, trembling, her gaze locking with his as they stared at each other.

For one split second Deanna had thought Luke was going to comfort her, that he was going to share his grief with her and allow her to share hers with him. Then he had slammed that door shut before she could get a toehold. But he believed her about the baby. At least he'd given her that much. That was all he would give her. His actions made that abundantly clear.

She knew that Luke thought nothing had changed between them just now, that he had successfully guarded himself from any feelings he still had for her. But she knew better. In that one infinitesimal moment in time, he had given her hope. The very fact that he believed her about her miscarriage told her that Luke's mind and heart weren't completely closed to the truth.

Deanna wiped her eyes with her fingertips, all the while watching Luke, waiting for him to say or do something. The next move would have to be his.

"It'll be daylight soon," he said. "We might as well head for home."

Deanna nodded agreement as she continued staring at him. He grasped her arm and pulled her toward the door. After grabbing her purse, she followed without protest. Outside pink dawn eased upward into the dark gray sky. The motel sign flashed on and off. A train whistle sounded from miles away, a lonely, forlorn moan. The highway that went straight through Stone Creek was deserted, not a single vehicle in sight.

Luke walked Deanna to her car. She fumbled in her purse for her keys, then snatched them up in her hand and tried to unlock the Mustang. Her fingers trembled. Luke covered her hand with his, steadying her, then inserted the key in the lock and opened the door.

He shifted back and forth from one foot to another, like a pawing bull raking his hooves into the earth. "I've got a ranch to run, so I won't have much time to help you play detective."

"I'll take whatever time you can give me." He wouldn't look at her now—now, when she so desperately needed to see his eyes and try to understand what he was thinking and feeling.

"It might be a good idea if you moved to Montrose," he said, staring over her shoulder. "If you were close by, it would make things easier for me. We could work around my schedule."

"What would Kizzie say about my moving into the house?"

"I wasn't planning on moving you into Kizzie's house."

Was he suggesting she live in the cabin where they'd first made love? Surely not. Luke hadn't been the sentimental type, not even when he'd loved her.

"Where would I stay?" Deanna asked.

"There's a small guest house on Montrose. It's not used much, but Alva could get it ready for you by tonight." Continuing to look past her across the road, Luke thrust his hands into his pockets and spread his legs apart. "Your staying in the guest house would be more convenient, all the way around. There wouldn't be any need for us to come back into town to the motel."

Deanna realized that Luke had no idea that he'd just given her another fragment of hope. If he wasn't going to continue publicly humiliating her by making her meet him at the county's most visible motel, then he had already softened his heart just a little toward her. He might never love her again, but Deanna prayed that he would one day forgive her. She wanted this for Luke more than for herself. He needed to forgive her even more than she needed his forgiveness.

"Where is the guest house located?" she asked.

"You take the road up to the main house, then turn left and go around back. It's within spitting distance.

There's one bedroom, a bath and a living room–kitchen combination.''

"I'll go back to Mother's and pack," Deanna said. "I'll meet you at the guest house around six this evening, if that's okay with you."

"Make it seven," Luke said. "I have supper with Kizzie most nights. Afterward, I'll come over and we can discuss just how we're going to go about finding out who killed your father."

Luke turned from her, heading for his truck. Deanna rushed after him and grabbed his arm. He stilled instantly, glanced over his shoulder and narrowed his eyes into slits.

"Thank you, Luke. I know this won't be easy for you."

He pulled away from her touch, then grinned mockingly. "It won't be easy for you either, babe."

He walked away, got in his truck and started the engine. Deanna stood there and watched him drive off down the road. She didn't move until the truck's red taillights disappeared from view.

There was so little of the young man she had loved left in Luke McClendon. The man who had ravaged her last night, the man who had been unable to comfort her this morning, was a stranger to Deanna. Had her betrayal and his years in prison erased any kindness, any compassion from Luke's heart? If so, she was responsible for his turning into a hard, cold, ruthless loner.

Was it possible that she and she alone had the power to help Luke reclaim his soul and find peace within himself?

Deanna closed the door to her bedroom and sighed with relief. She had thought someone—more than

likely her mother, if not her mother and brother—
would meet her at the front door, demanding to know
where she'd been. She was thankful for even this short
reprieve before she had to face her family. It was only
a matter of time before they found out that she'd spent
the night in a motel with Luke. She dreaded facing
them, and on top of that she had to tell them she was
moving to Montrose.

Deanna stripped off her clothes, taking care to stuff
her tattered blouse into her suitcase. She didn't want
anyone to see that torn piece of material. What had
happened between Luke and her last night was nobody's business except theirs. She knew that despite
his desire for the whole county to know they had spent
the night at the motel together, Luke would never tell
a soul what had transpired between them, behind closed
doors.

After turning on the shower, Deanna stepped into the
glass cubicle and allowed the warm water to cascade
over her. She could still smell Luke on her body—that
strong, unique scent that was his and his alone. At the
thought of him, her body tightened and released, sending a tingling sensation upward from her feminine core.
Luke had taken her, found his own release and deliberately left her unsatisfied last night. Her body ached
with need, craving Luke. She closed her eyes and imagined what it would have been like if he had made love
to her with the wild, sweet abandon that had given
them both so much pleasure all those years ago.
Deanna leaned her head back against the glass wall and
sucked in a long, low cry of anguish and longing. After
all this time, she still wanted Luke McClendon. Luke

and no one else. It had always been that way and she was afraid it always would be.

Luke didn't bother going home. Even though there was a good chance Kizzie would be up and making coffee, he parked his truck and went straight to the stables. He saddled Cherokee and rode the big dun stud away from the main house and up into the nearby hills. He needed to be alone, needed to escape from civilization and find some peace of mind. But Luke knew he could never have any real peace, that contentment eluded him and happiness was an impossibility. He tried to fight the wildness in him and sometimes he won—other times the wildness won. But there was an emotional deadness inside him that he feared the most. Nothing would bring to life that dead spot deep within him.

Deanna had killed something in him fifteen years ago, something that nothing and no one could resurrect. Five years in Huntsville's brutal prison, following Deanna's betrayal, had destroyed what little gentleness or compassion there had been in him. And even now, as the head of the McClendon family, ruling Montrose as his father and grandfather had done, Luke still felt unworthy. There was a part of him that knew he didn't deserve love and happiness, that he didn't deserve a good woman and children of his own. He was a hard, mean son of a bitch. A good woman wouldn't want him, and certainly wouldn't want his children.

Oh, Luke I wanted your baby more than anything on earth.

Damn Deanna! And damn his stupidity for believing her. And that was the problem—he did believe her. He believed she had wanted his child. And if that was true, then there was a possibility that everything else she'd said was true, too. Maybe she *had* loved him. Maybe her mother had threatened her. Maybe she honestly couldn't remember what had happened the night Rayburn Atchley was murdered. Was it possible that he'd hated Deanna so much for testifying against him that he hadn't allowed himself to even consider that she might have been telling the truth?

Luke guided Cherokee deeper and deeper into the hills, not even aware of where he was going until he came upon the burned-out ruins of the cabin. He dismounted, dropped the reins and walked over to a nearby live oak tree, its crooked limbs reaching toward the sky. He remembered the day he had set fire to the place and stood at a distance, watching it burn. The day after he had been released from prison. Baxter hadn't said a word to him. But it wouldn't have mattered if his father had cursed him for destroying the old cabin. Luke had done what his soul demanded, no matter how dark and warped that soul had become. All his anger and hatred had been centered on that pile of old logs, that ramshackle, one-room cabin, where he and Deanna had made love the first time and numerous times afterward. He had tended the fire, keeping it confined and not allowing it to spread. All he'd wanted was to wipe their meeting place from the face of the earth. But now, ten years later, the rock chimney still standing, the remains were as vivid a reminder of what he'd lost as the cabin itself had been.

God, he wished she'd never come back to Stone Creek! He had made a life for himself, one he was used to, one that suited his needs. He had accepted the fact that he would always be alone, always be unloved. He didn't need Deanna Atchley coming back into his life and messing around with his mind and his emotions. He hadn't thought himself capable of hurting a woman the way he'd hurt Deanna last night. He hadn't harmed her physically. Even in his foulest moods, he wasn't enough of a bastard to do that. But he had humiliated her by using her the way he had. He had thought if he could make her feel as helpless and degraded as he had felt when he first went to Huntsville, it would ease the raw pain eating away at his guts. But afterward, he'd felt ashamed that his brutal soul had urged him to take his revenge on Deanna in such a way.

Hell, he shouldn't regret what he'd done. He should be feeling in control and loving the power he had over her now. Instead, he felt out of control, on the verge of losing his sanity. He had spent fifteen years hating Deanna, wanting her to burn in hell for what she'd done to him, and now here he was preparing to help her and making plans to have sex with her as often as possible. That's where he'd made a fatal error—thinking he could have sex with Deanna without it meaning anything to him.

He could lie to her. He could lie to the whole damn world. But he wouldn't lie to himself. He had slept with his share of women in the past fifteen years, had scratched an itch and kept his emotions totally uninvolved. But Deanna was different. Even now. And he should have known she would be. He had loved her once, loved her with a passion that overruled every other aspect of his life. He would willingly have laid down his life for her. A man—any man, even Luke McClendon—couldn't love a woman that deeply and think even hatred and an unquenchable thirst for revenge could make him immune to her.

Luke turned from the cabin ruins and sought out the

clearing that overlooked a large section of Montrose, from the hills to the pastures and beyond to the horizon. Sitting down on a rock ledge, Luke watched the morning come alive. The fog lifting from the hilltops. The sunlight dappling the green with gold. The breeze ruffling through the wildflowers. The sky bursting with various shades of blue, tinged with pale pink and cream.

Even at this distance he heard the rippling waters of the stream that ran through the north section of Montrose. This was his—all of this—as far as the eye could see. Ruling Montrose should be enough for any man—more than enough for a quarter-breed bastard son. So why wasn't it enough for him? Why did he feel so empty inside, so in need of something that was missing?

"Don't be a fool," he said aloud, but only Cherokee and the birds in the trees heard him. "Don't you dare trust Deanna Atchley again."

Deanna placed the last garment in her suitcase and closed the lid. She hadn't brought much with her when she'd come from Jackson. Just the basics. It would be easy enough to take her one case downstairs and put it in the car before anyone saw her. If there was some way she could get around having a confrontation with her family, she'd take that route. But that wasn't possible. She hadn't come home to run away from the truth—not any longer. She had come home to find the truth and face it.

Deanna lifted her makeup case off the bed and set it on the floor beside her suitcase. A soft knocking at the door alerted her that someone other than she was awake in the Atchley household. Nerves quivered in her stomach.

"Deanna, may I speak to you, please." Phyllis's voice held that slightly superior, slightly aggravated tone that she had perfected over the years.

"Yes, Mother." Deanna sighed, dreading the thought of facing her mother. "The door's unlocked. Come in."

Phyllis, her blond hair perfectly coiffured, her long mauve nails an exact match for the mauve silk pantsuit she wore, stood in the doorway thoroughly surveying her daughter. Deanna suddenly felt as if she were on the auction block.

"What do you think you'll see by staring at me that way?" Deanna asked.

"I was looking for the bruises that Luke McClendon no doubt left on your body." Phyllis's nose wrinkled as if she'd smelled something unpleasant.

A lead weight dropped to the bottom of Deanna's stomach. So, her mother already knew that she'd spent the night with Luke. "I can assure you that I have no bruises on my body." No bruises. But a badly battered heart. And her pride that had been severely damaged.

"How could you?" Stepping into the bedroom, Phyllis slammed the door behind her. "Home only a few days and you've already run to him like some bitch dog in heat! My God, Deanna, what sort of hold does that man have over you?"

"How did you find out?" Deanna asked.

"What difference does it make?" Phyllis clenched her jaw, then breathed deeply through her nose and exhaled in a disgruntled huff. "I received an anonymous phone call, if you must know. How do you think that made me feel, having some voice over the phone tell me that my daughter had spent the night at the Stone Creek Motel with Luke McClendon!''

"Obviously, it made you angry."

"Angry? Yes, I'm angry. But I'm ashamed of you and for you. I've worked long and hard to get past what happened with you and Luke and—and your father's death. People had finally quit talking about it. But now you've come home and run straight into that man's arms. We will be the talk of the whole county again."

"I spent the night with Luke because he asked me to," Deanna said. "And I'm going to move into a guest house on Montrose, today, because Luke has asked me to."

"Have you lost your mind? Oh, God!" Phyllis covered her face with her hands, as if shutting out the sight of her daughter. "If you're willing to take up where you left off with Luke McClendon, then you're still mentally unstable."

"Listen to me, Mother. I'm quite sane. My relationship with Luke is really none of your business. It's no one's business but his and mine."

Phyllis grabbed Deanna's arm. "What does that man do to you to make you lose your good sense? Don't you know that he hates you? He'll use you and toss you aside like yesterday's trash."

"Luke has offered to help me regain my memory of the night Daddy was killed. That's more than my own family is willing to do." Deanna jerked free of her mother. "I need Luke's help. I believe he's the key to my regaining my memory. And Luke needs me as much as I need him." Looking Phyllis straight in the eye, Deanna braced herself mentally and emotionally. "I know Luke hates me and I know why. His hatred didn't stem solely from my having testified against him at his trial.''

''What other reason could there be?''

''You tell me, Mother.''

''I don't know what you're talking about.''

''I'm talking about the fact that you told Baxter McClendon that I'd had an abortion.'' Deanna stepped forward, right in Phyllis's face, and glared at her. ''How could you have done it? How could you have lied to Luke's father that way, knowing that Luke might believe I'd actually gotten rid of his baby?''

''I had no choice.'' Backing away from Deanna, Phyllis wrung her hands. ''Baxter threatened to hire a private detective to find you. He wanted his grandchild. He would have discovered that you were at Millones and then the whole world would have known that you were...that you were...''

''The whole world would have known what? That your daughter had suffered a severe nervous breakdown and miscarried, and was confined to a private clinic in California?'' Deanna's lips curved into a soft, sad smile. ''You preferred for Luke to believe that I had deliberately aborted his child, for his hatred of me to fester inside him, than to have told Baxter McClendon the truth. A truth you still haven't been able to accept.''

''What mother could accept the truth that her daughter was insane?''

''I wasn't insane,'' Deanna said calmly. ''I had a nervous breakdown. I witnessed my father's murder. I lost part of my memory. My own mother threatened to have my child aborted. I was forced to testify in court against the man I loved. And I lost a child I desperately wanted. Is it any wonder I suffered a mental break-down?''

"Everything that happened to us—to you—was that damn Luke McClendon's fault! If he'd stayed where he belonged—"

"I chased after him, Mother, and you know it." Deanna laughed, the gesture freeing her to say things she'd never been able to say. "I wanted him from the first minute I saw him and I decided that I'd have him, come hell or high water. I chose Luke to be my first lover because I was wild about him." Deanna grabbed her mother by the shoulders. "Do you hear me, Mother? I was wild about Baxter's quarter-breed bas-tard. And you know what? I still am."

"Then go to him, damn you. Maybe the two of you deserve each other!"

"I hope we do," Deanna said. "I sincerely hope we do."

"If I thought I could stop you—"

"Ah, but that's the beauty of it. You can't stop me. You have no power over me, not anymore." Deanna released her mother, picked up her suitcase and makeup bag and walked around Phyllis and out into the hall. She paused momentarily and glanced back into her bedroom. "I'm going to regain my memory, if at all possible. Somehow, someway, Luke and I are going to find out who really killed Daddy."

"You're going to be sorry," Phyllis said. "You're going to hurt not only yourself by doing this, but others as well. And if you think Luke will ever forgive you, you're wrong. Once he's gotten what he wants, he'll kick you out."

"I hope you're wrong. I hope, for his sake more than

mine, that Luke will eventually forgive me. And as far as him kicking me out—he won't have to. Once I know the truth and clear Luke's name, I'm going back to Jackson.''

Chapter 6

"Not once have I tried to tell you how to live your life." Kizzie McClendon planted her hand on her hip, then lifted her other hand and pointed her index finger in Luke's face. "Not when you burned down Baxter's granddaddy's old cabin. Not when you rode out of here and stayed gone for a week at a time. Not when you refused to come to dinner when I had company. Not when you found your comfort with the likes of Corrine Watkins. But moving Deanna Atchley into the cottage behind the house is more than I'm going to take."

"You don't have to see her while she's here," Luke said. "I'll tell her plainly that she's to stay away from you and any family members that happen to come by."

"Do you think I'm upset because I don't want to see the girl? Do you think I hate her the way you do?" Kizzie huffed loudly. "You listen to me, boy. I could kiss Deanna Atchley's fancy behind every day if I thought her being here was a good thing for you."

"She can't hurt me," Luke said. "You've got to love somebody before they can hurt you. And I haven't loved Deanna in a long, long time."

"That's the problem, son." Taking a deep breath, Kizzie clenched her fists, then opened her palms toward him in an obvious impulse to reach out and comfort. "You haven't loved anybody in a long, long time. Hate is what rules you now. I've watched that burning anger eat away at you, eroding every human emotion inside you. You might help that girl find out who really killed her daddy, but in the process your hatred could well destroy both of you. I can't bear to see that happen."

"What if I promise that I won't let it happen?"

"But it's already happening," Kizzie said. "Do you think I don't know that you spent the night with her at the Stone Creek Motel? I had four phone calls before noon today from people who couldn't wait to let me know what they'd heard."

"I was hoping you wouldn't let it upset you."

"If I didn't know you met her there just so everybody in Luma County would be aware of what the two of you were doing, then I wouldn't have gotten upset. But your hatred made you want to shame that girl, made you do something I'd wager you're none too proud of today."

"Kizzie, I—"

"No!" She held up her big, bony hand in a gesture for him to back off. "You have every right to bring whomever you want to Montrose. I think you're making a big mistake, but if you're determined to do this... You just remember that I don't approve of her coming here and I'm warning you that unless you deal with your feelings for that girl, you'll wind up worse off than you are now."

"I don't have any feelings for her. I'm going to help her because I want to set the record straight. I want to clear the McClendon name. I would have thought you'd want that, too."

"In case you've forgotten, hatred is an emotion. It's the flip side of love. And often there's a very fine line between the two. You hate Deanna because you loved her so much it nearly killed you when she betrayed you, when she took her family's side instead of yours. But mark my word, Luke, buried somewhere deep down inside you, past all that dark, sick, tortured misery, is the root of that love. And that's what you hate the most—the fact that you can't rid yourself of your feelings for her, despite everything that happened all those years ago."

"You're wrong. You're dead wrong!"

But a small voice inside Luke's head taunted him. *Maybe Kizzie's right.*

"Deanna's moving into the guest house tonight. And I don't want to hear another word about it!" He stalked off, stormed out and slammed the door behind him.

Following Luke's directions—up the road and around the main house—Deanna found the guest house easily. The cottage was a small limestone structure, with an arched doorway leading to a porch and a small rock patio encircling it, similar to the one at the main house. Luke stood in the open front door, his left shoulder braced against the facing. Apparently, he wasn't going to keep her waiting this time.

Deanna parked her car on the left side of the rock cottage, got out and opened the trunk. Silent and watchful, Luke made no move to help her with her suitcase. After adjusting her purse and makeup bag over her shoulder, she set the suitcase down on the patio, grabbed the leather strap and rolled it along behind her as she approached her temporary home.

It didn't matter that she wasn't staying at the main house, that Luke had relegated her to a place where she assumed unwelcome visitors were sent. Visitors with whom the family didn't want to share their home. Luke's inviting her to Montrose had been a concession; she had no problem with meeting him halfway. Anything was better than another rendezvous at the Stone Creek Motel.

"I had Alva air out the place," Luke said as she approached. "She put fresh linens on the bed and stocked the refrigerator."

So she wasn't going to be joining the family for meals, either. Deanna knew she shouldn't be surprised. Luke had invited her to Montrose for his convenience, but he wanted to keep her separate and apart from his family. The tables were turned now. Once she had been the one who'd been afraid for her family to know she was involved with Luke. Now, he obviously didn't want their relationship flaunted in his stepmother's face.

"Thanks." She stopped several feet from the entrance and looked her fill at Luke.

Big, broad, ruggedly handsome Luke. Apparently, he had showered and changed clothes after working all day. His clean, faded jeans sculpted his lean hips and long legs. The short-sleeved black-and-white-striped shirt revealed his strong, muscular arms, tanned to a rich copper by the sun. His black hair, cut conservatively short, appeared a deep blue-black in the bright porch light.

Butterflies danced in Deanna's stomach. Just looking

at Luke made her weak in the knees. It always had. She guessed it always would.

"Have you had supper?" he asked.

"Yes, I had dinner with Patsy Ruth Dawkins and her family. You remember Patsy Ruth, don't you?"

"Yeah, I remember her." Luke stepped out of the way when Deanna came toward the door. "I've seen her and her husband and kids in town a few times. How many have they got now? Three? Four?"

"Four. Two boys and two girls."

Luke let out a long, low whistle. "Four kids, huh? She's not much older than you, is she?"

"Two years. She was the best friend I ever had," Deanna said. "Neither of us had sisters, you know. Just big brothers."

"Speaking of big brothers—how did Junior take the news that you were moving onto Montrose?" Luke asked.

"I didn't see Junior before I left the Circle A," she said. "I'm sure Mother will tell him where I am. You'll be pleased to know that Mother was furious."

Deanna walked past Luke and into the guest house. The main room, a living room–kitchen combination, was neat, plain and clean. She could well imagine Kizzie McClendon decorating this cottage. It possessed the same no-nonsense style that epitomized the woman herself. A dark, plaid sofa had been used as a divider between the two areas, and the only other furniture was a matching chair and two small tables. A milk jug filled with fresh wildflowers sat in the center of the wooden kitchen table. Deanna's breath caught in her throat as impossible thoughts filled her head. Had Luke? No, of course he hadn't. Kizzie? Surely not. The housekeeper wouldn't have been told that the McClendons' guest wasn't to be given any special treatment. Then who?

Luke closed the door. Whirling around to face him, Deanna dropped her makeup bag and purse on top of her suitcase. "This is very nice. I should be quite comfortable here."

"Our housekeeper, Alva, doesn't know everything about you. About us. She just knows you were trouble for this family once," Luke said. "She's been working for us less than two years now. Margie retired and moved up to Montana to live with her daughter."

"Margie is the one who used to pack all those wonderful picnic lunches for us, isn't she?"

Luke's face hardened. His eyes narrowed to slits as he glowered at Deanna. Apparently, he didn't want to be reminded of the happiness they'd once shared—before her father found out about their love affair.

Luke turned and opened a door to his left. "The bedroom and bath are in there. You might want to go ahead and put your things—"

"Am I not allowed to talk about any of the good times?" she asked. "I may have lost my memory of some things, but I do remember what it was like when we first fell in love. How we—"

"Yeah, I remember what it was like, too." Luke kept his back to her. "We had to sneak around to see each other. You didn't want your parents to know about us. You were too ashamed of me for us to have real dates like other couples."

"I wasn't ashamed of you!" Deanna left her belongings in the middle of the living room floor, crossed the room and came up behind Luke. Her hand hovered over his shoulder. She wanted to reach out and touch him, but she was afraid of how he might react if she did.

"You *were* ashamed of me," he said in a low, pained voice, then turned slowly and looked at her, his eyes hard and cold. "But knowing I was a worthless bastard quarter-breed, you still couldn't stay away from me, could you? I realized you were bad news the first time I saw you sitting beside your daddy at the rodeo down in San Antonio. Baxter told me to stay away from you, that your daddy would have my hide if I messed with you." Luke chuckled, the sound rough and agonized. "I should have listened to my father and run you off when you came sniffing around. But you were bound and determined to have me, weren't you, babe?"

He knew exactly what to say to hurt her and he'd done it on purpose. If he was getting any pleasure out of her pain, she couldn't tell. As if made out of stone, his face didn't reveal his emotions.

Not moving an inch, Deanna stood her ground, looking directly at her tormentor. "Yes, you're right. I was bound and determined to have you. I never wanted anyone else. Not ever. You made me feel things I didn't understand, but they were things I wanted to find out about with you. With you, Luke. Only you. I loved you more than—"

"You wanted me! You'd gotten everything you wanted all your life, hadn't you? Mommy and Daddy's baby. Spoiled little rich girl, who got the hots for the wrong boy. But my being *unsuitable* didn't stop you. You just had to prove to me and the whole world that Deanna Atchley always got what she wanted. Well, you got me all right. You got me good."

"I *was* spoiled and selfish and used to getting my

own way," Deanna admitted. "You're right about all that, but what you're choosing to forget is that I was only seventeen and I had never disobeyed my parents. Not ever. I risked everything to be with you because I loved you."

"Is that what you call it? Love?"

"Don't, Luke, please don't…" She laid her hand on his arm. "Don't destroy what few beautiful memories I have by telling me that what we shared wasn't love."

He slung her hand off his arm. "If you had loved me, you would have left with me that night I came to the Circle A and asked you to marry me. If I hadn't stayed around begging you to come with me, your father never would have caught us together." Clenching his jaw tightly, Luke closed his eyes, shutting out the sight of the woman who had betrayed him. "And if you had loved me, you wouldn't have gotten on the stand and testified against me at my trial."

"I wanted to leave with you, to run off and get married, but I knew that if I did, my daddy would have tracked us down and killed you." Deanna shuddered. *This is so much more difficult than I'd thought it would be—facing Luke and telling him the truth.* "He'd already beaten you within an inch of your life only a couple of weeks before. I couldn't…" She could tell by the expression on his face that Luke didn't understand what she was trying to explain. "I've already told you that I barely remember the trial, but I do know that I was afraid not to testify. I was afraid of what my mother might do to me and to—to our baby."

"We're never going to remember the past the same, are we?" Luke moved away from her and opened the front door. "There's no point beating a dead horse."

"I'm sorry." Deanna rubbed her hands up and down

her hips, a deliberate effort to keep from reaching out to Luke. "I never meant for my loving you to hurt you so much."

"Good night, Deanna. I'll see you tomorrow and we can get around to the business at hand. But while you're waiting for me to find time for you, think about who else had a motive and an opportunity to kill your father."

"Think about—"

"Between the time I picked up that pitchfork and the time your father was found murdered couldn't have been more than fifteen minutes. So who else was around—on the Circle A—who might have wanted to see Rayburn Atchley dead?"

Luke left, closing the door quietly behind him. Deanna stood there staring off into space, Luke's words reverberating in her head. Who else was around on the Circle A? Who else? Who else?

Her mother. Her brother. Benita. And Eddie. And a few ranch hands. As far as she knew, none of them had any reason to kill her father. Or had there been someone else on the ranch that night? Someone hiding in the shadows, waiting for a chance to strike?

Wearing only a pair of jeans, Luke walked out onto the back porch. He hadn't been able to sleep. His bed looked like he'd been fighting someone in it—or ravaging someone. He flung open the back door and went out onto the patio. The guest house was less than a city block away. It was usually empty—the last person he remembered staying there was a distant cousin of Kizzie's who had come uninvited for a two-week stay. That had been nearly two years ago.

Tonight, Deanna Atchley was sleeping in the old

maple four-poster, cuddled under the handmade quilt Kizzie had labored over so patiently. And he could have been lying there beside her. He could have taken her again, vented more of his frustration and anger. But he knew that even if she had allowed him to touch her, he would have been the one who regretted it the most. He couldn't have sex with Deanna again and risk her getting the upper hand. He'd always been wild for her, hot to get her beneath him. She had held a power over him no other woman ever had—or ever would.

Without realizing he had wandered so far from the main house, Luke found himself outside the guest cottage. He wanted to be inside, in her bed, releasing his frustration and finding satisfaction in the arms of his enemy. For that was how he had thought of Deanna all these years—as his enemy. She had wounded him, his heart and his soul, in a way no one else could have. And he had hated his enemy, hated her with a burning rage. But the Deanna he had known—had loved beyond all reason—didn't exist any longer. The spoiled, pampered little rich girl had grown up and Luke had no idea who she was now. Had she changed as much as he had? Had the years been as unkind to her as they'd been to him? What had happened to her fifteen years ago and where had she gone?

The answers to those questions shouldn't matter to him. But they did matter. And so did Deanna. He realized it wouldn't take much more persuasion on her part to have him doing the begging and pleading. For him to be the one looking at her with sympathy and concern in his eyes, instead of the other way around.

I'm sorry. I'm sorry. I'm sorry. He could hear her voice repeating the words over and over, like the mournful lyrics to an old blues song. Maybe she was sorry for what she'd done. Maybe she did want to make amends. But what she didn't realize was that she was too late—much too late. All the apologies in the world couldn't make things right. Even if they discovered the identity of Rayburn Atchley's real killer, nothing would change. Deanna had betrayed him. He had spent five years in prison. Their child was dead. And as long as he lived he would be Baxter McClendon's quarter-breed bastard, who wasn't worth being loved.

Luke moved silently as he turned the corner of the cottage, his common sense telling him he was a fool. What the hell was he doing hanging around outside? If he wanted her, all he had to do was knock on the door and wake her. She wouldn't reject him, not as long as he didn't humiliate her again. If all he wanted was sex, she'd give it to him. At the thought of taking her, his body hardened.

The bedroom window was open and the white curtains fluttered in the night breeze. He glanced inside, but could make out only dark shapes and shadows in the moonlight.

"Damn!" Luke cursed under his breath. Sometimes he went weeks, even months, without a woman. And here he was panting after Deanna as if he couldn't go a night without having her. This raw, hot need had been what had nearly gotten him killed once. He wasn't going to give in to his need for her, no matter how hard that need drove him.

Luke turned to walk away, but before he'd taken a step, a loud, terrified scream rent the night air. Luke stiffened immediately, the hairs on his neck rising. Deanna! Deanna had screamed! He rushed over to the long, narrow bedroom window and looked inside.

"Deanna?"

He noticed movement—the outline of Deanna's body—on the bed. Then she moaned deeply.

Luke raised the window farther, flung one leg over and vaulted into the bedroom. He stumbled over a chair, cursing when his big toe hit the chair leg.

He found the lamp on the nightstand and turned it on, filling the room with a soft, dim light. That's when he saw her, sitting in the middle of the bed, trembling, tears streaming down her face. Good God, what had happened to frighten her so?

Luke sat down on the bed, reached out and pulled Deanna toward him. She slapped at him, fighting him, then looked at him through misty eyes and sobbed wildly as she threw herself into his arms.

"Oh, Luke...Luke. It was horrible! Horrible!" She clung to him, her sweat-soaked body quivering.

He threaded his fingers into her hair and grasped the back of her head, lifting her upward so that he could see her face. "What was horrible? What happened, Deanna?"

"The dream," she gasped. "I had another one of those dreams."

"One of those dreams?"

"About—about the night—" she licked off the tears clinging to her lips "—the night Daddy was killed."

"Was it a dream or a memory?" Luke asked, his big hand cradling her head.

"A dream," she said. "But it might be a memory, one that I won't let myself remember when I'm awake."

"Want to tell me about it?"

Deanna pulled away from him and wiped her face with her fingertips. "What are you doing here?"

"I was out taking a walk and heard you screaming."

Deanna glanced at the clock on the nightstand. "You were out taking a walk at two o'clock in the morning?"

"Yeah. It's not unusual for me. I roam around Montrose all hours of the day and night. Just ask anybody."

Deanna grabbed his arm. "Luke, the dream was so real."

"Do you want to tell me about it?"

Deanna scooted to the edge of the bed, slid her feet off the side and sat beside Luke. "Mother was in the dream. And Eddie."

"Eddie Nunley?"

She nodded. "Mother was screaming and crying. And Eddie was telling her that she had to get hold of herself, that she couldn't fall to pieces."

"Where were Eddie and your mother?" Luke asked.

"We—they were at the stables on the Circle A. And Daddy was there, too. He was lying on the ground with—with—" Tears lodged in her throat, choking her.

Luke slid his arm around her shoulder, but didn't draw her into his arms or look directly at her. "He was lying on the ground with the pitchfork stuck in him."

Deanna gulped down a deep breath. "Yes. And I was just standing there staring at him. Mother slapped me. She was nearly hysterical. Eddie said…Eddie said…"

"What did Eddie say?" Luke squeezed her shoulder.

"He said, 'Dammit, Phyllis, can't you see she's in shock? We need to call the sheriff and then get a doctor over here to see about Deanna.' And then—then we were in the courthouse, at your trial. And you were sitting there, looking at me, accusing me with your eyes. And I wanted to tell you why I was there, why I had to tell them what I knew. But I didn't say anything.

I just picked up the pitchfork and rammed it into your chest! Oh, God, Luke, I killed you!''

She fell apart in his arms, sobbing, clutching his naked shoulders, saying *I'm sorry* over and over again.

Luke didn't want to feel sorry for her. Dammit, he didn't want to feel anything. Not even hatred. Not anymore. All he wanted was to feel numb. Blessed numbness. He had survived five years at Huntsville by keeping his emotions numb, by burying them so deep he sometimes wondered if he had destroyed everything but the hatred. Now he knew he hadn't.

"You didn't kill me, Deanna." He lifted her hands off his shoulders and laid them on his bare chest. "I'm very much alive."

She glanced up at him, her blue eyes swimming with tears. And more than anything on earth, he wanted to take away her pain and fear.

"Feel my heart beating." He pressed her right hand over his heart.

"But I did kill you. That day in the courtroom. I could see it in your eyes. Your beautiful green eyes were void of any life. I destroyed the man I loved."

"You didn't destroy me," he told her. "I survived."

"Did you, Luke? Did you?"

He realized that Deanna was eaten alive with guilt. She blamed herself as much as he had always blamed her. Wherever she'd been these past fifteen years, whatever she'd been doing, she had been living with that guilt. Maybe she'd been trying to run away from her feelings, her memories, just as he had.

"What else do you remember about my trial?" Luke asked, his breath tickling her lips.

"Only your eyes. That's all, I remember. I saw your dead eyes staring at me and I knew you hated me."

Luke licked her lips, softly, tenderly, running a damp line around her mouth. Deanna sucked in her breath. Her hands spread out over his chest. He eased the thin straps of her gown off her shoulders, then circled the back of her neck with his hand and drew her toward him. Deanna sighed his name. Luke eased her onto the bed and came down on top of her.

Chapter 7

"Luke, please don't. Not again. I don't think I could bear it." Deanna looked up at him, his big body hovering over her, his eyes glowing with desire. And something else? No, it wasn't possible. Luke couldn't be looking at her the way he used to, with a passionate yearning, so strong and powerful—and yet so very loving.

Luke slipped his fingers underneath the straps of her gown and slowly slid the satiny material down over her breasts, exposing them to his view. Lowering his head, he took one jutting nipple into his mouth and laved it with his tongue. Deanna moaned as tingling pleasure spiraled from her breast to her feminine core. Clutching the sheet beneath her, she quivered when he moved to the other breast and gave it equal treatment.

Was he loving her or tormenting her? Was his aim to give her pleasure?—or simply to torture her before he took her roughly and uncaringly, as he'd done last night.

She shoved against his chest. He stopped, lifted his head and looked at her.

"I know that I agreed that you could...that we would have sex whenever you wanted me, but not... not the way it was last night. Please." She knew her fate was in his hands. Not because he was bigger and stronger and capable of physically forcing his will on her. Luke never would do that. Not even this hard, cold, ruthless Luke who was little more than a stranger to her. But he could bend her mind to his will, take her if he wanted her and she would be powerless to stop him. Because she wanted him, wanted him touching her, loving her, plunging himself into her. She had been wild about him since the first moment she saw him, and heaven help her, nothing had changed. Just one look, one touch, one word and she was his. And he knew it.

"Not like last night," he said, the words a low growl.

Luke lifted himself off her, and for a split second she thought he was going to leave her. But he didn't. He slipped his hands under her hips and dragged her gown down and off, baring her body completely. She lay there before him, naked and exposed, her nipples tight, her breathing ragged. He made no move to remove his jeans. He didn't even unzip them.

Before she had a chance to think about what was happening, Luke straddled her hips, burying his knees on each side of her. She shuddered. He grasped her wrists and drew them over her head, pinning them to the bed. Her chest rose and fell as she breathed deeply, the act offering her breasts to him. She watched him carefully, wondering and waiting and hoping. If this man was the old Luke—her Luke—he would pleasure her until she was half out of her mind, then he would make love to her like a madman until they were both spent completely. But this wasn't the old Luke. This was the new Luke—the man her betrayal and five years in prison had created.

Lowering his head, he covered her lips in a hard, hot kiss. She cried out, the sound captured by his mouth. He thrust his tongue inside, then retreated. When he repeated the act, Deanna rose up off the bed, her body pressing intimately against his. He was aroused, his sex pulsating against her through the barrier of his faded jeans.

He ravaged her mouth, kissing her until she was breathless, until she was ready to beg him to take her. But when he removed his lips from hers, he didn't prepare himself for sex. Instead, he ran his hands down her arms and back up, then over her breasts, lifting them, examining them.

"Luke, please—" She tried to shove him away, but couldn't budge him. He was too big and strong.

"Hush, babe."

She struggled, thrashing her head from side to side, tugging on her wrists, twisting her body. "No, don't. I—"

"Hush!" he said roughly, then flicked his thumbs across her nipples and bit softly into her shoulder.

Deanna shivered. Every nerve in her body came to full alert. She ached with the wanting, with the need for fulfillment. Was he going to bring her to the very edge and then walk away, leave her hurting, the way he had last night?

His mouth replaced his thumbs, playing with and

then tormenting her nipples. He caressed the curve of her hip with one hand, while he held her waist with the other. When he slipped his hands between her legs, she knew his destination. Without hesitation, she opened her thighs for him. As he stroked the dark V of her hair that protected her feminine core, Luke continued caressing her breasts with his tongue. Laving, nibbling, sucking. And all the while, Deanna lay beneath him, her arms at her sides, her palms opened flat against the bed.

The pleasure was almost beyond bearing, but a dull aching doubt throbbed inside her head. Was he going to stop abruptly and leave her wanting? Was this loving just a form of punishment for her?

His fingers danced over her intimately, seductively, playing with her, toying with the tiny kernel that pulsed beneath his touch. Turning her head to the side, she moaned into the sheet. When he eased his finger inside her while his thumb stroked her, Deanna cried out as her hips lifted in a pleading gesture. Asking for more. Needing all he had to give.

"Easy, babe. Easy."

Luke smoothed his other hand down over her stomach when he removed his fingers from inside her. He flipped her over onto her stomach. She gasped.

His tongue began a snake dance across her shoulders, slowly licking over and across and then down. No one had touched her like this in years—not since the last time Luke made love to her. She had forgotten how wonderful it was to have a man worship her body, taking his time to savor every inch. While he painted a moist path over her back and buttocks and thighs, his fingers explored, entering and retreating, then entering again. She was mindless with need by the time he turned her over again and began a similar waltz from her collarbone down over her throbbing breasts, into her navel and onto her inner thighs.

Deanna flung back her head, pressing it into the bed. If he didn't take her—and soon—she would die. How much more of this torture did he think she could endure?

Reaching up, she caressed his chest, her fingertips rubbing his male nipples until they peaked. He groaned, the sound deep in his chest.

"I want you," she told him. "I want you so much."

"You want this!"

Scooting off the bed and onto his knees, he dragged her with him. When he lifted her legs and placed them over his shoulders, Deanna tried to protest, tried to beg him not to take her any further before he deserted her. But the moment his mouth covered her, tasting her, his tongue darting out to seek and find her richness, all coherent thought left her mind.

His hard, insistent tongue and soft, loving mouth brought her to the edge. Her body tensed, waiting for that one final stroke that would release her. But Luke kissed her inner thigh, leaving her aching painfully.

"No, Luke. Oh, please. No."

She tried to rise from the bed, to reach out and touch him, but he held her in place by covering her breasts with his big hands.

"Don't fight me!" Luke's voice was harsh and ragged.

Sweat coated his face and bare chest. He looked like a man who had taken part in a heated brawl.

The moment he pinched her nipples, she cried out. His mouth returned to her, moving around and about, inside and out, creating a great tidal wave of energy.

And once again, just as she started to peak, Luke eased off and left her panting for more.

She struggled, thrashing and twisting, pounding her fists into the bed. She had begged him not to do this to her, not to—oh, oh, oh. His mouth encompassed her. His tongue massaged steadily until her body tightened like a thin wire coil. And then Luke gave her that final stroke, that much needed caress that plunged her headlong into an earth-shattering climax. All the while she unraveled around him, he continued his attentions to her, drawing every ounce of tension from her body. Luke lifted her legs off his shoulders and pushed her gently toward the center of the bed. The aftershocks of her release tingled through her. She held out her arms for him. She wanted to give him as much pleasure as he'd given her. She needed to feel him moving inside her, taking her with fast fury.

But Luke stood and turned his back to her. Lifting her head, she watched him move toward the open window.

"Luke?"

"Go back to sleep, Deanna."

"But you—you aren't going to—to..."

"No," he said. "I'm not going to."

He crawled back out the window and disappeared into the darkness. Deanna rushed to the window, wanting to call him back. He had given her such intense pleasure and taken nothing for himself. She felt as if she had used him, as if—

At the realization of why Luke had pleasured her without taking anything for himself, Deanna cried out. Covering her mouth with both hands, she slid to the floor and rocked back and forth as tears misted her eyes. *So, that was the reason why.* Her heart rejoiced at the thought that there was hope for Luke, that he wasn't completely, irrevocably lost.

His giving her pleasure had been a form of apology. Even if he didn't know it yet, Luke was sorry for the way he had treated her at the motel. He had needed to vent his anger that night, to seek revenge by humbling her the way he had been humbled fifteen years ago. If he was the unfeeling monster others had warned her he had become, he wouldn't care that he had brutalized her emotions, that he had used her for his own satisfaction. But he did care. His actions tonight proved it. He had given her fulfillment, but not himself.

Luke had given, not taken. A complete reversal of his actions at the motel. A payment in kind.

Deanna hugged herself as tears of relief trickled down her cheeks. What was going on in Luke's mind? How had he rationalized what he'd done? Did he have any idea that he had revealed a secret part of himself to her, that she realized some of the old Luke still existed inside the supposedly heartless man he was today?

For the first time since she had returned to Stone Creek, Deanna thought it was possible that things would work out all right. With the revealing nightmares continuing and Luke agreeing to help her, she had a good chance of regaining her memory. If she could clear Luke's name, he might be able to forgive her. And if Luke forgave her, he would, at long last, be free.

Deanna lay down in bed and pulled the sheet up to cover her naked body. She closed her eyes and sighed. Go to sleep, she told herself. It'll be morning soon. A new day. Tomorrow. And sometime, Luke would come back to the guest house—back to her.

* * *

Luke's alarm went off at five o'clock. Groggily he opened his eyes just enough to see the digital box, then slammed his hand on top of it, shutting off the buzzing noise. He'd gotten what, less than two hours' sleep? Well, it wouldn't be the first time he had functioned without a good night's rest. He showered and dressed hurriedly, then made his way through the dark house into the kitchen. The timed coffeemaker that Alva prepared nightly before she went to bed held eight cups. He'd drink at least three before he checked on the six hands who would be at work by five-thirty. He was glad Montrose wasn't in the dairy business. If they were, he'd have to get up before the crack of dawn and so would his hands. Milking on the ranches was done before daylight.

Four of the Montrose hands lived on the ranch. The two bachelors, Jim and Herb, shared quarters in the old renovated bunkhouse and the two married men, Les and Bud, who'd been with the McClendons for nearly twenty years, lived in houses a couple of miles down the road. The two college kids, who worked part-time, lived in town and came out after their classes every day. He knew when he'd first hired Randy and Chris that they'd both wanted to *play* cowboy, and he'd wondered if they'd stick with it. They had, and had turned out to be valuable employees.

Luke poured himself a cup of high-octane brew and shoved open the back door. He stepped off the back porch and onto the patio, breathing in the cool, sweet morning air. Felt like rain. He glanced toward the sky, gray and overcast. Looked like rain, too.

His gaze traveled from the red-streaked horizon down to the guest cottage. There wasn't a light on in the place. Deanna was probably still asleep. At the very thought of her, his body hardened. That's the way it had always been. Every time he got near her, his sex got hard and his head got soft. He hadn't given a damn about anybody's feelings in a long time, except maybe Kizzie's. But Kizzie left him alone, didn't bother him with demands or needs he couldn't meet. Deanna was altogether different. She needed things from him, and as time passed she'd start demanding more and more. The sexual satisfaction he'd given her earlier this morning wouldn't be enough. She'd start making female noises about feelings. She'd want them to talk about what they thought and how they felt.

He could tell her that he thought she was the sexiest woman he'd ever known and that he felt like having sex with her morning, noon and night.

What he couldn't admit to her—what he could barely admit to himself—was that he had no intention of ever having sex with her again. After what he'd done to her at the motel, he had owed her the fulfillment he'd given her this morning. But that had to be the end of it. If he allowed himself to give in to his needs and take Deanna whenever he wanted her, she would soon be the one calling the shots. She possessed some kind of wicked control over him when they were lovers, and he had sworn that no one—least of all Deanna Atchley—would ever again have that kind of power over him.

But she would wonder and probably ask why he'd changed his mind about their having sex as payment for his help. He'd just have to think of something to tell her. Something that would ruffle her feathers enough to keep her from asking any more questions about his feelings.

*   *   *

Deanna awoke to the sound of rain. A slow, steady downpour. The kind that usually lasted all day. She stretched languidly, enjoying the feel of the cool cotton sheets against her skin. She hadn't slept naked in a long time, nor had she slept so soundly or awakened so contented. She wondered if Luke would come to see her before he had breakfast this morning. He would have a lot to do before he enjoyed the first good, hot meal of the day. But maybe he would make time to drop by and say hello. And maybe he would stay long enough for— No! She couldn't dwell on Luke making love to her the way he used to do. That was asking for too much. But a kiss wasn't out of the question, was it?

Deanna got up, went into the bathroom and turned on the shower. The bath was small, almost cramped, but the fixtures were fairly new and the room was spotlessly clean. Rummaging around in her makeup bag, she found her raspberry-scented body wash. Pressing her nose against her shoulder, she breathed in the rich, musky scent that was a combination of herself and of Luke. She almost hated to wash away the smell of him, that unique earthiness. Her body tingled with remembrance. Luke's hands caressing, his lips possessing, his tongue delighting.

She stepped under the warm water flow, tossed back her head and smiled. She felt deliciously content. Lathering her body with the fragrant wash, she shivered slightly. Her breasts were tender from Luke's ardent attention. Just the thought of his mouth on her body created a moist throbbing between her thighs.

After her shower, Deanna inspected her clothes, wanting to choose something perfect, something that would please Luke. She picked up a pair of hot pink slacks and a matching silk blouse. Luke had always loved her in pinks and reds.

Later, she discovered the kitchen was indeed stocked—fully stocked. There was enough food here to feed four people for a couple of weeks. While she busied herself with preparations for coffee and toast, she turned on the small radio sitting on the window ledge over the sink. Finding a local country music station, she set the dial.

Maybe she'd have scrambled eggs to go along with the toast. She was starving. She broke the eggs into a bowl, added a dash of milk and a pinch of sugar, then whisked them until they were fluffy. She wished Luke was here, sharing the morning with her. She would have fixed him a big, country breakfast for his man-sized appetite.

Don't do this to yourself, Deanna. Don't pretend that just because Luke offered you a sexual apology in the dark hours of early morning, things are all right between the two of you. Nothing has changed, not really. He still hates you and still blames you for sending him to prison.

But did he still want revenge against her? Only time would tell.

Nothing had changed for her, either. She still needed Luke's help. No matter what happened between them, she couldn't forget why she was here, in Stone Creek, at Montrose. Nothing could ever be all right for her, or for Luke, until they knew the truth. Finding her father's real killer had to take priority over everything else.

Deanna emptied the scrambled eggs onto a plate, buttered her toast and poured herself a cup of black coffee. She added a teaspoonful of sugar and stirred.

She tried to recall the nightmare she'd had last night, but already the dream was fading. Her mother had been there, and so had Eddie. But that might not mean anything. She'd been told that Eddie was the one who'd found her kneeling over her father's body. Had her mother really been there, too, when Eddie had found her? Had Phyllis actually slapped her? If so, why? Was it possible that they had thought she'd killed her father?

"Did I kill him?" Deanna asked aloud. Was it possible that she actually rammed the pitchfork through her daddy?

She had loved her father and in his own fashion, he had doted on her. Lord knows, he had bought her anything money could buy. But he'd gone mad when he'd found out that she was pregnant with Luke's baby. He had struck her. He'd never even spanked her before that day. And after he'd knocked her to the ground, he'd rounded up Eddie and Junior and gone after Luke. They'd found him alone on the range that evening and, outnumbered three to one, Luke had had little chance of escaping Rayburn Atchley's wrath.

Kizzie had called her from the hospital that night, to tell her that Luke had been horsewhipped and was in serious condition. Deanna had tried to go to him, but her parents had kept her guarded day and night to prevent her from leaving the Circle A.

Suddenly the warm, fluffy eggs in her mouth tasted like cardboard. Deanna swallowed, then washed them down with the coffee. She'd lost her appetite. Recalling the past often did that to her. Remembering, with regret, never became any easier.

The phone rang; Deanna jumped. Maybe it was Luke phoning her. Maybe he wanted her to join him for the afternoon. She'd love to ride over Montrose with him, just the two of them alone together.

She picked up the receiver, anticipation in her voice. "Hello."

"Deanna?"

"Junior?"

"What the hell are you doing over there at Montrose?" he asked, sadness in his voice. "You're asking for trouble, honey. Don't you know that? Come on home where you belong."

"Did Mother ask you to call me?"

Phyllis knew that Deanna and Junior had once been very close, that if Deanna had ever listened to anyone, it had been her big brother. Did her mother actually think Junior could dissuade her from her chosen course of action? Maybe once, years ago when she'd been very young and very weak, but not now. No one made her decisions for her. No one told her what she could and couldn't do. A part of the healing process from her nervous breakdown had been taking responsibility for herself and her actions.

"Mother's concerned about you. She's afraid of what Luke McClendon might do to you."

"Mother's concerned about herself," Deanna said. "She's not afraid of what Luke might do to me. She's afraid of what Luke and I might find out about Daddy's death."

"Sugar, you can't mean to imply that Mother knows something about Daddy's death and has kept it a secret all these years." Junior sighed loudly. "Why can't you just accept the fact that Luke killed Daddy? I know he might have had cause, seeing as how Daddy nearly beat him to death."

"And you just stood by and did nothing when

Daddy whipped Luke. You could have tried to stop Daddy.''

"Hell, Sis, you know nobody stopped Rayburn Atchley when he was in one of his moods. Not even Mother could handle the old man when he went into one of his rages.''

She knew Junior was right. Their father had never been abusive to her, but she'd been aware of his temper. She'd seen her father whip Junior until blood trickled down his legs. And she'd seen her father slap her mother and curse her. Why she had been spared, she didn't know. Spared, that is, until he'd found out about her love affair with Luke.

"I've already told Mother that I'm staying here at Montrose until I regain my memory. Until I know who really killed Daddy.''

"Deanna—''

"Don't say it was Luke. I know it wasn't.''

"How can you know, when you don't remember anything from that night after Luke picked up the pitchfork and headed straight for Daddy?''

How *did* she know? Why had she always been so sure Luke was innocent, despite his having reason to want to see her father dead?

For years she had tried to forget that horrible night. Now, she wanted to remember. Needed to remember. For herself. And for Luke.

Suddenly Deanna could see her father standing tall and proud, his cheeks red with anger, his mouth curved into a snarl.

"You get off my property, boy, and you stay the hell away from my little girl," Rayburn shouted. *"If I catch you anywhere near anything that's mine, I'll take my*

whip to you again and the next time I'll kill you for sure.''

Rayburn snapped the whip he held in his hand.

''No, Daddy. Don't. Please don't hurt Luke. I promise I won't go away with him. I'll never see him again.''

''Do you mean that, Deanna?'' Luke asked. ''Are you willing to give up all our plans just because your father forbids us to be together?''

''You heard her,'' Rayburn said, snapping the whip again. ''She doesn't want anything else to do with you, you filthy redskin bastard.''

Moving toward Luke, Rayburn wound the whip, preparing to use it. Deanna stood between her father and Luke, pleading with Luke to go and begging her father not to hurt Luke. Rayburn shoved her aside, knocking her to the ground. Luke backed up toward the stables, reached out and grabbed a pitchfork leaning against the outer wall.

''You'll never whip me again, old man! I'll kill you first.'' Luke started walking toward Rayburn.

Deanna screamed. Luke drew closer and closer. Rayburn's face paled, and he backed away as Luke walked toward him, the pitchfork aimed at his heart.

Within a foot of Rayburn, Luke stopped and glared into the man's face.

''Please, Luke, don't!'' Deanna cried.

Luke froze to the spot, gripping the pitchfork with white-knuckled ferocity. Deanna's heart ceased to beat for one second.

Then Luke threw the pitchfork into the ground and walked away.

''Deanna, are you there? What's wrong?'' Junior demanded. ''Why don't you answer me?''

Gripping the telephone in her hand, Deanna dropped to her knees. She gasped for air. She had remembered! Dear God, she had remembered that Luke had tossed the pitchfork aside and walked away.

Somewhere deep inside her, she'd always known that Luke hadn't killed her father. But now, she remembered.

"Deanna! Dammit, if you don't say something, I'm coming over there to Montrose right now."

"Don't," she whispered. "I'm all right."

"What's wrong with you?" Junior asked.

"Nothing. Absolutely nothing. I'm fine." Deanna laughed. "I'm better than fine."

"You're not making any sense. Are you having some kind of spell or something? I thought you said you were all right now, that you didn't have any mental problems."

"I remember," she told her brother. "I remember seeing Luke throw the pitchfork into the ground and walk away. He left the Circle A. He didn't kill Daddy."

"Are you telling me that you actually remember that happening?" Junior asked. "You didn't dream it? You honest to God remember that Luke didn't kill Daddy?"

"Yes, Junior, I honest to God remember."

"Do you remember anything else? Do you remember seeing somebody else around, somebody that might have used that pitchfork on Daddy?"

"No." Deanna let out a long, labored sigh. "But I will remember. I know I will. And when I do, we'll be able to clear Luke's name and whoever really killed Daddy can be punished for what they did."

"I—I suppose I don't have any reason to think you'd lie about this, even if you and that...even if you and

Luke are sleeping together. You wouldn't pretend to remember things about that night, just because you're still in love with Luke, would you?''

"No, Junior, I wouldn't lie about something this important." She didn't bother to deny that she was sleeping with Luke or that she still loved him. After all, she'd had sex with Luke since her return to Stone Creek. And maybe she did still love him.

"You're going to tell Luke that you remember, I suppose."

"Of course I am." Deanna smiled, cherishing that one tiny memory from her past—the memory of Luke throwing aside the pitchfork and walking away. "And you tell Mother and Eddie that my memory is coming back. After all these years, I'm finally going to remember the truth."

"Be careful, Sis. Remembering the truth might be dangerous."

"What?" Had she heard Junior correctly? Was he trying to warn her about something?

The dial tone hummed in her ears. Junior had hung up on her! Well, it didn't matter. She'd talk to her brother later. Right now, she needed to talk to Luke.

She dialed the number for the main house and waited for someone to answer. Excitement bubbled up inside her, threatening to explode into laughter and happy tears.

"McClendon residence," a female voice said.

"May I speak to Luke McClendon? This is Deanna Atchley. I'm a guest of Mr. McClendon's. I'm—"

"The lady in the guest house?"

"Yes."

"I'm sorry, but Mr. Luke isn't here. He's checking the fences. Would you like to leave a message?"

"Does Luke have a cellular phone?" Deanna asked.

"He keeps one in his truck. Is this an emergency, Ms. Atchley?"

"An emergency? Well, no, not exactly." She could wait until Luke returned to the house for lunch, couldn't she? "Just ask Luke to call me when he comes home for lunch."

"Sure will."

Deanna hung up the phone and whirled around and around, laughing giddily. She had remembered something vitally important. Something that was the first step in clearing Luke of her father's murder.

She just knew that, one by one, all her memories would return. Her mood sobered quickly as she thought of the grief remembering might bring. She had to prepare herself to face the truth, whatever that truth might be. Someone other than Luke had killed her father and that someone could be a member of her own family.

Luke stood on the back patio, looking at the guest cottage. Alva had mentioned earlier in the day that Deanna had asked to see him, but ranch duties had caused him to skip lunch and work well into the evening. Besides, a part of him had been reluctant to return to the guest cottage, to face Deanna again. It would be the easiest thing in the world to go to her, to wake her from her sleep, to apologize for coming by so late. He could say he hadn't realized it was nearly midnight. Would she welcome him with open arms? Would she fold herself around him and take him to her bed?

His body hardened as images of Deanna filled his mind. He couldn't let her do this to him. He didn't dare give in to his desire to possess her completely, to make love to her.

Luke McClendon didn't make love. He had sex. What he needed was to simply release some of his tension. Just about any of the *ladies* of his acquaintance would do. All cats were black in the dark, weren't they?

I'm not driving into town at this time of night. Deanna Atchley isn't going to run me off my ranch. Maybe I am aching to be inside her. Maybe I'd kill right now to have her long legs wrapped around me. But I can handle her. I don't need to tomcat around to stay away from her.

Luke walked out to the stables, saddled Cherokee and rode out for the hills. He'd spend the night alone, on his land, and by morning, he'd be completely in control again.

Nothing has changed, he told himself. I still hate Deanna. I still can't trust her.

And you still want her, a taunting inner voice reminded him.

Chapter 8

Deanna chose her tightest, most body-molding jeans, dragged them up over her hips and stuffed her red-and-blue plaid shirt under the waistband, then looped a wide leather belt around her waist. Inspecting herself in the dresser mirror, she lifted her ponytail, fluffing it with her fingers. Then she unbuttoned the top three buttons on her blouse and spread the material apart just enough to expose her cleavage. She hadn't dressed provocatively, just to tempt a man, since she was seventeen and dying to get Luke McClendon's attention. After all these years, she wanted to gain the attention of the very same man.

He never had responded to the message she'd left him yesterday, and she'd be damned if she'd call him back and beg him to see her. She'd known Luke wouldn't make anything easy for her, but she had hoped he'd keep his word and try to help her. So far, she was batting zero.

She had spent the day alone. Waiting for a knock at the door. Waiting for the phone to ring. Well, she was tired of solitary confinement and she was tired of being ignored. Bits and pieces of her memory kept coming back. Fragments. Like tiny pieces of an intricate puzzle. And she wanted to share that puzzle with Luke. She needed him to help her put the pieces together, so that the whole thing made sense.

Luke might not love her anymore. He might even still hate her. But the one thing he couldn't deny was that, on some level, he still wanted her. The only weapon in her arsenal was sex, and if using it was what it took to get Luke's attention, then she'd use it. And the world be damned!

Montrose covered eighteen thousand acres and Luke could be anywhere on the ranch. She just hoped he was close by, but it didn't matter where he was, he wasn't going to escape her. If it took her all day and half the night, she'd find him.

Deanna made one final adjustment on her shirt, then straightened the small gold hoops in her ears. With her chin tilted, her head held high and her shoulders squared, she walked out of the guest cottage and marched straight over to the main house. She knocked at the back door several times before someone answered. A short, squat middle-aged woman opened the door and peered out.

"Yeah, what can I do for you?"

"I'm Deanna Atchley. I'm staying in the—"

The box-shaped, dark-eyed woman stepped out onto the porch. "Yes, ma'am, Ms. Atchley, is there something you need?"

"I'd like to know where Mr. McClendon...where Luke is."

"Well, as far as I know he's over at the corral. Mrs. McClendon told me she was headed over that way to watch Luke gentling one of the new mustangs."

"Thank you, Mrs....Mrs....?"

"Name's Alva."

"Thank you, Alva."

"Do you know how to get to the corrals?" Alva asked.

"I can probably find them."

Alva smiled broadly, then gave Deanna specific instructions on the location of the corrals.

The afternoon sun was Texas-hot, but still cool this time of May compared to what it would be like in July. She had pulled her hair up in a ponytail and chosen a short-sleeved shirt so she'd be more comfortable. She'd decided against shorts. Shorts would have been too obvious. Luke had always said she had the sexiest legs in the world. No, the jeans were a better choice. Sexy, but subtle. She just hoped she wasn't making a mistake, going after Luke this way. But what other choice did she have? He wouldn't come to her.

She had chased him once and he'd loved being caught. Was it foolish of her to hope that she might be that lucky a second time?

From yards away, Deanna caught a glimpse of Kizzie standing outside the corral, watching her stepson as he gentled the black mustang. Approaching Luke would be easier if she didn't have to face his stepmother first. The woman had made no attempt to welcome her to Montrose. And why should she? Kizzie probably hadn't wanted her on Montrose in the first place.

When Deanna approached the corrals, Kizzie turned abruptly, shading her eyes with her hand. She turned her back on Deanna and focused her gaze on the action inside the corral.

Deanna hesitated. Apparently, Luke's stepmother wasn't going to be friendly. Deanna breathed deeply, then released the breath and marched directly over to Kizzie.

"Good afternoon, Mrs. McClendon."

"Hello, Deanna," Kizzie said in a sharp tone.

"Beautiful day today."

"Right pretty weather for May." The sharpness in her voice dulled slightly.

"I was looking for Luke," Deanna said. "I stopped by the house and Alva told me where I could find him."

"You should have known Luke wouldn't be at the house at three-thirty in the afternoon. There's too much work to be done on this ranch for him to stay inside while the weather's this cool."

"Alva said he was gentling a new mustang."

Deanna glanced out into the corral and her breath caught in her throat. Luke stood in the middle of the corral rubbing the horse's neck and head. She didn't know who was the more magnificent, or which was the untamed beast. The mustang wasn't an elegant horse by any means, but there was a wild beauty about him just as there was about Luke.

Luke's old jeans were faded and dusty. He had rolled the sleeves of his chambray shirt up to his elbows and had cocked his Stetson back away from his forehead. Sweat stained the armpits of his shirt and dotted his forehead.

"Luke's got a way with animals. Just wish he was half as good with people," Kizzie said softly.

Deanna made no reply. Indeed she didn't know what

to say. Kizzie was right. Luke did have a way with animals, especially horses, but he was as wary of other people as they were of him. He was a man alone, separated from the rest of the world by some invisible barrier that he had erected to protect himself.

Deanna watched as Luke touched the stallion's ears and then his muzzle. Slowly, cautiously, he eased his thumb into the left corner of the horse's mouth. The mustang relaxed his lips and opened his mouth for the man with the magic touch.

Deanna shuddered as a shiver raced through her. Luke had such big, hard hands, but his touch could be tender and loving. With a horse. And with a woman. Closing her eyes, she could feel and see Luke making love to her. Slow, sweet love. The kind of loving that could last all night.

"He's going to try putting a bridle on that wild boy today," Kizzie said. "He's been working with him for a couple of weeks now. That's been one stubborn horse. Luke even had to use molasses the first couple of times to get him to open his mouth."

"Molasses?" Deanna moved closer to the edge of the fence where Kizzie stood.

"Don't tell me you don't know that old trick." Kizzie chuckled. "You stick a little molasses in a horse's mouth, let him taste it and then before you know it, he's working his mouth and opening his lips."

"Oh, I see."

"Notice how Luke's got him haltered and the lead rope draped over his left arm? Luke's training the horse to lower his head to Luke's comfortable working level."

Well, at least now Kizzie was talking to her in a pleasant tone. She didn't want Luke's stepmother against her, but she had no idea how to win the woman over.

"You're very fond of Luke, aren't you." The words were a comment, not really a question.

Snapping her head around, Kizzie glared at Deanna. "Yeah, you could say that. I love Luke like a son. I didn't at first. He wasn't an easy person to like, let alone love. But when I looked past all that huffing and puffing he did, I realized what a lost soul he was. If ever a boy needed to be loved and accepted, Luke did."

"You and your husband welcomed him into your family. You did everything possible to—"

"You destroyed him. He's never been the same since the trial. He wouldn't let us come to Huntsville to see him, you know. And he never answered a one of my letters."

"But why—"

"A man that doesn't care about anyone can't ever be hurt. During those five years in prison, Luke finished the job of isolating himself from human emotions. He came home to us, but he's never been a part of us. He won't let himself be."

"I hope that when we can prove who really killed my father, Luke will be free from the past and can learn to reach out to the people who love him."

"Do you love him, girl? Is that what this is really all about?"

Deanna was taken aback. She'd never expected the woman to see so deeply into her heart and find those hopes and dreams she had buried there long ago.

"I don't know," Deanna said. "A part of me still cares about Luke...the Luke I knew and loved fifteen years ago."

"He's not the same. You've seen what he's like now." Kizzie grabbed Deanna's arm. "I don't know what scares me the most—you hurting him or him hurting you. Either way, it'll finish him off. And I can't bear to see that happen."

"I'm not going to hurt Luke. I promise you that." Deanna patted Kizzie's hand.

Jerking her hand away, Luke's stepmother turned her attention back to the corral. "With a little work Luke could even lower that wild boy's nose all the way to the ground. The mustang has learned to yield to that pressure now."

Luke held the headstall in his left hand, with the reins draped over his right arm, while he lowered the mustang's head. He raised his left hand and the headstall up to meet his right hand and the horse's forelock. Then he transferred the top of the headstall from his left hand to his right, simultaneously grasping the forelock in his right hand.

Deanna watched, amazed at the ease with which Luke handled the stallion. Not only did Luke know exactly what he was doing, he considered the horse's feelings every step of the way. Was it easy to care about animals, knowing they wouldn't love you and then leave you? Wouldn't betray you. Wouldn't rip out your heart.

Luke held the headstall and forelock with his right hand, then raised the bit to the horse's mouth with his left hand. As he rubbed the stallion's gums and tongue with his left thumb, he waited patiently for him to open his mouth. He didn't force any action. Didn't rush in any way.

There was such patience and caring in the way Luke managed the horse. He had touched her, loved her—

once—and just as this horse was doing, she had given him whatever he'd asked of her.

After letting the mustang take the bit into his mouth at his own speed, Luke gently pushed the horse's ears forward and the headstall over them, one at a time. Then he adjusted the headstall and the throat latch.

The horse worked his mouth, running his tongue over and under the bit. Luke petted the big animal, speaking low and soft to him. Deanna wondered if he was praising the stallion, telling him what a fine beast he was.

She remembered when Luke had praised her, his words sincere. Strange how she was standing here wishing that Luke would treat her the way he treated that horse. With gentleness and patience and understanding. And with respect.

Deanna turned away, no longer able to look at Luke, to think about what it might have been like for them if she'd had the courage to run away with him that night. If only she hadn't been so afraid. For Luke. And for herself. If she had gone with him when he'd begged her to go, what would their lives be like now? She'd be Luke's wife and the mother of his children.

When Deanna started to walk away, Kizzie grabbed her arm. "I thought you wanted to see Luke."

"I did, but—"

"Don't you think I've watched him with the horses and wished, just once, he'd show me, or one of his brothers, or even a stranger, the same kind of caring he lavishes on those animals?"

"I wanted to tell Luke that more of my memory has returned," Deanna said. "I remembered that Luke threw the pitchfork into the ground and walked away.

He asked me, one last time to go with him, and when I refused, he left the Circle A that night.''

"Oh, mercy! You actually remember Luke walking away, leaving your father alive?''

"Yes, and I've been waiting for Luke to come to see me so I could tell him. I even left him a message to call me.''

"He's stubborn as a mule. He's not going to meet you halfway, you know." Kizzie released her hold on Deanna's arm. "Stay until he finishes up with the mustang, then talk to him. Tell him what you remembered." Kizzie walked past Deanna. "I'm going back to the house. You two will need to be alone.''

Luke glanced up and saw his stepmother leaving. He called out to her, but she just waved and kept on going. He tried to avoid eye contact with Deanna. He'd known for quite some time that she was watching him.

"Luke." Deanna waved at him.

He nodded his head but didn't respond verbally. While she returned to the fence, he watched her. Damn but she looked good. Tight jeans encasing those long, slender legs. Legs that went on forever. Legs that had wrapped tightly around him when they'd made love. And a shirt with just enough buttons open to tempt a man's gaze. Nobody could convince him that she hadn't known exactly what she was doing dressing that way. She was out for bear and had set her trap accordingly.

"Luke, when you finish up here, I need to talk to you.''

"I don't have time," he told her. "When I get through here, I've got to ride out and check the water troughs and windmills. That's something that has to be checked at least every other day. I didn't get around to it yesterday, so it has to be done today.''

''I'll ride out with you and we can talk.''

Deanna was temptation personified. He didn't love her. Hell, he didn't even like her. But he sure did want her. How could a man dislike a woman—hate a woman—and still want her to the point of madness?

''Go over to the stables and ask Herb to saddle Fair Weather for you. I'll come on over in a bit.''

''Thank you, Luke. I wouldn't have bothered you, but…well, I have something important to tell you.''

A cold shudder racked Luke's body, then he looked away, turning his attention back to the mustang. The last time Deanna had said that she had something important to tell him, she'd told him she was pregnant.

Deanna had kept up with Luke as they covered as much of Montrose as was possible in one afternoon. He hadn't said more than two words to her while they checked the water troughs and windmills. And she had kept silent, waiting for the right moment to tell him what she had remembered. But as the hours passed, she grew impatient. When she'd waited as long as she could stand it, she asked Luke to stop.

''Please, Luke, can't we talk now? I really do have something to tell you. Something I think you'll want to hear.''

''When I finish up, we'll ride up there—'' he nodded toward the hills ''—and talk.''

An hour later, they rode up into the hills—the glorious hills that were alive with the blush of springtime. A profusion of wildflowers, especially bluebells, lined the paths and covered the fields, adding a purple hue to the land. The sun lay low in the western horizon, an orange fireball descending from the heavens.

She hadn't ridden into the hills on the northern side of Montrose in fifteen years, not since the night she'd met Luke at *their* cabin and told him that she was going to have his baby. But Luke wasn't taking her toward their cabin. He led her up the path and to the right. The old cabin lay to the left of the well-worn route.

When they reached the summit, a high ridge that overlooked the ranch, Luke dismounted, but he made no effort to assist Deanna. He used to help her off her horse, lift her into his arms and carry her to the ground, eager and passionate, his body hungry for hers. Now, he didn't even pay her the courtesy of offering his hand. Deanna dismounted and followed Luke, who stood on the ridge, gazing out over Montrose.

With his back to her, he said, "So what's so important that you had to tag along with me while I worked?"

"If you'd bothered to return my call, to drop by and see me for a few minutes, I wouldn't have had to track you down today!"

"I told you, when I agreed to help you, that I wouldn't have much time for you. This is a working ranch and my job comes first with me."

She grabbed his arm, her fingers biting into the hard muscle. "Dammit, Luke, I'm not a fool. Don't you think I know why you're avoiding me?"

His big body tensed. The muscles under her hand tightened. "I've been busy. I haven't been avoiding you."

"You're afraid of me. Afraid I might make you feel something. And you couldn't handle that, could you? You're a big, strong, tough guy who doesn't need anybody, but you haven't got the guts to risk caring about anyone or anything!''

Knocking her hand aside, he turned on her, his eyes wild, his jaw tight. Deanna backed away from him. He reached out, took her shoulders in his big hands and glared at her. She trembled beneath his touch. For one instant, she was actually frightened. Luke looked so fierce when he was angry.

''You think you've got me all figured out, don't you, babe?'' He practically growled the words. ''You'd like to think that I still give a damn. That I still care about you. Well, I don't. You don't mean anything to me.''

''Does anyone?'' She wriggled, trying to free herself from his tenacious hold.

''No. No one and nothing, except Montrose.''

''Not even the truth? Doesn't the truth mean something to you?'' she asked.

He dropped his hands away from her shoulders, but continued glowering at her. ''What are you talking about?''

''The truth, Luke. You know—telling it like it is. Facts. What really happened.''

''If you've got something to tell me, say it!''

''I had another memory flash,'' she said. ''While I was talking to Junior.''

''So?''

Why did Luke have to be so nasty to her? Why couldn't he understand that he wasn't the only one who had suffered? *Because, nitwit, he has no idea what you went through at Millones. For all he knows, you've spent the last fifteen years happy as a lark.*

''I remembered that you grabbed the pitchfork and told Daddy that he'd never whip you again. You started walking toward him. And I think Daddy was actually scared. He backed away from you. And you—you walked toward him, then you threw the pitchfork into the ground and kept on going. You glanced back over your shoulder and asked me to come with you. I wouldn't go, so you left.''

Luke stared at her as if he wasn't quite sure what to make of what she'd told him. ''That's exactly what happened,'' he said. ''But what I don't know is whether you've suddenly just remembered that vital piece of information or whether you've known all along.''

''You think I've known all along! That I lied on the witness stand. That I let you go to prison when I could have saved you.'' Deanna rushed at him, her fists lifted against him. When she was within a foot of him, she halted. Her breathing ragged, her face hot, she stared at him and saw all the doubt and distrust in his eyes. She lowered her arms.

''I don't know,'' he said calmly. Too calmly. ''You tell me, Miss Atchley.''

''Do you honestly think that I would subject myself to your abuse if I wasn't desperate to remember everything that happened that night? Why would I be willing to put myself at your disposal night and day, allowing you to treat me any way you want to, if the truth—the whole truth—wasn't vitally important to me?''

''Maybe you've got a guilty conscience. Maybe after all these years, you actually do want to set the record straight. But you've got to admit that it seems odd that you couldn't remember a damn thing about me walking away, leaving your father alive and well, fifteen years ago, right after it had happened. But now, suddenly, after all this time, you can remember I didn't kill your old man.''

"Why can't you believe me?" She held out her hands beseechingly. "Don't you know that I'd never lie to you, that I'd give my life if I could change the past. I loved you so much. I..." Emotions so strong they nearly choked her created a blockage in her throat, preventing her from talking.

"You're good, lady. I'll give you that. You know how to twist the knife so it hurts the most, don't you!"

Deanna gasped, gulping in air. "If you don't *care,* how can I hurt you? If I don't still mean something to you, then how is it possible for me to affect you so strongly?"

"You want to know what you mean to me, Deanna? You really want to know?"

"Yes."

"Then get on your horse and follow me. I'll show you exactly how I feel about you and why you still have any effect on me at all."

Deanna was bewildered by his statement, amazed that he was no longer denying that she did affect him, that he did have feelings of some sort for her.

Without saying a word, she mounted Fair Weather and waited for Luke. When he stared at her, the corners of his mouth lifted in a hint of a smile. A dangerous, deadly smile. And Deanna's stomach tightened into knots. Where was he taking her? And what was he going to do to show her exactly how he felt?

Within a few minutes, she realized where he was taking her. The moment they turned off the path and went right, her heartbeat rolled like thunder in her ears. This passage led straight to the old cabin. The cabin where she and Luke had made love for the first time. Their rendezvous spot, where they had spent hours alone, loving each other, talking to each other, making plans for their future.

Dear Lord, if he was taking her there, did he actually still care, did he want to tell her that they could find a way to forgive each other and—no, she didn't dare hope for more. But he knew that the cabin represented their young, passionate love. Even Luke wouldn't be cruel enough to take her to their most special place on earth to her and tell her that he hated her.

Although she wanted to hurry, wanted to fly to the cabin, Luke took his time. Before they reached the crook in the trail that led off directly in front of the cabin, Luke slowed, then stopped and dismounted.

"This path's not clear the rest of the way," he said, his voice void of any emotion. "We'll have to walk."

She nodded agreement, then dismounted and followed him. He picked his way through the brush that had grown to cover this northwest dirt path. Why was this trail so overgrown? Hadn't Luke or anyone else been up here in years? Or did he usually take the other route, up the back side of the hill from the northeast?

Luke shoved aside the limbs on a tall bush in order for them to pass. The closer they drew to the cabin, the more intense Deanna's feelings of apprehension grew. Something was wrong. Terribly wrong.

And then she saw the site where the old cabin had stood for over a hundred years. She moved past Luke, as if in a trance. Realization struck her hard, like a lethal blow from a fighter's fist. So this was why Luke had brought her here.

Covering her mouth with her hands, she stifled a scream. The only thing left standing was the rock chimney, a lone survivor of an obliterating fire. She walked through the charred ruins, barely able to believe what she was seeing.

"Oh, Luke, what happened? Did lightning strike the cabin and catch it afire?"

"No," he said.

"Then what happened?" When she stared into his hard, green eyes she saw the truth and that truth hurt her in a way nothing had in a long, long time. "You— you did this, didn't you? You destroyed *our* cabin."

"It was the first thing I did when I got home from Huntsville." Luke joined her inside the ruins, his booted feet crunching over sticks and dried leaves and the vegetation that had overrun the sooty remains. "I rode up here, cleaned the land around the cabin, dug a protective trench around the place and then doused the cabin with kerosene, lit a match and watched it burn. I made sure the fire didn't spread beyond the cabin."

"Why, Luke? Why burn the cabin? Your great-grandfather built that cabin. It meant so much to you. It was our—" She paused as realization dawned. He'd burned it because it had once been their place.

"You wanted to know how I feel about you." Spreading out his arms, Luke turned his head from side to side, inspecting the destruction his hatred and bitterness had caused. "Take a good, hard look at this place and you'll know what I think of you."

She had thought Luke couldn't be this cruel, but now she knew better. He had wanted to hurt her, wanted to destroy any illusions that there was hope for them to forgive and forget. Luke didn't want to put the past behind him. He intended to use it as a shield to protect himself from her.

She struggled not to cry, not to show any sign of weakness to Luke. He was like a wild animal poised to attack again if she seemed vulnerable enough for him to come in for the kill.

"What's happened to you to turn you into such a ruthless monster?" She stared at him, tears swimming in her eyes. "When I met you at the motel and allowed you to use me and humiliate me, I knew you were filled with hate, but I thought—I had hoped that by letting you vent your anger and take revenge, I could give you back a part of yourself. Give you back your soul. But I see now that you're beyond help. Anyone's help. Even mine."

Like the trapped animal she was, Deanna ran—away from Luke and away from the pain inside her. With tears blinding her, she couldn't see where she was going. Didn't care where she was going. She'd been a fool to think that by discovering the truth about her father's death, she could gain Luke's forgiveness and set things right.

"What's wrong? Can't you face the truth?" Luke called after her. "I'm not the one who still cares. You are. You're the one hurting, not me."

Deanna stumbled, but caught herself before she fell. She had to make her way back to her horse and leave this place. Swiping her eyes, she dashed away her tears too late to see the downed tree limb just as she fell over it. She landed with a dull thud, the wind momentarily knocked out of her. She gasped for air, and when her lungs filled again, her chest ached.

Before she could move, she felt strong hands grasping her, turning her over onto her back. She gazed up into Luke's dark green eyes. She saw him study her carefully as if making sure she was okay. But once he ran his hands over her face and body and was assured she had suffered no injury, the concern disappeared from his eyes, replaced by an angry, mercenary look. This wasn't the Luke she had loved. The wild, passionate boy who had been capable of tenderness and compassion. No, this man was a stranger.

He dragged her up and onto her feet, all the while keeping his arms around her. She trembled from head to toe, still badly shaken from the fall and frightened by this man who had so easily ripped out her heart.

"Why the hell did you have to come back!" He clasped the back of her head with one hand as he held her in place with the other. He lowered his head and took her mouth in a savage kiss. Deanna stood there— shocked, frightened and yet strangely aroused by his brutal kiss. He plundered and pillaged, thrusting his tongue inside, pressing her body into his as he gripped her head in his big hand.

She had no fight left in her. Luke had drained every ounce of life from her by his cruelty. She let him maul her with his mouth and hands, making no protest by word or action to indicate she wanted him to stop.

When he cupped her buttock and lifted her up and into his arousal, she shivered, her body responding traitorously to his intimacies. He lowered her to the ground, his lips madly covering her face and neck. He hovered over her like a giant, large and powerful. Stunned by his passion, dazed by her own acceptance, she stared up at him and saw desire burning in his eyes.

He wanted her as she wanted him. He was as powerless as she was over the driving need that forced his actions. He could hate her. He could willingly hurt and humiliate her. He could deny that she meant anything to him. But he could not hide his body's reaction to hers.

"Oh, Luke," she whispered and reached up to touch his face.

The moment her hand made contact with his beard-stubbled chin, his body jerked and he closed his eyes, as if trying to shut out the pity he obviously saw on her face.

Rising from the ground, he lifted her up and into his arms. Deanna draped her arm around his neck and laid her head on his shoulder. Silent and strong, Luke carried her down the path to where their horses waited. He set her on her feet, then grasped her hand in his.

"The only power you have left over me is this." He placed her hand on his crotch, pressing her palm against the bulge in his jeans. "And I know dozens of women who can ease this ache. I don't even need you for sex. I got what I wanted from you at the motel the other night, so I won't be bothering you with my unwanted attentions anymore."

"Luke, I—"

"Oh, I'm not kicking you off the ranch," he said. "Feel free to stay on as long as it takes for the rest of your memory to return. That shouldn't take long, should it? Just look how quickly you remembered seeing me walk away and leave your father alive that night. Heck, within a week, your memory should be fully restored."

Luke lifted her up and into the saddle, then handed her the reins. "Who really killed Rayburn? Was it good ole Eddie? Was it Junior or maybe even Benita? Or did your mother actually sully her hands and plunge that pitchfork into the old bastard herself?"

Deanna shook her head sadly. "No matter what I say, you won't believe me, will you? You're so eaten alive with hatred that you aren't willing to give me the benefit of the doubt. Dammit, Luke, what are you so afraid of? Are you scared that I may actually be telling the truth? That I didn't mean to betray you? That after all these years, I still care about you?''

Luke slapped Fair Weather on the rump and set the chestnut mare into motion. Deanna didn't glance back as she rode away, up the path and down the hill.

Luke watched her until she disappeared from sight, then he mounted Cherokee and headed in the opposite direction. He wasn't going home tonight. Hell, he might not ever go home again. Not as long as Deanna was staying in the guest cottage. He had told her that he didn't need her for sex anymore and the look on her face had been almost as priceless as it had been when she'd first realized the old cabin was gone forever.

He wasn't going to feel guilty for hurting her, and he knew he had. He had taken the knife out of his own heart and plunged it into hers. What he didn't understand was why the pain wouldn't go away. Why did he hurt even more now than he had before he'd gutted her with his cruelty? She deserved what he'd done to her and more, didn't she?

Luke accelerated Cherokee's speed, racing him across the open range. All the while memories chased him like demons. Memories of Deanna's face when he'd told her he had burned their cabin to the ground. If she didn't still care about him, seeing the cabin ruins wouldn't have hurt her so deeply. But he'd known before he took her there how she would react. He'd counted on it. He had known Deanna still cared.

And God help him, so did he.

Chapter 9

Standing on the front porch of the guest cottage, Deanna stared at the main house. It was after nine o'clock, so Luke would have been up for a good four hours now. She wondered where he was and what he was doing. Yesterday when she'd taken a walk around the inner sanctum of Montrose, she had overheard two young hands talking about old man Cooley finally selling Hercules to Luke. Apparently for the past year, Luke had been trying to persuade Otis Cooley to sell his prize bull. Maybe that's where Luke was, she thought. Gone to bring Hercules home to Montrose.

Whatever else he was doing, Luke was doing a good job of ignoring her. He hadn't spoken to her in over a week—not since the evening he'd taken her to the old cabin site. The evening he'd made it perfectly clear that he didn't want anything to do with her. She supposed he'd expected her to pack her bags and leave Montrose, but she'd been hell-bent on staying.

It had become apparent that Luke didn't want to help her, that his distrust of her outweighed his need to discover the truth. She realized that perhaps her only hope of learning the identity of her father's real killer lay in regaining her memory of that fateful night. To pass the time, she rode Fair Weather up into the hills every day, but always avoided the remains of the cabin. She didn't think she could bear to see it again without crying. It had never entered her mind that Luke might have destroyed their special place. If there had been any doubts in her mind that Luke truly hated her, he had erased those doubts.

But she could endure Luke's hatred, his avoidance of her, his cold, bitter glares whenever he saw her wandering around the ranch—she could endure almost anything—because she knew it was only a matter of time until her memory returned. All of it. Every lost fragment. Dr. Kirkland had been right—facing Luke, confronting her love for him and her guilt over what she'd done had acted as a catalyst, accelerating the return of memories her mind had blocked for fifteen years. Every day, she remembered something new. Tiny pieces of a giant puzzle, but added together they represented a part of her life that trauma had destroyed. More and more flashbacks from the trial haunted her. Testimony of the key witnesses—Eddie Nunley and Phyllis Atchley, who swore they'd seen Luke running away and found Deanna huddled over her father's lifeless body. She hadn't questioned the validity of their sworn statements—not once in all these years. But now she did. She didn't know why—not yet—but she knew that her mother and Eddie had lied. They hadn't seen Luke. She knew they hadn't! Somewhere buried in her subconscious was that memory—the memory that Luke had left long before Phyllis and Eddie had come to the stables. If only she could recall the details. But the harder she tried to bring them forth, the deeper the memories buried themselves.

If only Luke would talk to her, tell her what he remembered about that night… If only he would live up to his end of the bargain and really try to help her.

Who was she kidding? Luke had gotten what he'd wanted—her subjugation and her humiliation. And he'd allowed her to stay on in the guest cottage. The way he looked at it, they were finished. Maybe he was right. Maybe staying on here at Montrose was foolish. Her memory seemed to be returning steadily, even if only in bits and pieces. She could stay with Patsy Ruth, who'd given her an open invitation. Or she could go home to the Circle A. Junior called her every day. To check on her, to make sure she was all right, he'd said. "Why don't you come home where you belong?" he'd asked her more than once. "Don't let Luke McClendon hurt you any more than he already has."

Even with her brother and her best friend from childhood both advising her to leave Montrose, to give up on saving Luke from himself, she found it hard to say goodbye to a dream. Yes, a dream. For the past ten years—since the day she'd left Millones—she had dreamed of being reunited with Luke. In her dream, he always forgave her, always loved her again, always promised her a future with him. If she left Montrose, she would have to stop dreaming the impossible dream. And without that dream, she had nothing.

She had to talk to Luke, to give him one last chance. But if he turned his back on her again, she would leave Montrose. She'd taken all she could stand. And without any hope of Luke changing his mind about her, there was no point in staying. He wasn't going to help her. And he certainly wasn't ever going to care about her again.

On her way to the stables, Deanna rounded the side of the barn and came upon Luke corralling a big Beefmaster bull. Was this the famous Hercules, the bull Luke had been trying to buy for over a year now?

A potbellied elderly man stood behind a shiny new Ford pickup. He scratched his head, mussing the sparse white strands that barely covered the round bald spot in the center. If the animal was Hercules, then the man had to be Otis "Ole Man" Cooley.

Maybe Luke would be in a good mood this morning, now that he had captured the prize. Years ago, when Baxter McClendon was alive, Luke had told her how much he loved Montrose, how desperately he wanted to be a real part of the family and how he longed to follow in his father's footsteps and take over the reins of the eighteen-thousand-acre ranch. Montrose was a family-owned cow-calf operation with a herd of around twelve hundred cattle. Herefords mostly. And a few registered Longhorns. And now a Beefmaster bull.

"If he gives you any trouble, pull one of these on him," Old Man Cooley said as he dragged a pitchfork out of the back of his truck. "My pappy never went into a corral with a bull unless he had his protection. Done the same all my life."

Luke glared at the pitchfork. Deanna's heart skipped a beat. Damn that old man. Didn't he have any idea what he'd just said to Luke? Obviously not. Mr. Cooley was probably eighty years old and half senile and it never entered his mind to consider the fact that Luke had been sent to prison for killing a man with a pitchfork.

The longer and harder Luke glowered at the pitchfork the longer Deanna gazed at it. Within minutes she
felt a strange tug, as if something was drawing her into
a whirlwind. Her head spun around and around. Dear
Lord, was she going to faint?

*The pitchfork in Mr. Cooley's hand grew larger and
larger until it was the size of a tree and then he disappeared altogether. Blood dripped from the pronged
weapon. Rivulets of red liquid poured onto the ground.*

*Luke turned his back on her and walked away. No,
Luke, please, come back. Don't abandon me. Save me,
Luke. Please, save me.*

*Suddenly her father towered over her, his eyes shoot-
ing hot beams of fire into her. She cried out from the
burning rays of his gaze.*

"No, Daddy, please. Don't. Don't!"

*His big fist rammed into her belly. She doubled over
and fell to the ground. The pain shot through her like
a knife blade.*

*Junior and Benita helped her to her feet, but she
drew away from them quickly. Both of them were covered in blood. Her daddy's blood.*

*Her mother slapped her, screamed at her, damned
her for bringing the curse of Luke McClendon into
their lives.*

*"Leave her alone, Phyllis," Eddie said. "Can't you
see that she's in shock. Don't worry about her. She'll
do what you tell her to and say whatever we need for
her to say."*

The world spun around her, as if she'd been caught
up inside a tornado. Memories flashed by like ten-
second segments on a television screen.

Her father lying on the ground, the pitchfork stuck

in his chest. Benita crying softly. Junior staring off into space. Her mother arguing with Eddie.

And then she wasn't on the Circle A anymore. She was at the Luma County courthouse, testifying against Luke at his trial.

He looked at her with dead eyes. And she knew he hated her. "Please don't hate me. Please. I can't remember. I can't. Mother forced me to take the stand. She threatened to kill our baby if I didn't. Don't hate me."

The courthouse disappeared into a swirling gray mist.

A kind hand stroked her brow. A soft voice assured her that she would be all right. A nurse. The nurse at Millones, comforting her after she'd lost her baby. Luke's baby. Their baby had died.

She cried out, pleading with God not to take her baby. It was all she had of Luke.

"It's all right, Deanna," the nurse said. "You can have other babies someday."

But not Luke's babies. Not ever Luke's. And if I can't have Luke's children, I don't want any other babies.

"Luke! Luke! Luke!" She screamed his name repeatedly.

Deanna screamed his name. Luke snapped his head around and looked in Deanna's direction. What the hell? The expression on her face scared the hell out of him. She was in a trance, her eyes glazed over and her face deathly pale.

"I heard she was crazy," Old Man Cooley said. "That Atchley girl who saw you kill her pappy. She disappeared after your trial, didn't she? I always figured she was in the looney bin somewhere."

As he climbed the fence, jumped down and ran toward Deanna, Luke ignored Otis Cooley. Deanna swayed on her feet as she stumbled in a haphazard fashion.

"You ought to get that gal into town to see a doctor. She's touched in the head all right." Otis tossed the pitchfork back into the truck bed.

Deanna's knees buckled. She grasped out into thin air. "Luke. I'm sorry. Please, Luke." She crumpled like a starched lace doily dropped into warm water.

Luke caught her before she hit the ground, then lifted her into his arms and headed toward the main house.

"She ain't dead, is she?" Otis asked.

"No, she just fainted," Luke called out to the old man. "Our business is finished, isn't it, Mr. Cooley? You can go on home now. And take your damn pitchfork with you!"

Luke tromped across the yard, through the arched porch openings and straight for the front door. Holding an unconscious Deanna close to his chest, he leaned over and pressed down on the pewter door handle.

Kizzie swung open the door. "Oh, Lordy. What happened? We heard Deanna screaming." Alva stood directly behind Kizzie.

Luke swept past them, taking Deanna straight into the living room, where he deposited her on the sofa. Kneeling beside her, he shoved the honey-brown strands of hair away from her face.

Kizzie placed her hand on Luke's shoulder. "What happened? Is she hurt?"

"She had some kind of spell," Luke said. "Right before she passed out, she looked like she was in a trance."

"Where was she?" Kizzie asked. "And what brought on this spell of hers?"

"Should I call for an ambulance?" Alva gathered her apron into her hands, knotting the edge into a wad.

"Not yet," Kizzie said. "Go get a damp cloth and we'll see if we can bring her around."

Luke stroked Deanna's cheek and called her name. "Come on. Wake up. You're safe."

"Luke, did she fall and hit her head?" Kizzie squeezed his shoulder.

"No. I caught her before she hit the ground. She came nosing around out there by the barn while I was corralling Hercules. Old Man Cooley pulled a pitchfork out of the back end of his truck and—"

"That stupid old fool! What was he thinking, hauling out a pitchfork in front of you and Deanna?"

"To give the old coot the benefit of the doubt, I don't think he even remembered anything about Rayburn Atchley's murder. Not until Deanna started acting funny. Then he said something about he figured she'd been in a looney bin all these years."

"What a ridiculous thing for him to have said."

"Deanna was acting mighty strange," Luke admitted. "I think she was having one of those memory flashbacks. She kept saying odd things."

"What things?"

"I didn't pay much attention. At first, I thought she was talking to Mr. Cooley. Then I heard her say something like, 'No, Daddy, don't,' but I just ignored her. She also said, 'Don't hate me.' Then a few minutes later she screamed my name over and over again."

"That poor girl."

Luke glanced up at his stepmother and realized that she believed Deanna was worthy of her pity. He looked back at Deanna. She couldn't have faked this. Whatever had happened to her had been real.

She hasn't been lying to you, a voice in his head whispered. She really has been suffering from partial amnesia for fifteen years. And she honestly wants to remember. She wants to clear your name.

"Here's a nice cool cloth." Alva handed the damp rag to Kizzie, who in turn gave it to Luke.

He washed her face gently, then patted her cheeks. "Come on, babe. Wake up."

"Luke?" she said groggily.

"I'm right here." He clasped her hand in his.

"Luke, please…" Her eyelids fluttered.

"It's all right, Deanna. I'm here with you and I know seeing Mr. Cooley holding that pitchfork unnerved you a little."

She opened her eyes, then closed them. "I remembered…I…I think I—"

"Don't worry about remembering right now. Just take it easy. You passed out on me and scared Kizzie and Alva half to death."

She opened her eyes again. "I'm sorry, I didn't mean to— Oh, Luke, I remembered being in the hospital after I lost our baby. The nurse told me I could have other babies. But I didn't want any other baby. Only yours." She tried to sit up.

Luke grabbed her shoulders and pressed her down onto the sofa. "Just lie there and rest." His chest tightened. His jaw clenched. Pain stabbed him square in the gut.

She gripped his hand. "But don't you see. The memories are getting stronger and stronger. And they're all coming at once. A bit of this memory and a bit of that one. My mind is like a cracked dam with all these tiny holes spewing water.'' She reached out and clutched both of his forearms. ''I wish the dam would burst and I'd remember everything.''

''You will, babe. You will. Just not right now. You're too weak to try to remember any more about the past.''

''But I have to remember,'' she said. ''Don't you understand? If I can't remember what happened, you'll never be free. You'll go on hating me, go on feeling unloved and unworthy. I have to remember. For your sake, Luke.''

He pulled away from her and fled the living room.

''Luke.'' Deanna tried to sit up again.

Kizzie sat down on the sofa beside Deanna and helped her into a sitting position. ''Give him some time alone. He'll be back. I think you finally got through to him.''

''You believe me, don't you?'' Deanna gazed incredulously at Kizzie.

''Yes, I believe you. And I think Luke does, too.''

''I never meant to hurt him. Never. I loved him, but I was so afraid of Daddy, and then Mother threatened to—''

Kizzie patted Deanna's cheek. ''Don't excite yourself so, girl. You're just coming around from a dead faint. No need to try to explain your whole life to me in five minutes.''

Deanna lifted her head from the sofa, testing to see if she was able to sit up. ''I think I'm all right. I'd like to sit up now, please.''

Kizzie helped her sit, then motioned to Alva. ''Go in the kitchen and pour up a shot of whiskey and bring it to me.''

"Think you're going to be all right now, Miss Deanna?" Alva asked.

"Yes, thank you. I'm feeling much better."

Kizzie shooed Alva out of the room, then turned her attention to Deanna. "As soon as Alva brings the whiskey, I want you to drink it and then I'll walk you back over to the cottage and stay with you for a while. I don't think Luke will be ready to see you or talk to you right away."

"I was looking for Luke this morning when I came upon Mr. Cooley, right after he'd delivered Hercules. I'd decided to tell Luke that I was leaving Montrose, that I'd given up on him."

"And now, do you still want to leave?" Kizzie asked.

"I don't know." Deanna rubbed her aching forehead. "I want to help Luke. He's in so much pain and I know that a great deal of it is my fault."

"Not all of Luke's problems are your fault." Kizzie shook her head sadly. "Luke's life started out all wrong, with no father and a young half-Cherokee mother trying to make it alone in the white world. All Luke knew for fifteen years was that he was a quarter-breed bastard whose mother didn't earn enough money to put food on the table half the time. That boy grew up wild and lonely, without any self-confidence. After she died and he came looking for the man she'd told him was his father, he was prepared for rejection. I don't think he knew how to handle the fact that Baxter and I accepted him into the family so quickly. Or that Baxter legally recognized him as his son less than a year after he showed up on our doorstep."

"Yes, I know all about Luke's childhood, but he had just begun to fit in, to think of himself as a real

McClendon, when…when my father…'' She couldn't bring herself to say the words.

''When your father took a horsewhip and nearly beat my boy to death.''

''Luke might have been predisposed to being a loner, filled with rage and hatred, but if I hadn't betrayed him, if he hadn't spent five years in prison, then—''

The front door flew open just as Alva returned from the kitchen. Kizzie and Deanna glanced up at the dusty cowpoke standing in the entrance foyer.

''Les Cunningham, dust off them boots before you come in this house,'' Alva scolded the middle-aged man.

''Sorry about your clean floors, Alva, but I've got to see Luke. Right now.'' Les removed his sweat-stained Stetson, then nodded when he saw Kizzie in the living room. ''Good day, Mrs. McClendon.''

''What seems to be the problem, Les?'' Kizzie asked.

''Well, ma'am, I need to see Luke.''

''Alva!'' Kizzie motioned the housekeeper to her. ''Bring me that whiskey, then go tell Mr. Luke that Les is here and it's urgent.'' Cocking her head to one side, Kizzie gazed at the ranch hand. ''That is right, isn't it, Les? This is an urgent matter?''

''Yes, ma'am, it most definitely is.''

Alva rushed over, handed the shot glass to Kizzie and hurried off to find Luke. Kizzie gave the whiskey to Deanna.

''Drink it all. Now.''

Deanna followed her instructions. The straight whiskey burned as it went down and landed in her stomach like a fireball. She coughed a couple of times and gasped for air.

Luke appeared suddenly and Deanna wondered where he'd been and what he'd been thinking. There was a tired, pained look in his eyes.

"What's this urgent matter, Les?" Luke asked.

"Well, you might ought to come with me, Luke. Out to the eastern range. I got Bud keeping an eye on things. Seems somebody done gone and shot about twenty head of our cattle. Killed with a rifle, I'd say, at long range. Just left them lying out there."

"When did you discover the dead cattle?" Luke glanced into the living room straight at Kizzie.

"Just a while ago. Me and Bud was checking for new calves when we come up on the cattle. God, Luke, who do you think would want to kill our cattle like that? Wasn't nobody hungry or they'd have killed one and taken the meat. Somebody did this for pure meanness."

"You go on with Les and have a look," Kizzie said. "I'll call Tyler and tell him what's happened."

Luke glanced quickly at Deanna. Kizzie nodded understanding.

"I'll take care of our guest, too."

Luke didn't say a word to Deanna before he hurried out the front door with Les Cunningham.

Somewhere deep inside, in her gut, she wondered why anyone would want to hurt the McClendons. And the only answer that came to her was the Atchleys. But why? Why would her family want to harm Luke's family—now—when there was no reason. Or was there?

"You just sit here and take it easy," Kizzie said. "I've got to call Tyler. As the sheriff, he'll have to investigate the crime. And as a McClendon, he has a stake in anything that happens on Montrose."

"Who would have committed such a senseless act?"

Deanna wanted any explanation that would eliminate her fears about her family's involvement.

"I don't know. But when Luke finds out, there's going to be hell to pay."

"Well, Mama, I sure am glad you talked me into staying for dinner." Tall, lean Tyler McClendon leaned back in the chair and patted his firm stomach. "I don't get many home-cooked meals."

"If you came to visit more—" Kizzie said.

"I have a job, Mama, and it's not here on Montrose."

"It is today," Luke said. "We've got twenty head of cattle that were buzzard bait when Les and Bud found them. I've got to know who killed those animals and why."

"Well, big brother, you've made your share of enemies over the years," Tyler said. "Anybody you pissed off recently?"

"You think somebody got mad at Luke and killed twenty head of our cattle to get back at him?" Kizzie glared at her son, disbelief in her eyes.

"There's got to be a reason for such senseless slaughter." Tyler lifted his iced tea glass. "Whoever killed those animals did it to make a point and my guess is their point is to hurt this ranch, this family."

"What are the odds you'll find out who did it?" Deanna asked.

"Well, that depends." Tyler bestowed a warm smile on their dinner guest. "If we can figure out who Luke or even Grant or I ticked off, we might come up with a list of suspects. Or this person or persons might strike again."

"What do you mean they might strike again?" Kizzie asked.

"Depends on how pis—er, how ticked off they are. Could be this was a one-time thing. Or it could be just the beginning."

"I don't know anyone who'd want to hurt this family," Kizzie said. "What could any of us have done to someone to deserve this kind of payback?"

Luke's gaze met Deanna's and she knew instantly that he suspected the same people she did. But what would her family hope to accomplish by harming the McClendons?

Tyler caught the visual exchange between Luke and Deanna. He cleared his throat. "Do y'all think the Atchleys are involved?"

"After all these years, why…?" Kizzie gasped as realization dawned. "They're scared Deanna's going to remember the truth about who killed her daddy."

"If that's true, then they must already know who killed Rayburn," Tyler said.

"But how's killing off our cattle going to keep Deanna from remembering?" Kizzie asked.

"I don't know." Tyler finished his tea, then set the glass back on the table. "Besides, we could be barking up the wrong tree. The Atchleys might not have a thing to do with the cattle being shot."

"It could have been Andy Sales," Luke said. "We got in a fight about a month ago and he threatened to make me sorry that I'd ever crossed him."

"Andy Sales?" Tyler chuckled. "Bet you whipped his ass good, didn't you, big brother. What was the fight about? Corrine Watkins?"

"Tyler, I won't have that woman's name mentioned

at my dinner table.'' Kizzie folded her arms belligerently across her chest.

''I don't get in fights over women,'' Luke said. ''Andy claimed I cheated him when I played poker with him for those mustangs of his. He wouldn't sell the horses, but said he'd play me for them.''

''Well, the man was a fool!'' Tyler said. ''Apparently, he didn't know what Grant and I found out at an early age—never play cards with Luke.''

''Could be he decided to take revenge,'' Luke said.

''Well, we aren't going to settle this tonight.'' The minute Kizzie stood, her sons rose from their seats. ''Looks like we might have to wait and see. I'm tired out. We've had a big day, in more ways than one. Think I'm going to head on to bed.''

Tyler kissed his mother on the cheek, but Luke only nodded to Kizzie.

''One of you boys will see Deanna to the guest house, won't you?'' She looked directly at Luke. ''She's been a mite under the weather today and I don't want her—''

''I'd be delighted to walk Deanna over to the cottage,'' Tyler said.

''Thank you.'' Deanna smiled weakly at Luke's stepbrother. ''But that's not necessary. I'm perfectly all right. I can see myself home.''

''No way.'' Tyler offered her his arm. ''My mama wants you escorted and I'm your man. If you're ready, we can take a stroll before I see you to the cottage.''

Deanna hesitated, waiting for Luke to make an objection, but he didn't say a word. When she glanced at him, he looked away.

She took Tyler's arm. ''Thank you. I think I would like a nice stroll before turning in.''

The minute Tyler and Deanna walked out the front door, Kizzie turned to Luke. "Well, what do you make of that?"

"I'd say Tyler finds Deanna to be a beautiful, interesting woman," Luke said. "And God knows Tyler has a way with the ladies."

"So, you don't mind him walking Deanna to the cottage?"

"Why should I mind?"

"I don't suppose you should, if she doesn't mean anything to you," Kizzie said. "A woman can take only so much rejection before she gives up and starts looking elsewhere." With that, Kizzie left Luke standing alone in the living room.

He sucked in a deep breath, then released it. Deanna had wanted him to walk her to the cottage, not Tyler. He'd seen the silent plea in her eyes. Why the hell hadn't he said something? Why hadn't he told his little brother that Deanna was his woman and that if anybody was going to walk her home, he was?

Because she wasn't his. She hadn't been his girl since they were kids. He had no claim on Deanna. Not anymore.

He'd sworn that she would never get under his skin again. That he'd never allow her to have control over him the way she once had. And yet here he was, jealous of his own brother. The very thought that Tyler might hold Deanna's hand, might put his arm around her, might even kiss her good-night, tortured Luke.

But why did he care? What difference did it make? God only knew how many men there had been in Deanna's life and in her bed during the past fifteen years. Even as an inexperienced girl, Deanna had been an adventurous, eager lover. She had enjoyed sex far too much to have remained celibate all these years.

But those men were nameless faces in the past. Tyler was in the present—the here and now. And he was his brother, dammit!

He couldn't just sit around the house and brood. If he did, he'd go out of his mind. He had to get away, had to escape. And the sooner the better.

"Beautiful night," Tyler said as he walked alongside Deanna. "We could use a little rain soon. Been over a week now and as hot as it's getting, things could start drying out."

"Do you think my family's responsible for those dead cattle?" she asked.

Tyler stopped abruptly and turned to look down at her. "I honestly don't know. But you're asking the wrong man if you want somebody to defend your family. I'm Luke's brother, and I might have been only fifteen when he went to prison, but I know who was responsible for putting him there."

"I was." Lowering her head, Deanna stared down at the ground.

Tyler lifted her chin. He smiled. Deanna liked his smile. Warm and kind, like Kizzie's wide-mouthed grins.

"You were just a kid yourself—what, seventeen? I was in the courtroom the day you testified. Grant and me. And I saw how scared you were. If you hadn't been testifying against Luke, I'd have felt sorry for you."

Deanna laughed mournfully, then tossed back her head and clicked her tongue. "I remember, you know. Now. I remember seeing Luke stick the pitchfork in the ground and walk away. Why couldn't I have remembered that fact fifteen years ago?''

"Even if you had remembered, do you think your mother would have allowed you to take the stand and tell everybody that Luke didn't kill your father?" Tyler released her chin. "She wanted Luke out of your life and seeing him convicted of manslaughter was one sure way to do it. Besides, if she was covering up for the real murderer—"

"You think she did just that, don't you?"

"I think that if you ever regain all your memory, we'll know for sure. That's the only way we'll clear Luke's name and make the guilty party pay for what he or she did."

"My brother calls me every day, pleading with me to come back to the Circle A, to leave Montrose and Luke." Deanna grasped Tyler's arm. "They don't want me to remember. They're afraid that if I stay here, my memory will return and they won't have any control of me. They want me back home with them so they can— Oh, God, Tyler, what if this was a warning to me? What if killing Luke's cattle was a way of saying that if I know what's best for Luke, I'll—"

"You're jumping to conclusions." Tyler slipped his arm around her shoulder and hugged her to his side. "Don't borrow trouble, honey. It'll find you soon enough."

Luke stood on the porch, watching Tyler put his arm around Deanna's shoulder and hug her. Every possessive instinct in Luke urged him to fly out across the yard, rip Deanna from Tyler's arms and beat the hell out of his own brother.

All he could think about was that she was his. It

didn't matter that he'd spent fifteen years hating her, or that she had betrayed him, or that he was still as unworthy of Deanna Atchley as he'd been at twenty. Nothing mattered except claiming the woman he wanted, the woman his body demanded belonged to him.

Luke rounded the house, avoiding the evening strollers. He headed straight for the stables, saddled Cherokee and rode off into the night. He could escape the sight of Deanna in his brother's arms, but he could never escape the memories that haunted him. Memories of a girl who had once said she would love him forever—and then some. Memories of a woman who had said, *but I didn't want any other baby. Only yours.*

Chapter 10

Luke pulled his pickup truck alongside the sheriff's car parked at the side of the house. What was Tyler doing here at seven in the morning? Surely he didn't already have new information about the senseless cattle slaughter yesterday. No, more than likely Tyler had come back because of Deanna. Luke had expected more loyalty from his brother. Didn't Tyler know how he felt about Deanna?

Luke hopped down out of the truck cab, slammed the door and stared at Tyler's car.

How the hell should Tyler know what his big brother's feelings for Deanna Atchley were, when Luke himself didn't know? Did he still hate her? Yes. And no. Did he want her? Definitely yes.

Since Luke hadn't put a brand on Deanna since she'd returned to Stone Creek, maybe Tyler thought she was fair game. He'd have to set his brother straight on the matter. He'd have to do it this morning.

When Luke walked into the kitchen, he found Tyler sharing breakfast with his mother, who paused to look up and smile.

"Any signs of trouble this morning?" Kizzie asked. "No more dead cattle anywhere?"

"Everything seems to be fine," Luke told her. "Les and Bud are still out checking on cattle, while Jim and Herb handle things here. I've instructed Les to hire a couple of part-time men to help out for the time being. Until we see whether yesterday's incident was a one-time happening or just the beginning."

"Deanna seems concerned that her family is somehow involved," Tyler said. "She's awfully worried about—"

"Just how long did you stay over at the cottage with Deanna last night, after you walked her home?" The question shot out of Luke's mouth like a high-speed bullet.

Tyler grinned. Kizzie glanced back and forth between her two boys, a look of concern in her eyes.

"What business is it of yours, big brother, how long I stayed?" Tyler sliced into his pancakes and shoved a huge bite into his mouth.

Luke glared at him, but didn't respond. He poured himself a cup of coffee, removed his plate from the oven where Alva had placed it to keep warm, and sat down at the table.

Tyler swallowed, then took a swig of coffee. "I didn't spend the night, if that's what's bothering you."

"Tyler," Kizzie cautioned.

"There are plenty of other women around," Luke said. "Stay away from Deanna." Luke added salt and pepper to the scrambled eggs Alva always prepared for him.

"Didn't know you still had a claim on the lady," Tyler said.

"I don't." Luke picked up his fork, clutching it tightly.

"Then you're hardly in a position to put up No Tres-passing signs around her, are you?"

Luke squeezed the fork so hard that he bent it. When he realized what he'd done, he tossed it onto the table, scooted back his chair and started to stand. "Dammit, Tyler—"

Kizzie reached over and grabbed Luke's forearm. "No fighting at the breakfast table, boys. Remember my rules."

Luke sat back down. "Yes, ma'am."

"Sorry, Mama," Tyler said. "And, Luke, I didn't mean to rile you." He grinned sheepishly. "Well, maybe I did, just a little. I wondered how you felt about Deanna and I knew you weren't likely to tell me if I asked. Not the truth, anyway."

"What do you mean by that?" Luke glared at his brother.

"You've spent a lot of years professing to hate Deanna Atchley, so I figured if I asked how you felt about her now, you'd tell me you still hated her. And I wouldn't have believed you. So I had to needle you a little, to get a reaction, so I'd know."

"And what do you *know?*" Luke asked.

"I know you're very possessive of the lady, and that you're jealous of me and probably any other man who even looks at her."

"You're crazy!"

"Am I? You saw me put my arm around her last night, didn't you? How did that make you feel?"

"Boys, that's enough of this. Tyler, Luke's feelings for Deanna are none of your business."

"What's going on with Luke and Deanna may turn out to be the sheriff's business, if her family is behind the killing of Montrose cattle."

Tyler wiped his mouth on his napkin, eased back his chair and stood. He leaned down and kissed Kizzie's cheek. "I'm going to check around a bit more out where the cattle were shot. See if I can find anything that might help us out. But I think I'll stop by and say good-morning to our visitor in the guest cottage before I drive on out."

Luke gritted his teeth. Damn Tyler for making him see red! Even though he knew what Tyler was doing, he still couldn't help rising to the bait. Luke knew what kind of effect Sheriff McClendon had on the ladies and he didn't want Deanna succumbing to his little brother's charms.

"If I come up with anything, I'll stop back by and tell you." Tyler lifted his hat off the counter, placed it on his head and walked out the back door.

Luke dived into his breakfast like a starving man. If he kept his mouth full, he wouldn't have to talk to his stepmother, who sat there inspecting him, probably waiting for a reaction.

"After what happened yesterday, you've got to know that girl's been telling the truth all along," Kizzie said.

Luke swallowed a mouthful of food. "She could have been acting."

Kizzie huffed disgustedly. "Nobody's that good an actress and you know it. Why can't you admit that Deanna means what she says? She really did have partial amnesia all these years. She honestly wants to re-

member what happened when Rayburn was killed because she wants to help you."

"Well, she's a little late to help me, don't you
think?"

"I don't know, son. Is she? Are you too far gone
for anybody to help you?"

Kizzie's words cut deeply, reopening a wound that
had never really healed. When he'd first come to Montrose, seeking the man his mother had told him was his
father, he'd been a lost boy—lonely, afraid and angry.
He'd been just about too far gone then. Baxter and
Kizzie's acceptance and efforts to bring him into the
family fold had saved him. But after he'd spent five
years in Huntsville, he had become far more hardened,
much angrier, and much more of a loner. Even his family's support hadn't kept him from turning inward,
afraid to ever care about or trust anyone again. Not
even the people who obviously loved him.

"I'm going to see if I can catch Tyler before he
heads out." Luke rose from his chair.

"He cares about you, you know," Kizzie said. "The
only reason he needled you the way he did, is because
he cares."

Luke nodded. "I don't think I can change my
ways." Without another word or a backward glance,
he walked out onto the porch and looked over at the
cottage, just in time to see Deanna open her door and
invite his brother inside.

Deanna propped the wicker clothes basket, filled
with her dirty laundry, on her hip, then grabbed the
knob and pulled the front door closed behind her.
When she'd heard a knock at her door this morning,
she had hoped it was Luke. She'd been waiting for him

to come to her. But instead, Tyler had been on her doorstep. All smiles and charm, Tyler was the kind of man any woman would be interested in—unless she was already in love with his big brother. And she *was* still in love with Luke. She had to be or she wouldn't still be here on Montrose, enduring his stony silences and bitter tirades.

Tyler hadn't stayed long, just long enough to be friendly and reassuring. Two things Luke certainly didn't know how to be. When Tyler had left her, she'd caught a glimpse of Luke stopping Tyler beside his car. She'd been too far away to hear their conversation, but when Luke got in the car with Tyler and rode away, she decided it must have had something to do with the dead cattle.

"Morning, Miss Deanna," Alva said as she opened the kitchen door for Deanna. "Mrs. McClendon said when you came over to do your washing, she wanted to talk to you."

"Oh? All right. Where is she?" Deanna headed for the laundry room.

Alva followed, grabbed the wicker basket from Deanna and placed it on top of the washer. "You run along into the office. Mrs. McClendon's working on the payroll. I'll take care of these things for you."

"I can do my own washing. There's no need—"

"Hush up and go on." Alva swatted Deanna away.

"Thanks. I'll go find Kizzie and see what she wants."

"My bet is she wants to talk to you about Mr. Luke. He must have been in some state this morning. He bent one of the forks so bad I had to throw it away."

"Luke bent... Was he upset about something?"

"That man is always upset about something." Shooing her with her hands, Alva smiled warmly. "Go on now."

Deanna found Kizzie behind the big oak desk in the office, a manly room with leather furniture and wood paneling. Pausing in the doorway, she cleared her throat. Kizzie looked up and smiled.

"Good morning," Kizzie said. "Come on in."

"I don't want to disturb you, but Alva said you wanted to see me."

"Yes, I did." Kizzie motioned toward a leather wingback chair to the right of the desk. "Sit down, Deanna."

Quivery sensations tapped on Deanna's nerves, alerting her to danger. Emotional danger. There was a look of sadness in Kizzie's eyes that warned Deanna this conversation was going to be about Luke.

Deanna took the seat indicated to her, crossed her legs at the ankles and laid her folded hands in her lap. And waited.

Kizzie laid aside the papers in her hand. "You look tired, girl. Didn't you get any sleep last night?"

Deanna was surprised by Kizzie's personal interest in her well-being. Luke's stepmother hadn't been friendly and welcoming. In fact she'd been cool and distant ever since Deanna had come to Montrose.

"No, I didn't get much sleep. I'm afraid between all the memories bombarding my mind and my concern about what happened to your cattle, I wasn't able to rest very well."

"Have you had more of your memory return?"

"Yes, some. One thing in particular that I'd like to tell Luke."

"Well, when you and I finish our conversation, I suggest you go find Luke and tell him. He's working with that mustang again today and started work with another one. He has a way with animals, almost as if he can get inside their heads and know what they're thinking.''

''Yes, he does.'' Deanna paused, but when Kizzie just stared at her, she said, ''Do you think Luke will see me today?''

''Don't give him a choice. Just go out to the stables and tell him whatever it is you want him to know. Usually the direct approach is the only one that works with that boy.''

A tentative smile trembled on Deanna's lips. ''All right. I'll give the direct approach a try.''

''Deanna—'' Kizzie leaned forward, placing her hands on top of the desk. ''I want you to know that I believe you. About your loss of memory and about your wanting to clear Luke's name. I'm willing to give you the benefit of the doubt, girl. You'd better not disappoint me. And you'd better not hurt Luke.''

''The last thing I want is to cause Luke any more hurt than I already have.''

''All right then, here's what I want from you.''

Kizzie slapped her hands together. Deanna jumped, startled by the action.

''Luke's been lost to us—Lord almighty, he's been lost to himself—ever since he came home from Huntsville. Baxter and I did everything we knew to help him, but he wouldn't let us reach him. He won't let anybody get close enough to help him or hurt him. Nobody except you. You're right thinking that you're Luke's last hope, his only hope.''

''Mrs. McClendon, I'm afraid that—''

''Call me Kizzie. If you and I are going to work

together to help Luke, then we should be on a first-name basis, don't you think?''

"I'm afraid that Luke won't let me help him. He hates me and he'll never trust me. No matter what I say or do."

"That may be true," Kizzie said. "But I don't think Luke is as immune to you as he'd like to be. You're the one weakness that might cause him to lower his defenses. If you can save that boy from himself…if you can convince him that he's a man worthy of love and respect, I'll be indebted to you forever."

Deanna scooted to the edge of the chair seat, slumped her shoulders and stared down at the hardwood floor. With her head still bowed, she lifted her eyes and looked at Kizzie.

"If I could do what you're asking, I would. But no matter how hard I try, Luke won't give an inch. He's determined to go on punishing me. He won't let himself feel anything for me except hatred."

"That's where you're wrong. Luke cares for you whether he'll admit it or not." Kizzie smiled crookedly, as if trying not to laugh. "Luke and Tyler nearly came to blows over you at the breakfast table this morning."

"What!"

"Luke warned Tyler to stay away from you. A man doesn't warn another man, especially his own brother, to stay away from a woman, unless he's got feelings for her."

Hope soared in Deanna's heart, but then she realized Kizzie might have misunderstood Luke's attitude. "Maybe—maybe Luke didn't want to see his younger brother get involved with a woman like me. That could be the reason—"

"No. I was there. And I'm telling you that Luke still cares about you and you've got to use his feelings for you to help him. Do whatever you have to do to reach him. Use whatever methods are necessary. You go out there to the stables and be waiting for him when he gets through working with the horses. And you tell him about what you've remembered. Make him listen to you."

"I'll try, but—"

"I don't know if you and Luke are sleeping together." Kizzie avoided eye contact with Deanna. "And I don't want to know. It's none of my business. But I can tell you this, girl, a man's at his weakest and most vulnerable when he's making love to you." Kizzie smiled then, and her eyes glowed. "I remember what his daddy was like. I knew just how to persuade Baxter to come around to my way of thinking."

"Are you telling me to seduce Luke?" Deanna asked.

"Do you still love my son?"

Kizzie's question was direct and honest and she deserved no less a reply. "Yes."

"Then prove to him that you love him, and if seducing him will help convince him, then, yes ma'am, I'm telling you to seduce him!"

Deanna felt like a voyeur, where Luke couldn't see her standing behind a tree, watching his every move. Kizzie was right about his special way with animals. He seemed to possess an instinct that enabled him to communicate with the horses. There was a gentleness in his voice when he spoke to them. A kindness in his touch when he stroked their big bodies. If he could bestow such tender care on these animals, then he was

still capable of showing the same care to human be-
ings—to his family and to her. He had simply chosen
not to risk being rejected and hurt. Luke was afraid,
and he had every reason to be. How many times in his
life before and after he came to Stone Creek had he
been rejected and scorned? How often had people's
thoughtless words ripped away at his pride and self-
worth?

She had come so close to giving up on Luke. She
would have left Montrose yesterday if Old Man Cooley's pitchfork hadn't triggered the most powerful
memory flashback she'd ever had, and this morning
she'd intended to tell Kizzie that she was going to pack
and leave before nightfall. But after Kizzie's pleas for
her to help Luke, Deanna knew she had to give him
one last chance.

Luke removed his Stetson, ran his fingers through
his damp hair and gazed up at the hot morning sun.
Replacing his hat, he opened the corral door and strut-
ted toward the stables. Luke possessed a regal bearing,
tall and straight, his shoulders back and his head held
high. Did he have any idea what a magnificent man he
was? Deanna's stomach fluttered wildly at the very
sight of him.

When he approached the stables, Deanna slipped out
from behind the tree. "Good morning."

Luke stopped, glanced back over his shoulder and
frowned. "It's nearly noon." Without another word,
he walked into the stables.

He wasn't going to make this easy for her, but his
frosty attitude was what she had expected. The direct
approach, she reminded herself. Just march right in
there and have your say.

She followed Luke inside, catching up with him just as he neared Cherokee's stall. "I need to talk to you."

"I don't have time," he told her. "I'm heading out to—"

"Whatever you're heading out to do can wait. What I have to say to you won't wait."

He turned and faced her, giving her a stern, disapproving look. "All right. Let's hear it. But make it quick."

"I didn't sleep much last night. I kept thinking about what happened yesterday before I fainted and then afterward...the memories kept swirling around in my head and I started remembering other things."

"What things?"

"Eddie knows who killed Daddy," she said.

"What makes you think he knows?"

"Because he wiped off the pitchfork while it was still...still stuck in Daddy's chest, and...and he told Mother that they had to make sure there were no fingerprints left on it."

Luke looked at her coolly, giving nothing away. "You just remembered this? Last night? This morning?"

"About four o'clock this morning," she said, realizing Luke still didn't trust her.

"So, are you saying that Eddie Nunley killed your father?"

"No, I'm just saying that he knows who did." She took a tentative step toward Luke, her hands reaching for him.

He eased away from her, avoiding physical contact. "Okay, so you've told me the urgent news. Now, leave me alone. I've got work to do."

He was dismissing her! Damn him! He was dismissing her and her memory as if neither was of any importance to him. Did he honestly think she was pretending that she had just remembered? "Don't you see that this means we're one step closer to knowing the truth? If we confront Eddie...if I tell him that I remember what he did and what he said—"

"You think he's going to *admit* that he killed your father, or that he covered up for whoever did?" Luke laughed, a chilling, cynical laugh.

Deanna sensed the war raging inside Luke. He was torn between his desire to believe her and his fear that she was lying to him. "You aren't going to help me, are you? You don't care. You honestly don't care— about clearing your name, about the pain you've put your family through, about me and what I've had to endure because of what happened that night. All you care about is hanging on to your hatred and anger and self-pity."

Luke grinned and Deanna's heart stopped. Instinctively, she stepped back, sensing danger. "You can always ask my brother to help you. I'm sure Tyler would be more than happy to listen to your miraculous memory flashes. Hell, he'd probably even drive you over to the Circle A and question Eddie himself, if you asked him real nice."

"Just what do you mean by that?"

"You're still the same spoiled girl who always had to have her own way. The little flirt who had a dozen boys panting after her, just waiting for her to snap her fingers. I'm sure if you made Tyler the same deal you made me, he'd keep his end of the bargain. Kizzie's son has a sense of honor that I lack."

Deanna raised her hand. Luke caught it in mid-air. They glared at each other, their gazes locking.

Luke released her arm. "Don't ever try that again."

"You deserve to be slapped," she said. "You deserve a swift kick in the butt. You're stubborn, mule-headed—"

"Call me all the names you want to. It won't change the facts."

"And just what are those facts?" Deanna rubbed her arm where Luke's big hand had gripped it so tightly.

"You tell me. Just how many conquests have you made over the years? I might have been the first to get in your pants, but I sure as hell wasn't the last, was I? In fifteen years, there must have been dozens of guys willing to do anything for you. How many unsuspecting men have you caught in your sweet trap, Little Miss Black Widow?"

The anger welled up inside her like lava on the verge of erupting from a dormant volcano suddenly brought to life. She had been a fool to think Luke McClendon could be helped, that he even wanted to be saved from his sad, lonely life. Agreeing to his terms had been a mistake. Coming to Montrose had been an even bigger mistake. Even if she remembered everything from the past, including the identity of her father's murderer, nothing would change between Luke and her.

Kizzie had been overly optimistic in thinking Luke still cared about her—the girl who had betrayed him—and she'd been dead wrong assuming that she and she alone possessed the power to save Luke's black soul. Only a miracle could save Luke now and Deanna was afraid she was fresh out of miracles.

She wanted to hurt Luke the way he kept hurting her. She wanted to rip out his heart and feed it to the buzzards.

She moved toward him, defiantly, determined to

show him that she didn't care about his feelings any more than he cared about hers. Looking him square in the eye, she said, "You want to know how many men there have been, how many lovers I've had since you?"

He stared at her, his jaw clenched, his body taut. She could smell the musky, manly scent of his perspiration. Could hear his quick indrawn breath. Could see his nostrils flare. Could feel the tension radiating from him.

"Nothing to say, big man? Maybe you really don't want to know about all my many sex partners, about all the men who have kissed me and held and caressed me and whispered sweet nothings in my ear."

The vein in Luke's neck throbbed. A slight flush of crimson brightened his deeply tanned cheeks. Involuntarily, unknowingly, he gripped his hands into fists.

"Do you want to hear about how I felt, what I did, what I said? Do you want me to describe in detail how they undressed me. How they ran their hands over my body. How they tasted every inch of me. How they—" Deanna ran her hand over her breasts "—pleasured me until I begged for them to take me completely."

Luke grabbed her shoulders and shoved her up against the stable wall. She cried out in surprise. Hot anger shot from his eyes, searing her to the bone.

He shook her soundly, then lowered his head so that his lips were almost touching hers. "Damn you for making me feel like this!"

Her heartbeat roared in her ears like a cyclone. Luke's powerful body surrounded her, encompassed her, consumed her as if she were a vaporous form. His sex pressed against her intimately, big and hard and demanding. She had wounded the lone wolf and now he was preparing to attack.

"Then you *can* still feel, can't you? You aren't completely dead inside." She tried to lift her arms to his neck, but he held her against the wall with the strength of his body while he grabbed her arms and pressed them back against the wall.

"Show me just what your legions of lovers taught you," he said, his voice a growling threat. "At the motel, you acted like you hadn't learned anything, that all you knew about sex was what I'd taught you."

"But you know better, don't you, Luke?" She ran her tongue quickly over his lips. She smiled when he sucked in his breath and his sex pulsed against her. "You know that a girl who loved sex as much as I did never would have spent the past fifteen years without a man...without dozens of men."

"That's right, babe." Luke nuzzled her throat as he leaned into her, rubbing himself against her. "I remember how you couldn't get enough of me. How you wanted me over and over again. You were a little wildcat."

"I wouldn't have needed love, would I, before I gave myself to a man? He wouldn't have had to mean anything to me before I took him into my body. After all, I didn't really love you, did I? It was just sex for me with you, just like it was with all those countless other men, just like it was only sex for you with the women you've had."

"You're lying! Damn you, you're lying. You loved me and I loved you. If I don't know anything else...if I don't believe anything else, I believe that."

"And how many other women have you loved since me?" She squirmed, moving her body against his, but she wasn't sure any longer whether she wanted to escape or get closer.

"I've never loved anyone else!"

He took her mouth then, with all the savage fury burning inside him. While he ravaged her lips, he eased his tight grip on her arms, allowing her to lift them up and around his neck. She stood on tiptoe, deepening the kiss herself, plunging her tongue into the fray. Giving as good as she got. Taking his heated passion and returning in full measure. Luke cupped her buttocks in his big hands and lifted her up and into him, only the barrier of their jeans separating his throbbing arousal from her aching femininity.

When he broke the kiss, both of them coming up for air, he licked a path from her lips to her throat. She quivered as urgent needs raced along the nerve endings throughout her entire body.

"Oh, Luke, you must know that there hasn't been anyone else. I couldn't give myself to a man without loving him."

He gave her neck a tiny love bite, then buried his face in her hair that lay across her shoulder. She grabbed a handful of his hair at the back of his head and forced his face up, making him look at her.

"And how could I love another man, when I've never stopped loving you?"

"Ah, babe. Don't..." He let the rest of his words trail off to nothing as he lifted her in his arms and carried her toward an empty stall in the back of the stables.

Deanna clung to him, breathless with anticipation, ready for anything and everything. Luke laid her down in the clean straw, then came down beside her. Hurriedly he unbuttoned her blouse and spread it apart, then undid the front hook of her bra and exposed her breasts. The moment his mouth touched her, she bucked up and against the hand he had slipped between her thighs.

There was no anger, no rage in Luke now, only passion. Only desire that equaled hers.

She worked frantically at the snaps on his shirt, finally releasing all of them. She slid her hands up under his shirt and over his back. Her hands stilled instantly when she felt the uneven texture of his skin in the scarred areas. Scars left by the sting of her father's horsewhip. She wanted to cry. Wanted to seek out his scars and kiss each one. He had endured the brutal whipping because of her, and yet he hadn't blamed her. Not then. He had come to her, begging her to run away with him. To marry him.

If only she'd taken the chance and gone with him. If only!

She caressed his back, his broad shoulders, his powerful arms and then she ran her fingers through the tufts of black hair in the center of his chest. He undid her jeans and eased down the zipper, his tongue moving downward, across her belly and to the edge of her bikini panties. She wanted this—needed it badly. Luke making love to her. Wild, sweet love. Hot and all-consuming.

She trembled when his mouth moved upward again to torment her breasts and then to seek out the pleasure of her mouth. A mouth eager to mate with his once more. He covered her body with his as his lips ate away at hers and he tugged on the waistband of her jeans, dragging them down to her hips. She struggled to unbuckle his belt. Luke shoved her hands aside, undid his belt and unzipped his jeans.

There was no time for words, only for action. No time for pleas or vows, only time for making love. At that precise moment, Deanna didn't care what came afterward—all that mattered was the here and now. Luke above her, on her, around her. Luke inside of her!

He eased her jeans and panties slowly downward, over her hips, down her thighs, over her calves and ankles. The moment he jerked them over her feet, he tossed them aside, then reached inside his briefs and freed his sex.

Deanna reached up for him, welcoming him, opening herself up for his invasion. He positioned himself over her, bracing his big body with his hands on either side of her shoulders. Lifting herself up to meet him, she inserted one hand between their bodies and encompassed his shaft. Luke groaned, low and deep, the sound guttural and animalistic.

"Luke! Luke, where are you?"

Kizzie's scream froze Deanna and Luke instantly.

"Luke, son, where are you?" his stepmother called out again.

"Damn!" Luke lifted himself up and off Deanna, zipped his jeans and started buttoning his shirt. He was aching. Hurting bad. What the hell was going on? It wasn't like Kizzie to scream her head off for nothing.

He glanced down at a disheveled and utterly sexy Deanna, who lay before him like an offering to the gods. She gazed up at him, puzzlement and unfulfilled longing in her eyes.

"I've got to answer her," Luke said.

"I know." Deanna nodded, then grabbed her panties and slipped into them.

Leaving her in the stall, Luke hurried out of the stables and called to his stepmother. Kizzie ran toward him, her face flushed.

"What's wrong?" he asked.

"Fire! The south pasture's on fire!"

Deanna stood in the stable door, nervously buttoning her shirt. Luke glanced over his shoulder at her.

"You've called the fire department?" he asked Kizzie.

She nodded. "Just as soon as Bud called in. But you know it'll take them a good thirty-five or forty minutes to get here. By that time we could lose a thousand acres."

"We'll have to create a firebreak. I'll take one of the tractors and get Jim to take the other one. What about the cattle? Is Bud—

"He and Herb are moving them. You go on, I'll come out in your truck."

"I want to go too," Deanna said. "Please."

Luke stared at her for a split second, then said. "You can ride out with Kizzie."

Chapter 11

On their way south, Kizzie and Deanna met up with Bud and Herb herding the cattle northeast. Kizzie waved at them and they returned her greeting. Deanna smelled smoke. Leaning over slightly she looked up and out the windshield. Her mouth opened on a silent gasp when she saw the dark, billowing clouds rising high into the sky.

Kizzie pulled Luke's truck to a halt, gazed out at the raging fire consuming the land and sucked in a deep breath. "Dear Lord," she exclaimed. "How did this happen? Couldn't have been lightning on a day like this and none of our hands smoke, so it couldn't have been a cigarette carelessly tossed aside."

Deanna had heard about grass fires, of course, but she'd never actually seen one. Thick, charcoal rolls of smoke rose from the earth, covering the blue sky like a hazy gray blanket. The roar of tractors hummed in her ears. Searching for the source of the sound, she saw Luke on a tractor to her left and the ranch hand she'd heard called Bud on the other tractor.

"What are they doing?" Deanna asked.

"Trying to create a firebreak." Kizzie opened the truck door and got out, her face lined with worry. When Deanna joined her, Kizzie turned to her and said, "They have to get a section plowed around the fire, in front of it. They remove anything that can burn from the surface, so the fire will die out when it reaches the break. If they can create the firebreak quickly, then Luke will probably set a small controlled fire at the edge of the break, so the two fires will meet."

"What happens if that fails?"

"Well, the fire department can drop dry chemicals from a helicopter if the fire's not under control by the time they arrive. I've seen grass fires destroy hundreds of acres and by the looks of this one, I'd say there's a good chance that's going to happen here."

"What about hooking up water hoses to the windmills and—"

"Won't work," Kizzie said. "It'd take hoses a mile long. Besides, the pumps generated by the windmills wouldn't produce enough water pressure."

"Oh." Deanna wondered how she could be so ignorant about ranch life, when she'd grown up on a ranch. But the Circle A, though a working ranch, hadn't been her family's main source of income, the way Montrose was for the McClendons. Deanna's grandfather had made his millions in oil, years before she was born. He had moved his family to Stone Creek and become a gentleman rancher, the place more of a hobby than anything else.

"At least we don't have to worry about the house and barns and stables." Kizzie shoved her tan Stetson back away from her forehead. If it was the western range on fire, we'd have twice the problems.''

"Is Luke in any danger?" Deanna asked. "I mean—"

"I know what you mean. And yes, of course, he's in danger. That's a wildfire out there, girl, and it's destroying our grazing land. Luke will do whatever it takes, even risk his life.'' Kizzie cocked her head to one side and looked at Deanna. "You and I are safe at this vantage point. The fire's headed in the opposite direction. Thank God, the wind's not high. That fire's burning fast enough without any help.''

"Can't we do anything to help?"

"Best thing we can do is stay out of the way.'' Kizzie reached over and grabbed Deanna's hand, clasping it tightly. "I know how you feel, worrying about your man. He's my boy, even if I didn't give birth to him.''

Clenching her teeth in an effort not to cry, Deanna squeezed Kizzie's hand, then released it.

"What's got me puzzled is how this fire got started in the first place," Kizzie said. "I'm wondering if this fire and the twenty head of cattle that were shot yesterday have any connection.''

Deanna's body tensed. "It makes sense, doesn't it, that whoever killed the cattle, also started the fire.''

"Somebody's out to get us—out to hurt the McClendons.''

"Or someone's trying to scare y'all. Maybe the cattle slaughter and this fire are warnings.'' Deanna listened, trying to hear the tractors' roaring engines, but all she heard was the crackling carnage of the rapidly moving, deadly fire.

"You're worried that your folks are behind what's happened, aren't you?"

"I know my family doesn't want me to remember what happened the night Daddy died. At first I thought maybe I had killed Daddy and they were trying to protect me, but now I know that isn't true. I can't remember who stabbed Daddy with the pitchfork—not yet—but it's only a matter of time until I do."

"And they're afraid that when you do remember, you'll reveal the killer's identity, that you'll turn against them in order to clear Luke's name. So, why kill our cattle? Why set a grass fire on the range?"

"I'm not sure, Kizzie, but I think maybe these things are warnings and they're meant for me."

Sweat drenched Luke to the skin. His shirt clung to his body. Rivulets of perspiration dripped from his sooty face. But he was smiling when he approached Kizzie and Deanna.

"We've got it under control," he said. "It burned off close to two hundred acres. Could have been a lot worse. If the grass had been drier or the wind had been high."

Kizzie handed Luke a thermos filled with water. He guzzled down the cool, refreshing liquid, then held up the container and poured the water over his head. He slung his head from side to side, showering the two women with the excess moisture.

He removed his shirt, wiped his face with it and then flung it over his shoulder. "I just can't figure out how that fire got started in the first place."

"Deanna and I figure it was deliberately set," Kizzie said. "Of course Chief Hobgood will check things out and let us know if he finds anything suspicious. And I've called and left a message for Tyler. If this was arson, then he'll be professionally involved, too."

Luke looked at Deanna. "Do you know what's going on?"

"No, not really, but I intend to find out."

"What are you going to do?" Kizzie asked.

"I'm going to the Circle A and talk to my mother."

Luke grunted. "You don't think Phyllis Atchley is going to admit anything, do you?."

"Luke, son…" Kizzie said.

"It's all right, Kizzie," Deanna told her. "Luke's right. If my mother was capable of covering up the true facts of my father's murder even if it meant sending an innocent man to prison, then she's more than capable of arranging to have someone kill off your cattle and set fire to your pastureland."

"You're not responsible for what your mother did in the past or for what she might have done now." Kizzie placed her arm around Deanna's shoulder.

"Maybe I am. I have to find out. And if I can stop her, I will."

Carlotta opened the front door for Deanna. "Señorita Deanna, your mama will be glad to see you. I will tell her you are here."

The housekeeper hurried off, while Deanna strolled around the living room and waited. Would her mother be glad to see her? She seriously doubted it. Not after Phyllis heard what she had to say.

"Deanna?" Phyllis, dressed casually in beige linen slacks and a brown silk blouse, hesitated in the doorway. "Darling, have you come home to stay?"

"No, Mother, I'm here on business."

"Business?" Phyllis strolled into the living room at a leisurely pace that was in sharp contrast with the agitation Deanna noted in her mother's eyes. "What do you mean? What business could we possibly have to discuss?''

''Old business that directly relates to some new business.''

''You're talking in riddles. I'm afraid I don't have any idea what you mean.''

Deanna studied her mother's face. ''I suppose you know that Junior calls me every day. I'm sure he reports to you like a dutiful son.''

''Your brother knows how concerned I am about you…about you living on Montrose, with that man.''

''His name is Luke McClendon.''

''I know very well what his name is.'' Phyllis reached for Deanna, but let her hands drop when Deanna sidestepped. ''When are you going to come to your senses and leave Stone Creek? You built a nice life for yourself in Jackson. I don't see why you had to come back here and stir things up.''

''I assume by 'stirring things up' you mean regaining my memory, and knowing without a doubt that Luke didn't kill Daddy.''

''I don't care what you think you remember, you're wrong. Luke ran your father through with a pitchfork. He was tried and convicted of the crime fifteen years ago. Let it be, Deanna. Please, don't—''

''What are you so afraid of? Who are you trying to protect? Yourself?'' Deanna took a step toward her mother, and looked her square in the face. ''Did you kill Daddy?''

Phyllis gasped and clutched her throat dramatically. ''How dare you accuse me of such a thing! I loved your father and he loved me.''

''Daddy loved half the women in the county. That had to make you hate him. Tell me something—did

you turn to Eddie for comfort? Was he a substitute
husband to you the way he was a substitute father to
me and Junior?''

Phyllis slapped Deanna. The sound reverberated
throughout the room. And then a deadly silence followed. Deanna rubbed her stinging cheek.

"You won't need to be informed, second hand, of
my latest memory flash. I'll tell you myself. I remember that Eddie wiped off the handle of the pitchfork,
while it was still stuck in Daddy's chest, and he told
you he had to make sure that there were no fingerprints
left on it. Whose fingerprints was he trying to remove?
His own? Yours?''

"No one is going to believe you," Phyllis said
calmly. "No matter what you tell the authorities, nothing will come of your revelations. After all, you spent
nearly five years in a mental hospital. A good lawyer
could destroy you on the stand.''

"Oh, a good lawyer—a good district attorney—destroyed me on the stand years ago. But I'm not that
same girl, Mother. I'm not afraid of you anymore. And
I'm not afraid of the truth.''

"Maybe you should be afraid," Phyllis said. "You
have no idea what your so-called truth could do to this
family.''

"I didn't come here to discuss what the truth might
do to our family. I came here to discuss what your fear
is doing to the McClendons! What do you know about
the Montrose cattle that were slaughtered and the grass
fire that was deliberately set to destroy their grazing
land?''

Phyllis's cold blue eyes focused on Deanna. "What
could I possibly know?''

"What do you hope to gain by wreaking havoc at

Montrose?'' Deanna asked. ''If you think you're going to force me to leave Luke—''

''I've done nothing, darling. I swear I'm not responsible for anything that has happened at Montrose.'' Phyllis smoothed her right palm over her left and entwined her fingers.

''Why should I believe you? Give me one good reason why I should trust you?''

''Because…because I'm your mother.''

Deanna laughed mockingly. ''I trusted you once. I made myself believe that everything you did was for my own good. But not anymore. You helped destroy my life! And for what? For whom? To protect yourself? Is that it, Mother?''

''You may not believe me, but I don't want to see you hurt. I never did.'' Phyllis slumped down on the sofa, her beautiful face pale and her bright eyes suddenly dull. ''You're my child and I do love you.''

''You don't know the meaning of the word love. If you loved me, you'd help me.'' Deanna knelt at her mother's feet. ''You know who killed Daddy.'' Her gaze locked with her mother's. ''If you love me, then tell me the truth. Tell me who killed Daddy and help me clear Luke's name.''

Phyllis drew in a deep breath. She opened her mouth to speak, but said nothing. Tears misted her eyes.

Deanna grabbed her mother by the shoulders and shook her soundly. ''Dammit, Mother, why are you so determined to destroy my life again!''

''I—I can't tell you what you want to know.'' Phyllis's words were a mere whisper, the one sentence a tortured utterance.

Deanna rose to her feet, then looked down at her

mother, whose head was bowed in a pathetic gesture of remorse. "You mean you won't tell me!"

Lifting her head, Phyllis gazed beseechingly at Deanna. "You owe some sort of loyalty to your family. We stood by you when you had a nervous breakdown. I saw to it that you got the best treatment available. I paid all your bills at that expensive private sanitarium because I couldn't bear the thought of my little girl being in a state facility."

"You put me in Millones because you didn't want anyone to know that your daughter was crazy or that you were the one who helped drive her crazy!"

"That's not true! I did what I thought best for—everyone."

"You did what you thought was best for yourself!" Deanna stormed out of the living room and into the foyer, almost colliding with her sister-in-law.

"Deanna!" Phyllis called out from the living room. "Please, darling, don't go."

"What's wrong?" Benita asked. "What happened?"

"Why don't you ask your mother-in-law?"

Deanna swung open the front door and ran outside, got in her car and drove away from the Circle A. She'd been stupid to think that confronting her mother would accomplish anything. She didn't trust her own mother. She wouldn't believe anything Phyllis Atchley said if she swore on a stack of bibles.

Her gut instincts told her that someone on the Circle A was behind the problems at Montrose—someone who wanted to warn her that remembering was dangerous. But was that someone her mother? She didn't want to believe her mother was capable of such ruthlessness, but if not her mother, then who? Junior? Benita? Eddie?

"Luke rode out after he took a shower," Kizzie said. "I don't know for sure where he went, but my guess is he's looking over the damage the fire did to the south pasture."

"I have to find him," Deanna said.

"How did your visit with your mother go?" Kizzie grasped Deanna's hands. "What did she tell you?"

"Nothing. Not about Daddy's murder. But either she killed my father or she's protecting whoever did." Deanna squeezed Kizzie's hands and looked into her keen, dark eyes. "She claims she doesn't know anything about the problems y'all are having here at Montrose. The cattle being shot. The grass fire. But I don't know if I can believe her. I can't trust my own mother!"

"Do you still think someone in your family is responsible?"

Deanna released Kizzie's hands, then paced back and forth in front of the fireplace. "Yes, I do. I think someone is trying to warn me to leave Montrose and stop trying to remember what really happened the night Daddy was murdered."

"Tyler called me about thirty minutes ago and he's on his way here now. Maybe he should go over to the Circle A and question your mother."

"There's nothing Tyler can do. Mother will deny everything. And we have no proof that anyone from the Circle A was involved in the cattle slaughter or the grass fire. But in my gut—" Deanna laid her fist over her belly "—I know that my family is responsible."

Kizzie moved up behind Deanna and placed her

hand on Deanna's shoulder. "I'm only now beginning to realize what it must have been like for you when your family found out that you were pregnant with Luke's baby. They must have put you through hell."

Deanna closed her eyes, trying to shut out the pain. She remembered all too well how her parents had reacted to the news. They had been bound and determined for Deanna to have an abortion.

Deanna patted Kizzie's hand that rested on her shoulder, then turned to face Luke's stepmother. "After I talk to Luke, I'm going to pack my things and in the morning I'll leave Montrose."

"No, you mustn't go. We can handle whatever your family dishes out. If you leave now, what will happen to Luke?"

"I'll eventually remember everything," Deanna said. "And when I do, I'll come back to Stone Creek and name the guilty person. But in the meantime, I have to—"

"Leaving is only a temporary solution," Kizzie said. "Don't you realize that if you're right about your family, then whoever was behind the fire and the cattle slaughter was warning you to keep your mouth shut. He or she was telling you that if you don't let sleeping dogs lie then the McClendons will pay the price."

"Then that's all the more reason to leave—to protect you and Luke and—"

Kizzie pulled Deanna into her arms and hugged her, then shoved her away. "I'm telling you to stay! We'll see this thing through to the end together. And Luke will tell you the same thing. You go on now, and look for him out toward the south pasture and if he's not there, then look up in the hills, near the site of the old cabin. I guess you know why he goes there so often."

Deanna nodded agreement, "If Luke says I should stay, then I'll stay. But if he wants me to leave..." She turned and hurried out of the house and toward the stables. All the while Kizzie's last words echoed in her mind. *I guess you know why he goes there so often. So often. So often.*

Yes, her heart sang. Yes, she knew. Despite the fact that Luke had burned the cabin to the ground, he was still drawn to the site because he couldn't forget the hours they had shared together, the moments of bliss they'd found in each other's arms. If he went there often, then no matter what he said or what he believed, he did still care.

Deanna saddled Fair Weather and headed out toward the southern range in search of the person who held the key to her future happiness.

When she didn't find Luke in the south pasture, she rode up into the hills, straight toward the site of the old cabin. Would she find him there—at their special place? Would he be glad to see her or would he be cold and distant? They had been on the verge of making love this morning—before the fire. The passion between them had been like old times. Hot, wild and all-consuming. But it had been loving. Not just sex. She had experienced both with Luke and she knew the difference.

She had to tell him and let him know that she planned to leave Montrose in the morning. Even if Kizzie had been determined for her to stay, she knew Luke wouldn't feel the same way. More than likely, he'd be glad to see the last of her. He'd probably even help her pack!

She saw Cherokee first, grazing not far from the

cabin site, and after she'd dismounted and walked though the tall brush, she saw Luke. He sat perched on a boulder about thirty yards from the ruins, staring at the old chimney. His big shoulders tensed. He turned his head slightly and looked back over his shoulder.

He must have heard her approach, she thought, and knew he had when their gazes met and held. He stood and walked toward her until only inches separated their bodies. Their eyes locked.

"How did you know where to find me?" he asked.

"Kizzie." Deanna cleared her throat. Luke was too big, too tempting and much too close. "Kizzie told me that you came up here a lot and that I should check for you here, if I didn't find you looking over the destruction to the southern range."

"I had no idea Kizzie knew that I came up here. The woman's too damn smart. She knows things she shouldn't."

Deanna nodded toward the large rock Luke had recently vacated. "Mind if we sit down? I have some things to tell you. Important things that can't wait."

Without uttering a word, Luke led Deanna over to the big rock, which was two-thirds enclosed by trees and shrubs. When she sat, he eased down beside her. Their hips almost touched.

"So talk," he said, but didn't look at her.

"I went to see my mother."

"And?"

"She denied everything."

Luke drew in a deep breath, his vision focused on the old cabin site. "Did you actually think she'd admit anything?"

Deanna wished Luke would look at her—really look at her—and see into her heart. "I believe that she killed

Daddy or she knows who did. And she does not want me to remember what happened.''

Luke snorted. "So you still think I've lost twenty head of cattle and had three hundred acres of grazing land temporarily ruined as a means to force you to leave town?''

"I'm sorry." She reached out and grasped his arm. He flinched, but didn't jerk away from her. "The last thing I wanted was to hurt you again, but it seems that that's all I can do. I—I'm leaving in the morning. But I'll come back, when I remember who killed Daddy. And sooner or later, I will remember.''

"Have you told Kizzie?''

"Yes.'' Deanna loosened her hold on Luke's arm, then dropped her hand away and let it rest, palm open, on the rock beneath them.

"What does she think about your leaving Montrose?''

Deanna wasn't sure she should tell Luke what his stepmother had said. She had no idea how he would react. But then she decided that there had been enough lies, enough secrets between them.

"She thinks I'm allowing my family to blackmail me again. Kizzie thinks I should stay here.''

Luke covered Deanna's hand with his. "She's right, you know. You're not going to help yourself, or me, by running away.''

The feel of Luke's warm flesh against hers sent shivers along her nerve endings. It was a small gesture, one of comfort, and yet it touched her more profoundly than Luke would ever know. Tears misted her eyes.

"But if I stay, someone in my family will continue the assault on Montrose. I have no idea what he'll do next.''

Luke squeezed Deanna's hand. "The last time you allowed your family's threats to dictate your actions, you testified against me in court. I went to prison for five years and you lost our child. Giving in to them was the wrong thing to do then and it's the wrong thing to do now."

"But I can't bear the thought of bringing more harm to you and your family." Deanna shot up off the rock. Tears gathered heavily in the corners of her eyes.

Luke stood, placing his big body behind her, and eased his hands from the top of her shoulders down to her wrists and back up again. Deanna shuddered. He slipped his arms around her and drew her up against his chest. Leaning back, the top of her head brushed his chin.

"I don't want you to go," he whispered against her ear. "Stay, Deanna. Stay and we'll see this through together."

"You believe me now, don't you? You know that I've never lied to you." Crossing her arms over her body, she hugged his arms around her.

"Yeah, I guess I do believe you," he admitted. "About the baby and about why you testified against me. You did suffer from some kind of amnesia after your Daddy was killed."

"I never meant to betray you, Luke." She held on to him for dear life.

Luke's jaw moved awkwardly, clenching and unclenching, as he fought to control his emotions. Emotions he had thought long dead. "Yeah. Yeah, I know."

"Does this change anything?" she asked. "Does it change the way you feel about me?" Her heart rumbled in her ears like the roar of a hurricane hitting the shore.

Please, dear Lord, please. Let him say he forgives me. Let him say that he doesn't hate me anymore.

"Yeah, it changes things. It makes me ashamed that I hurt and humiliated you that night at the motel." He shifted her in his arms, bringing her around to face him. He grasped her shoulders and looked directly at her. "I…uh…I hated you for a long time. I blamed you for everything that went wrong—"

"You had every right to blame me." Tears streamed down Deanna's face. "If I'd had the strength to stand up to my mother…if I hadn't fallen to pieces on the stand the way I did…if—"

"Shh…" Reaching up, he laid a finger over her lips. "We can't change the past. All we can do is try to right the wrong and not let your family win this time."

"But how can we—"

"You're staying here on Montrose, with me. And when we know who killed your father, we can put the past behind us. You can go back to your life in Jackson with a clear conscience. You'll have done all you could for me."

"But Luke, didn't what happened between us this morning in the stables mean anything to you? I'd thought that you might have realized that you still care about me. Just a little, anyway."

Luke jerked her up against him, forcing her to feel his arousal. "I want you. I want you so bad I stay awake nights aching for you. I need you, babe. I need you more than I ever did."

"Oh, Luke!" She wrapped her arms around him and spread kisses all over his face. "I need you, too. So very much."

Luke grabbed her face in his big hands, forcing her to look directly into his eyes. "Wanting and caring are two different things, Deanna. I want you. There's nothing I'd like more than to lay you down over there in the grass and make love to you. Right now. But I can't tell you that I care for you. Not the way you mean. And I won't lie to you. I don't know if I can ever care about anyone, ever again.''

She trembled from head to toe as huge sobs racked her body. ''I did this to you. I killed all the love in you.''

''Ah, babe, don't do this to yourself. You aren't the same girl who betrayed me anymore than I'm the same boy who loved you.''

''Make love to me. Now. Here,'' she pleaded. ''It doesn't matter that you can't say you care. Our needing each other is enough.''

''This isn't fair to you,'' he said.

''It doesn't matter.'' She pulled his hands away from her face and led him toward a shaded expanse of thick green grass. ''All that matters is this—'' she pulled her cotton sweater over her head, tossed it on the ground and then removed her bra.

Luke watched, mesmerized by each new inch of flesh Deanna revealed as she stripped away her clothes. His sex grew harder. He wasn't going to be able to resist her. She was what he wanted. All that he wanted.

Standing before him, naked and unashamed, Deanna held out her arms to him, inviting him to take what she was offering. To take all of her.

Luke swallowed the lump in his throat. ''You're a beautiful woman.''

He walked into her arms. And from the moment her body touched his, he was lost. Nothing else mattered but making love to Deanna. There was no past and no future. Only the here and now. And only the two of them.

Chapter 12

When Luke captured her in his embrace, she threw her arms around his neck, threaded her fingers into his hair and pulled his head down toward hers. Standing on tiptoe, she sought his mouth. His lips met hers in a kiss that robbed her of her breath and sent pinpricks of sexual longing throughout her body. Their tongues mated in a frenzy of need. Thrusting and retreating. Tasting and tempting. He cupped her naked buttocks and lifted her up and into his throbbing sex. She clawed at his shoulders, tugging on his shirt. He eased her slowly downward, against his body, allowing her enough freedom to grab the edge of his shirt and jerk open the snaps. She spread his shirt apart and pressed her breasts against his chest.

The last rays of sunlight cast a soft gossamer light over the trees and shrubs, over the wildflowers and green grass, and over their bodies. The smell of spring was in the air—fresh and alive, sweet and seductive.

The verdant beauty surrounded them as they stared at each other and saw their mutual hunger reflected in each other's eyes.

Placing her hands on him, Deanna felt the fast, wild beat of his heart. He was so completely, overpoweringly masculine. He was man, with all the faults and flaws, and all the strengths and perfections.

She gazed up into his eyes. "Luke."

He kissed her, ravaging her mouth, then nipped along the side of her neck. She moaned with pleasure. Her peaked nipples raked his chest as he maneuvered her body against his. She hurt with the wanting, her feminine core pulsating as moisture collected, preparing her body for his.

Luke lowered her to the grass, all the while tearing away his shirt. The jade-green bed beneath her was thick and plush, cushioning the hard ground. The aroma of rich earth and pungent evergreens permeated the air. A gentle evening breeze wafted over them, but did nothing to cool their heated bodies. Deanna shuddered. She had dreamed of this moment, of Luke taking her with the same passion as he had in the past. She reached up, unbuckled his belt and unsnapped his jeans. He straddled her hips. He unzipped his jeans and tugged them down so that the waistband rested on his hips. When he lowered his mouth to her breast, she reached inside his briefs and circled his erection. He groaned deep in his throat, then captured a begging nipple between his teeth. Deanna bucked up off the ground, her hips thrusting forward, her sex seeking his. She freed him, then led him to the apex between her thighs.

"I want you so," she said as she brought him into her body.

Luke plunged deeply. "Ah, Deanna."

She gave herself over completely to the desire that radiated through her, urging her to take everything she needed from him. And she needed so much.

"You're so wet and hot," he murmured, his words slurred with passion.

Luke braced some of his weight on his knees, but the bulk of him loomed over her, pressing into her with each forceful lunge. She loved the feel of him inside her, his big body surrounding her with his strength. She felt small and vulnerable and totally at his mercy, and yet more powerful than she'd ever felt in her life. The very fact that he was large and strong and dominant added to the excitement of his possession.

"Yes, Luke. Oh, yes!" she cried out with the passion she couldn't suppress. Her body was on fire, burning hotter and hotter with each renewed attack.

Luke cupped her buttocks, lifting them higher so that he could lunge deeper, seeking the depths of her. Harder and faster, his need driving him on, he pounded into her. Deanna clung to him, her hips undulating to the frantic rhythm he had set. Her soft moistness clenched and unclenched as pure sensation claimed her. She was a mass of feelings—wild, aching, spiraling feelings. She tightened around him. Her fingernails bit into his back. The coiled spring of sexual tension snapped and released a flood of overwhelming physical pleasure. Her body trembled uncontrollably with the heartbeat of her climax.

Her fulfillment triggered his. Moving furiously within her, he roared like a wild animal when fulfillment claimed him. Sweat coated their bodies as they clung to each other, their lips touching softly. Luke eased off Deanna. Draping his arm around her, he lifted her up and onto him. She lay there on top of him, her head resting on his shoulder. He kissed the side of her face and stroked her hip.

She wanted to tell him that she loved him. That she had never stopped loving him. But Luke wouldn't want to hear her declaration of love. Not now. Probably not ever.

This had to be enough. This glorious closeness she felt. This sexual bond that she was sure Luke had never known with another woman.

Kizzie maneuvered her Lexus into a parking slot at the post office, killed the motor and turned to Deanna. "Why don't I drop you by Patsy Ruth's after we get the mail? Luke could drive over and pick you up before supper tonight."

"I don't think so," Deanna opened the passenger door and stepped outside onto the asphalt parking lot.

Kizzie got out of the car, rounded the hood and caught Deanna by the arm. "There's no point in your sticking around Montrose all day, just waiting for something bad to happen. You're nervous as a cat, girl, and you're making me jittery."

"I'm sorry, but I know it's only a matter of time before another accident happens."

"Lord knows I wish Tyler could do something about this whole business." Kizzie stroked Deanna's arm. "This has got to be terrible for you, not being able to trust your own family. I'm just sorry we didn't realize how they treated you back when you testified against Luke. We didn't understand the whole situation."

And you still don't understand, Deanna wanted to say. Not the whole situation. No one outside her immediate family, and she included Eddie in that number,

knew that she had suffered a complete mental breakdown and spent almost five years in a sanitarium. The
same five years Luke had spent in prison.

"We're tempting fate, you know," Deanna said.
"My being on Montrose has already cost you twenty
head of cattle and hundreds of acres in grazing land."

Kizzie grabbed Deanna's shoulders. "Now, you listen here to me, girl. That twenty head can be replaced
and the grass will grow back on those acres. Clearing
Luke's name and giving him a chance at life again is
worth just about any risk. If he and his family are willing to take that risk, why shouldn't you?"

"Maybe I should leave. Maybe I—"

Kizzie gave Deanna a resounding shake. "Don't you
even think about running. You have to stand up to your
family. Show them that you aren't that weak, immature
girl who fell apart in front of the whole world and
doomed Luke to a manslaughter sentence. You need to
find your inner strength just as Luke needs to find his
self-worth."

Deanna nodded. "You're right. It's just I have this
gut feeling that something terrible is going to happen,
and it's going to be my fault."

"Don't borrow trouble. We can't predict if and when
something's going to happen. If we keep on worrying
like this, we'll be crazy as betsy bugs by the time whatever is going to happen happens."

"If only Tyler had found some proof of who killed
the cattle and set the fire."

"Whoever's doing your family's dirty work is smart
enough not to leave any evidence behind. My money
is on Eddie Nunley. What do you think?"

"Eddie's a smart man, all right," Deanna agreed.
"And he's devoted to my mother. I think he probably

loves her. I don't know that they've been lovers, but I suspect they have.''

"There have been rumors,'' Kizzie said. "Even before your daddy was killed.'' Kizzie tugged on Deanna's hand. "Let's pick up the mail and then stop by Wellington's and get the fixings for Alva's chocolate chip cake. It's Luke's favorite and she's going to teach you how to make it, isn't she?''

Deanna followed Kizzie into the small brick building that housed the post office.

"Alva believes that the way to a man's heart is through his
stomach,'' Deanna said.

"Yeah, that's partly true. His stomach and a part of his anatomy that's a little lower.''

Deanna laughed, releasing the tension that tormented her. Kizzie was right. She couldn't continue in this state of nervous worry. She was at the point now that the least little noise scared her senseless.

Kizzie spoke to two ranchers who were picking up their mail. When they stared at Deanna, Kizzie introduced her and didn't react at all when they murmured among themselves as she and Deanna gathered the Montrose mail, bought stamps and mailed a package.

The moment they walked outside, Kizzie huffed loudly. "Darn old busybodies. Hurt Medford and Earl Frost are worse than a bunch of women at a church social about gossiping. I'll bet meeting up with us just made their day. The whole county's buzzing with the news that you're living at Montrose.''

"They'll really have something to talk about when I remember who killed Daddy and can clear Luke's name.''

"Let's hope that happens real soon.''

Deanna and Kizzie made their rounds in town and headed home for Montrose. Distant thunder warned of impending rain.

"We sure could use a good soaking," Kizzie said. "Things are getting pretty dry."

"Are you afraid of another fire?" Deanna asked.

"Now, don't go reading anything into a harmless comment.
What you should do is find something to take your mind off things. You really should go visit Patsy Ruth or have her and that passel of kids out to the ranch."

"All right. All right." Deanna clutched the bundle of mail in her hands. "I'll drive over and spend the day with Patsy Ruth tomorrow. She's called several times and invited me. It's just…well, I suppose I think I should be at Montrose in case something does happen."

By the time Kizzie parked the Lexus at the side of the house, huge raindrops were plunking down out of the sky. She grabbed the sack of groceries, while Deanna held the mail against her chest, and the two of them made a mad dash toward the porch. Alva swung the door open, took the sack from Kizzie and stepped aside to allow them entrance. Deanna ran her hand through her damp hair and thought that it was probably curling around her face as it always did when it was wet.

"There was a phone call for you, Miss Deanna," Alva said.

"From whom?" Deanna asked.

"They didn't leave a name. But it was a man."

A sense of foreboding hit Deanna like a jolt of electricity. "Did he leave a message?"

"Sure did. And a right peculiar message it was."

"What was it?" Kizzie glanced at Deanna and the two women shared a moment of anxious anticipation.

"The man said, 'Tell Deanna Atchley she'll be better off without Luke McClendon.' Don't you think that's odd?"

Sour bile rose from Deanna's stomach, burning a trail up her throat. "A threat. Oh, my God!"

"Luke!" Kizzie cried.

"Where is Luke right now, Alva?" Deanna asked. "Did he let you know where he's working today?"

"Mr. Luke said to tell you, Mrs. McClendon, that he'd look over the mail after lunch. He planned to make the rounds checking the water troughs this morning."

"He could be anywhere," Kizzie said frantically, then turned to Alva. "Did he take his truck or ride Cherokee?"

"He rode Cherokee."

"Damn!" Kizzie paced the floor. "That means his cell phone is probably still in his truck."

"What's all the fuss about?" Alva asked. "Are you afraid something has happened to Mr. Luke?"

Pain welled up inside Deanna like a fast-growing tumor, filling her body, pressing on her lungs, pounding on her heart. The thought that her family could have harmed Luke, might have ordered his murder, ripped Deanna apart as swiftly and adeptly as any steel blade could have done.

"We have to find him!" Deanna grabbed Kizzie. "We have to find him before it's too late."

"I'll send out any of the hands I can find, then I'll take Luke's truck. You saddle up Fair Weather. I'll check east, you go west. I'll call Tyler from the cell phone and tell him about the message you received. Maybe he can have the call traced somehow.''

Her hands trembling, her stomach churning, Deanna nodded agreement, then rushed out the front door, Kizzie following her. When Deanna headed toward the stables, she heard Luke's truck come to life. She turned to wave goodbye to Kizzie, then noticed a lone horse and rider coming in from the east. Her heart thumped rapidly. Sweat coated her palms.

The horse galloped closer and closer. The man in the saddle was slumped over Cherokee's neck. It was Luke. And he was injured!

Deanna ran toward the big dun stallion as he approached the stables. Kizzie opened the door and jumped out of the truck.

''It's Luke,'' Deanna screamed.

Kizzie grabbed the horse's reins. Deanna clasped Luke's shoulder. He slipped sideways in the saddle. She reached for him, but his heavy weight was more than she could maneuver. He slid out of the saddle and off the horse, taking Deanna to the ground with him. She rolled him over onto his back, then lifted his wrist to check his pulse. Blood dripped from her fingers. She screamed.

''Lord almighty!'' Kizzie knelt down on her knees.

Together she and Deanna ripped open Luke's bloody shirt.

''He's been shot,'' Kizzie said. ''Twice! And he's lost a lot of blood. Thank the good Lord he was able to stay on Cherokee as long as he did.''

Deanna eased Luke's head into her lap. ''We have to get him to the hospital.'' Staring at his face, his closed eyelids, the blood oozing from his mouth,

Deanna caressed his cheek. "This is all my fault. I knew—"

"I'll try to find one of the boys to help us lift Luke into the back seat of my car. It'll take too long to get an ambulance out here." Kizzie rose from the ground, then hollered, "Alva! Alva!"

The housekeeper ran out onto the front porch and halted the moment she saw Luke lying in Deanna's arms. "What's happened to Mr. Luke?"

"He's been shot," Kizzie said. "Go call the medical center and alert them that we're bringing Luke in. Then call Tyler and tell him to meet us there. And see if you can get in touch with Grant, too."

Alva scurried back inside the house, while Kizzie began a search for the ranch hands. Within minutes Jim and Herb came running from opposite directions. They helped remove Luke's shirt, then Kizzie folded the soiled shirt and used it as a bandage to soak up more blood. Deanna crawled into the back seat of Kizzie's Lexus. Alva rushed outside, carrying a cotton blanket, which Kizzie grabbed and threw to Deanna. Jim and Herb loaded Luke into the back seat, careful not to jostle him any more than they could help. Holding his head in her lap, Deanna wrapped him in the blanket and brushed damp tendrils of hair away from his face.

"Oh, Luke," she whispered. "Please don't die, my love. Please." Tears filled her eyes; she blinked them away.

Kizzie shifted the Lexus into reverse, backed up and turned around. The car roared out of the driveway and down the long road leading to the main highway.

This has to be another nightmare, Deanna told herself. Sooner or later she would wake up and Luke would be all right. But she knew this was no nightmare. This was real. Someone had shot Luke—no doubt, their orders had been ''shoot to kill.'' She shuddered, her whole body reacting to the fear consuming her.

The ER staff had rushed Luke straight into surgery. That had been two hours ago! Two of the longest hours of Deanna's life. She knew one thing for certain—if Luke died, so would she.

Tyler sat down on the vinyl sofa beside Deanna, reached over and lifted her hand. ''Hey, he's tough, you know. The strongest, toughest guy around. A couple of bullets aren't going to get the best of him.''

''It was bad,'' Deanna said, squeezing Tyler's hand. ''He must have been shot from the back—'' she gulped for air ''—the holes in his...in his stomach and chest were exit wounds. Oh God, Tyler, those bullets ripped him apart inside!'' Tears poured from her eyes.

Tyler pulled her into his arms. She sobbed uncontrollably. Stroking her back, he soothed her with touch and with words. ''I know it's bad, honey, but you've got to believe Luke will survive this. He's survived so much already.''

''This is all my fault,'' Deanna cried.

Kizzie handed Deanna some tissues. ''Stop blaming yourself. This is not your fault. Luke wanted you to stay. He knew it was the right thing for you to do.''

''Was it?'' Deanna practically screamed the question. ''My staying here got Luke shot. Maybe killed.''

''Stop talking nonsense!'' Kizzie said. ''Luke isn't going to die. Do you hear me? And whoever shot Luke will be caught.'' Kizzie glanced at her son.

''I've got my deputies searching the area where we think Luke was ambushed,'' Tyler said. ''If there's any evidence out there, they'll find it.''

Deanna jumped up from the sofa and paced around the waiting room. "What's taking them so long in there? Why hasn't someone come out and told us how Luke's doing?"

"He was shot up pretty bad, you know that." Kizzie came up behind Deanna and placed her hand on her shoulder. "It could take them quite a while to patch him up."

"I spoke to Lassie Colby—you remember her, don't you, Mama? She was in school with Grant and me," Tyler said. "Anyway, she's a RN, working in the surgical intensive care unit. She's promised to keep a check on things in surgery and let me know something as soon as she can."

"If anything happens to my boy, I'll—" Kizzie clenched her jaw. Tears trickled down her wrinkled cheeks. She turned and walked away from Deanna.

"Now, Mama, don't think that way," Tyler said. "You leave whoever shot Luke to the law. I'll make sure the person or persons responsible are caught and punished."

"Tyler," a soft voice called his name.

Deanna's eyes flew open. Kizzie's head snapped around.

"Lassie." Tyler rushed to the door of the waiting room where a tall, slender blond nurse stood, a concerned look on her face. "Do you have any word on Luke's condition?"

Lassie clasped Tyler's arm and pulled him out into the hallway. Kizzie and Deanna exchanged frightened glances and instinctively moved toward each other.

Tyler came back into the waiting area. "The surgery's only half over. Luke's still alive...but—"

"But what!" Deanna demanded.

"But he's messed up something awful and things could go either way. Right now, they're giving him a fifty-fifty chance to pull through."

"Oh, God, no...no...no..." Deanna wrapped her arms around herself and doubled over. Rocking back and forth, she gasped for air. "He can't die. He can't die. I won't let him die. Not now." Deanna slumped down onto her knees. "Please, God! Please! Don't do this! Don't! Don't!"

Tyler lifted Deanna from the floor. Kizzie reached out and enfolded Deanna in her arms.

"It's all right, girl. It's all right. I know you love him, too. You just keep right on praying."

Each minute seemed like an hour and each hour like a day. Repeatedly, Deanna glanced at the round, glass-encased clock on the wall and wondered why the hands didn't move faster, why time passed so slowly. She tried to concentrate on the positive—Luke wasn't dead. He had a fifty percent chance of surviving.

With each breath she took, she uttered a silent prayer. Had she and Luke lived through hell, spent fifteen years separated, just to have their lives end this way?

Tyler returned from the snack bar carrying two cups of coffee. He handed one to his mother and then walked over and held the second cup out to Deanna.

"Drink it while it's still warm," he said. "It's black and strong."

Deanna accepted the offering. Taking the plastic cup in her trembling hands, she looked up at Tyler. "Thanks."

Tyler sat down on the sofa beside her. "I spoke to

Lassie again. She said surgery is almost finished and
Luke's still hanging in there.''

Deanna squeezed the soft cup so hard that warm liquid spilled over the sides and onto her hands. Tyler
grabbed the cup and set it on the round metal table to
his right, then jerked a handkerchief out of his pocket
and dried Deanna's hands.

She entwined her fingers and brought her folded
hands up to her mouth in a prayerful gesture.

Tyler patted the top of her hands in a comforting
gesture. ''I told you he was tough. Luke's a survivor.
He'll pull through. You just wait and see.''

The door to the waiting room opened. Kizzie rushed
toward the green-clad man who entered. Tyler helped
Deanna to stand.

''Mrs. McClendon,'' Dr. Stranahan said. ''Luke has
come through surgery, but it's still touch and go. If he
makes it another twenty-four hours, there's a good
chance of a full recovery. At this point, I don't think
there's any permanent damage. Luckily for him the
bullets missed his spine altogether.''

''When may I see him?'' Kizzie asked, then turned
and held out her hand to Tyler and Deanna. ''When
may we all see him?''

''He's being placed directly in intensive care,'' the
doctor said. ''Once we have him settled, his family can
go in to see him, but no more than two at a time. And
you'll have to keep your visits short.''

''Yes, I understand.'' Kizzie grabbed Deanna's hand
when she drew near.

''Thank you, Doctor,'' Deanna said.

Dr. Stranahan nodded, then turned to leave.

''Hold up a minute, will you, Doc,'' Tyler said, then
followed the doctor out into the hallway. ''I need to

speak to you. Not as Luke's brother, but as the Luma County sheriff.''

Kizzie dozed on and off as she lay on the sofa, but Deanna hadn't slept a wink. She sat in the green vinyl chair facing the door that led into the surgical intensive care unit. Every four hours, she and Kizzie were allowed inside for five minutes. Tyler had gone in the first time, and then he'd left the hospital. He hadn't said where he was going or why, but Deanna knew that he and his deputies would be searching for the crime scene. At this point, the medical evidence was all he had. There were tests to be run, things that, as the sheriff, Tyler had to do. He could help Luke more by doing his job than he could waiting around at the hospital.

Seeing Luke lying there, his big body connected to an endless assortment of wires and tubes, reassured them that he was alive, but also reminded them how close he was to death. He was breathing on his own and that in itself was a positive sign, but he had not regained consciousness, and that was a bad sign.

The cell phone in Kizzie's shoulder bag rang, waking her instantly. She jumped, then groaned. Rummaging in her purse, she found the telephone.

"Hello. Oh, Grant. Yes. Yes, he's still alive. The doctor said if he could make it for twenty-four hours after surgery he has a good chance of surviving. It's already been over twelve hours now."

Deanna stood, stretched her arms and strolled around the small waiting room. Twelve hours and counting. Twelve hours to pray and worry. Twelve hours of guilt and anguish. Twelve hours of pure torment.

Deanna went to the bathroom and before returning to Kizzie, she washed her hands, then splashed cold water in her face. In another hour, it would be time to go in and see Luke again. If only the staff would allow her to stay at his side. If only she could hold his hand and caress his cheek. If only she could be with him in case…in case… If he died, she didn't want him to die alone. Without her.

Tears lodged in her throat. She willed her emotions under control. Kizzie couldn't handle her falling apart. Luke's stepmother was a strong woman, but she already had enough to deal with.

Squaring her shoulders, Deanna marched out of the rest room and back into the waiting area. Kizzie glanced up and smiled.

"Grant was in Dallas when Tyler finally tracked him down. He's on his way home. He should be here in a few hours."

"Are you hungry?" Deanna asked. "I could run down to the snack bar and get something for you before we go in and see Luke again."

"Thanks, but I don't think I could eat a bite. Why don't you go get yourself something."

"I couldn't—"

The door to the intensive care unit opened and Lassie Colby emerged, a hesitant smile on her face. "Deanna?"

"Yes?"

"Luke came to for a couple of minutes and he called out your name," Lassie said.

Kizzie and Deanna hugged each other, tears misting their eyes.

"Is he still conscious?" Kizzie asked.

"No, but I think it's only a matter of time." Lassie looked directly at Deanna. "I think it would be a good idea if you were with him when he comes around again.''

''Oh, yes!'' Deanna released Kizzie and took an unsure step toward Lassie. ''Does that mean I can stay with him?''

''Go right on back,'' Lassie said.

Deanna rushed into the unit, hurried straight back to the cubicle surrounding Luke. He looked the same as he had four hours ago. His eyes closed. His body unmoving.

Lassie dragged a chair into the cubicle and placed it to the right of Luke's bed. ''Sit down there and take his hand. Talk to him. Sometimes that helps.''

Deanna sat, reached out and lifted Luke's hand into hers. He was warm and alive. A lone tear escaped from the corner of her eye and slid down the side of her face. His big, callused hand lay lifelessly in hers, but his strong pulse told her that life still coursed through his body.

''Luke, it's me. It's Deanna. Please, my love, open your eyes and look at me.''

There was no response. Lassie patted Deanna on the shoulder.

''I'll leave you alone with him. Don't give up. Keep talking to him.''

For endless minutes, Deanna babbled away, talking about everything and anything that entered her mind. She had no idea if her one-sided conversation was penetrating Luke's mind, but she wouldn't give up. If there was the least chance that her voice could get through to him and bring him back to consciousness, she'd talk continuously for the next ten years.

Deanna paused, took a deep breath and began recalling the story of how she and Patsy Ruth had been caught smoking cigarettes in the bathroom when they were in sixth grade.

Luke shifted in the bed. Just a slight movement. Deanna sucked in her breath, then continued talking. Luke's eyelids fluttered. Deanna kept talking.

"Deanna?" His voice was weak.

"Luke? Yes, I'm here. Right here with you." She squeezed his hand gently.

"Babe?" Luke opened his eyes.

"Yes!" She came up out of the chair, leaned over the bed rail and looked down into Luke's beautiful, fully open green eyes.

"Don't ever leave me again," he said, then closed his eyes.

"I won't," she told him. "I promise."

Chapter 13

Leaving most of the meal untouched, Luke shoved his breakfast tray aside. "This stuff is slop. I'll wait until I get home and have one of Alva's good meals." He threw back the covers, slid his legs over the edge of the bed and dropped his feet to the floor.

"Luke, be careful!" Deanna said, jumping up from the chair beside his bed. "You're still very weak."

"And I'm not going to get any stronger if I don't get out of this damn place and go home." Standing, he swayed slightly, then righted himself and pointed toward the closet. "Get my clothes. I'm sick and tired of this—" he pulled the loose hospital gown away from his body "—stylish attire."

"Sit back down and I'll get your jeans and shirt." Deanna reached up, placed her hands on Luke's shoulders and urged him to sit.

Nodding agreement, he slumped down on the edge

of the bed. "I thought Kizzie would be here by now. I'm ready to leave."

"I talked to Alva a few minutes ago. She said that Kizzie is on her way." Deanna retrieved Luke's clothes from the tiny closet and carried them over to him.

When she tried to help him, he knocked her hands away. "I can dress myself."

"Sorry!" She threw up her hands in defeat and moved away from him. "I just wanted to do something to—"

"Why don't you call somebody to come and get all these flowers," he said. "Have them spread around the hospital. There's no sense in taking them home."

"I've already made arrangements for that to be done."

"Well, then sit down and take it easy, babe," Luke said. "You've done more than enough this past week. You've hardly left my side since I woke up after surgery."

Luke watched her out of the corner of his eye, while he drew his jeans up his legs and over his hips. The first face he'd seen when he regained consciousness eight days ago had been Deanna's. Oddly enough, it had been the first face he'd wanted to see.

Neither he nor any member of his family had objected when Deanna had insisted on staying at the hospital with him. For all intents and purposes, she had been his twenty-four-hour-a-day nursemaid. She had bathed him, fed him and shaved him those first few days when he'd been unable to do anything much for himself. She had read to him, talked to him and watched television with him. And she had slept on a foldout chair-cot at his side every night.

And despite his and his family's efforts to convince

her otherwise, Deanna blamed herself for what had happened to him. Even though Tyler had no concrete evidence against Phyllis Atchley or anyone connected to the Circle A, there was no doubt in Luke's mind that whoever shot him had been working for the Atchley family.

Luke finished dressing himself, but when it came time to put on his socks and boots, he found bending over still painful. He glanced at Deanna, who was watching him closely. He grinned. She smiled back at him.

"Need some help, cowboy?" she asked.

Luke ran his hand over the bandage that covered his healing gunshot wounds. "Do you mind?"

Deanna knelt at his feet, picked up his socks and lifted his right foot. "I don't mind at all," she told him.

Luke looked down at Deanna while she slid his socks onto his feet and then struggled with his boots. A tight knot of emotion formed in his chest. *God in heaven, don't do this to me! Don't let me love her again. Don't you remember who I am? I'm Luke, Mae Keeler's quarter-breed bastard, who isn't worthy of being loved or respected, who doesn't deserve to be happy.*

His mother had left the Cherokee reservation in Oklahoma when she was seventeen and she'd never returned. She had lived her whole life, all thirty-three years, trying to fit into the white man's world. She had fought a losing battle and had taught her son that people like them—who were scorned for being different— didn't belong anywhere, wouldn't find the happiness other people had, weren't worthy of love and respect.

When he'd found a home with the McClendons,

been accepted by his new family and legally recognized by his natural father, Luke had thought his mother must have been wrong about him. Then Deanna Atchley had come into his life, professing her undying love and giving him hope. False hope. Life had taught him that he was better off alone.

"Well, I'm here," Kizzie announced as she breezed into Luke's hospital room. "I've taken care of all the paperwork, the nurse's aide is coming with the wheelchair and the car is parked out front."

"I'm not leaving here in a wheelchair," Luke said.

"Yes, you are," Deanna informed him sternly. "And when we get you home, you're going straight to bed. Doctor's orders."

Luke opened his mouth to speak, then glanced over at his stepmother and grinned. Kizzie knew, perhaps better than anyone, how he hated to take orders. When Kizzie winked at him, he laughed out loud.

"What's so funny?" Deanna asked innocently.

"Not a thing," Luke replied. "Why don't you go find that nurse with my wheelchair. I'm ready to get out of this place."

A month after Luke's homecoming, he was champing at the bit to return to his normal activities. But the doctor had told him he couldn't rush back into the heavy workload he'd had before he'd been shot. Deanna and Kizzie were having the devil's own time reining him in and keeping him occupied without letting him overdo.

Deanna had been living on Montrose for nearly two months now, and in that time she had gone from unwanted visitor to practically a member of the family. Kizzie's acceptance of and faith in her meant the world to Deanna. And although Luke's attitude toward her had softened somewhat, he kept a protective barrier between them. She realized that he was fighting his feelings, working overtime to keep his emotions in check. Luke wouldn't allow himself to love her again. Maybe he never would.

With each passing day, with each sweet hour spent with Luke, Deanna regained more and more of her memory. She remembered the trial and the weeks following, those painful days after she had lost not only Luke, but their child as well. She could recall almost all of the past—everything except the details surrounding her father's murder.

She decided the time had come to return to the Circle A. But she planned to steer clear of her family, if at all possible. She hadn't seen the stables at the Circle A since the night her father died, and had thought she'd never have the courage to return. Perhaps if she forced herself to go back to the very spot where her father had been killed, the horror of that night would return to her. As much as she dreaded the thought of confronting her fears, Deanna hoped this desperate measure would at long last completely free her mind and allow her to fill in that final missing piece of the puzzle.

Despite her reluctance to ever go near the stables, she had considered going there when she first arrived at the Circle A, over a month ago. Lack of courage hadn't been the main reason she'd stayed away. She'd realized, when she first came home, that she wasn't ready to take the last step in the journey of remembrance. Not then, when the memories had just begun. But even then, she had instinctively known that once all the other memories had returned, she would have to brave this final moment—this one excruciating trip back into a past her subconscious had hidden from her. Returning to the Circle A stables before she was ready—before the other memories had returned— would have been useless.

But now she was ready. *God help me. Please, help me.*

She hadn't told Luke or Kizzie what she'd planned. She knew Kizzie would be upset and Luke would forbid her to go. She'd fabricated a little white lie, telling Kizzie that she needed a day away from Montrose, away from an irritable, grumbling Luke, who hated being restricted by his slow recovery. She didn't think anyone would check on her whereabouts, to see if she was visiting Patsy Ruth as she'd said she was.

Deanna parked her Mustang half a mile from her mother's house and walked the rest of the way. Avoiding the driveway altogether, she trekked off into the woods and came around behind the stables. She didn't see a soul. Good. If she was lucky, she might be able to accomplish her goal without confronting any of the Circle A hands.

The stables had been well maintained, as had the ranch as a whole. Outwardly, the Circle A was as beautiful a ranch as anyone could find in the state, but Deanna knew that looks could be deceiving. There was a dark, deadly secret lurking behind the inviting facade.

She hesitated before rounding the east side of the stables. You can do this, she told herself. You can look at the very spot where your father lay penned to the ground by the prongs of a pitchfork. You can face the past. And you can remember.

Please, dear God, let me remember everything!

The morning sun drenched her with warmth, adding to the heat rising within her as her heart thumped erratically and her palms grew damp. Without thinking, forcing her body to move, she rushed toward the stables and stopped dead still just inside the open doors. Shutting her eyes, she leaned back against the wall and willed herself to be brave. She could be afraid. She could dread facing the truth. But she could not weaken and run. Too much depended on her remembering.

Opening her eyes, she focused on the interior of the stables, seeking and finding the exact stall that had belonged to her palomino, Dublin. That night, she had been alone in the stables when Luke arrived. He had called to her from outside. She had turned and run to him, going into his arms without hesitation.

Deanna retraced her steps from that night. She ran outside, mimicking her actions from the past. Stopping suddenly on the spot where she had stood, wrapped in Luke's embrace, she recalled pleading with him to leave the Circle A before someone discovered his presence.

"Come away with me, Deanna," he said. *"Leave here with me tonight. Let's get married as soon as possible."*

"Oh, Luke, that's what I want more than anything," she told him. *"To spend the rest of my life with you."*

"Then let's go, babe. Let's get out of here now."

"I can't. What if Daddy comes after us? He'll kill you, Luke."

"No, he won't. If he tries to keep us apart, I'll kill him first."

"Never thought I'd see you here," Eddie Nunley said.

Gasping, Deanna jumped at the unexpected sound of the Circle A foreman's voice. She turned and faced him defiantly, determined not to let him see the fear gripping her mind and heart.

"Hello, Eddie." She glanced at the stables and the nearby corrals. "The place looks the same."

"Does your mother know you're here?" he asked.

"No, I didn't inform her or Junior that I planned a visit."

"I'm sure she'd like to see you. You need to talk to her, DeDe, and try to work things out between the two of you."

Deanna searched Eddie's weathered face for the truth and saw that he was sincere. But his sincerity did little to appease her shattered nerves. She'd never been afraid of Eddie. In the past, he had been her friend, her substitute father, her protector. Eddie would never hurt you, she told herself. But a tiny grain of uncertainty formed in her mind, creating doubt and fear.

"I thought that if I came here, to where Daddy was killed, I might remember exactly what happened," Deanna admitted. There was no point in lying to Eddie when she was certain he knew why she was there.

"And have you remembered?" he asked.

"No, not yet. But I'm sure that I will." She looked directly into Eddie's faded gray eyes. "You know the truth, don't you, Eddie? You've known all these years. Who are you protecting? Mother?"

"Why can't you just leave things be, DeDe? Why'd you have to come back and dig up the past?" He removed his Stetson, raked his bony fingers through his rusty-gray hair and shook his head sadly. "Can't nothing change the past. Finding out what really happened won't give you back what you lost and it could cause a world of hurt for your family."

"What really did happen? Who killed Daddy? Did

you do it, Eddie? Did you kill him for Mother? Or did you kill him to protect me? Did you—''

Dropping his hat to the ground, Eddie grabbed her shoulders. Deanna's eyes widened. Her mouth opened on a silent cry. ''Dammit, gal, do you honestly think I'd have hurt a hair on Rayburn Atchley's head? The man was my best friend. I'd have died for him, but I would never have killed him.''

''Then who, Eddie? Who?''

He tightened his hold on her shoulders. ''The worst day of your life was the day you met Luke McClendon. If you'd never set eyes on that young heathen, nothing bad would've ever happened. You damned this whole family by taking up with the likes of him. Luke might not have rammed the pitchfork through Rayburn's heart, but he killed your daddy all the same, just like he destroyed this whole family.''

Deanna noted the rage in Eddie's eyes, felt the tension in his hard, callused hands that held her so tightly, and realized how desperate he was to protect the real killer.

''Did you shoot Luke?'' she asked, her pulse racing madly as fear surged through her body.

''You'd be better off without him,'' Eddie said.

''Oh, God!'' Realization of the truth hit her hard. Eddie, who'd been like a father to her, had indeed tried to kill the man she loved. She struggled to free herself from his hold, but he shoved her up against the fence behind her and glared down into her face.

''Are you willing to destroy your family—your mother and brother, Benita and little Lauren—for that bastard? He doesn't love you. He never did. He just saw you as some sort of prize. He knew he wasn't fit to kiss your feet.''

Deanna forced herself not to scream, not to fight, not to give in to the fear she couldn't hide. "What if I said yes, that I am willing to do anything for Luke? Would you try to kill me, too, Eddie?"

She saw the conflict in his eyes and wondered if she had pushed him too far. Was he trying to decide her fate right this minute? Was he contemplating whether or not to let her live?

Soft giggles came from close by. Eddie eased his hold on Deanna's shoulders and took a step back from her. Deanna glanced around him and saw Benita and Lauren walking toward the stables, mother and daughter talking and smiling.

"I'd never kill you," Eddie said. "You're an Atchley. You're Rayburn and Phyllis's little girl."

Eddie moved away from her just as Benita and Lauren drew close. Deanna's stomach lurched and for a moment she thought she might throw up.

"Deanna!" Benita rushed toward her, her hands extended in greeting. "I'm so glad to see you. You must go and talk to your mother and Junior. Please speak to them before...before—" Benita glanced at Eddie, then clasped Lauren's hand. "Go see that our horses are saddled, while I speak to your aunt Deanna."

Lauren obeyed her mother instantly. Benita took a hesitant step toward Deanna. "My daughter is an innocent child. You don't want to hurt her, do you? If you pursue your quest to clear Luke McClendon's name, you will be sorry. You hold the power to save or destroy your family."

"You know the truth, too, don't you, Benita? You know who really killed Daddy."

"Please, Deanna. Please—"

"Was there a conspiracy to frame Luke for Daddy's

murder? Did my entire family know the truth and allow an innocent man to go to prison?''

"You don't understand," Benita said.

"You're right," Deanna agreed. "I don't understand. Perhaps you can explain it to me."

Eddie, who had stood quietly to the side, stepped forward and grasped Benita's arm. "Lauren will be back out in a few minutes."

"Please, go speak to your mother," Benita said, then pulled away from Eddie and went inside the stables.

"Stay here on the Circle A, DeDe," he said. "Stay with your family. Fifteen years ago you knew where your loyalty lay."

"Fifteen years ago, I buckled under to my family's threats. I betrayed the man I loved because I was so afraid of my mother." Deanna lifted her chin, her eyes focused on Eddie's face. "But I'm not that same little girl. I'm not weak and frightened and easily manipulated. Tell that to my mother!"

Deanna walked away. Although she wanted to run as fast as she could to escape the Circle A, she reminded herself that she had to remain in control.

She half expected Eddie to follow her, but he didn't. When she slid into the bucket seat of her car, she locked the doors, breathed a sigh of relief and rested her forehead on the steering wheel.

She started the engine, turned her Mustang around and drove away from her family's ranch. In twenty minutes, she would be back at Montrose, on McClendon land—back where she felt safe.

The noonday sun glared down, creating hazy spots on the highway. Deanna's mind replayed the scene with Eddie and Benita. Over and over again she heard Eddie telling her that she would be better off without

Luke. The exact words of the phone message that had been left for her the day Luke had been shot. But she'd heard those words before that day. Someone had said them to her years ago. Eddie! Eddie had said those very words the night her father died.

"You'll be better off without him. Do you hear me, gal?" *Eddie shook her gently, then pulled her into his arms.* *"Ain't nobody going to hurt you. Me and your mama are going to take care of you. You just do what we tell you to do and everything will be all right."*

"But she will tell the sheriff what really happened," *Benita said.* *"She loves Luke McClendon. She knows he didn't kill her father. She saw what really happened."*

"Is that right, Sis?" *Junior looked pleadingly at her.* *"Do you love Luke more than you do us? Are you willing to see one of your own go to prison?"*

"Luke had every reason to want to see Rayburn dead," *Phyllis said.* *"Your father nearly killed that boy. Any jury would understand that Luke acted in self-defense. At most he'd get off with a manslaughter charge."*

Eddie hugged Deanna to his side. *"The best thing you can do is forget what happened here tonight. Put it out of your mind. We're going to have to call the sheriff and when we do, I want you to tell him that Luke McClendon rammed that pitchfork into your father."*

"No! I can't! I won't lie! Luke didn't kill Daddy!" She jerked free of Eddie's tender hold. One by one she looked at the group of people circling her. Eddie. Her mother. Junior. And Benita. She felt them closing in on her, their lips moving, but all she heard was the roar of her own heart. Everything began to swirl around

and around. Her legs felt like rubber. Suddenly every-
thing went black.

The Mustang swerved off the road at high speed,
taking a deadly course toward the fence enclosing the
pastureland to her right. Deanna realized, too late, that
she had lost control of her car. The Mustang hit the
fence, flattening it to the ground. Deanna slammed
down on the brakes. A huge live oak tree loomed in
front of her.

She heard herself screaming as the car came to a
thundering halt.

Chapter 14

The driver's-side air bag ballooned open, protecting Deanna, cocooning her with soft safety. Her heartbeat blared in her ears like a wild trumpet. Nausea rose from her stomach, burning an acidic trail upward and into her throat. She gagged on pure fear. She touched her cheeks, felt for the pulse in her neck and breathed a sigh of great relief. She wasn't dying. She wasn't even injured. Or was she? Commanding her trembling hands into movement, she unsnapped her seat belt, eased back the bucket seat, unlocked the door and got out of the car. Staggering on wobbly legs, she stepped away from the Mustang. The front end rested against the live oak's massive trunk. A sheet of onionskin paper wouldn't fit between the car and the tree.

Thank you, God. Thank you. Deanna dropped to her knees as gratitude overwhelmed her. There had been times in her life when death would have been a sweet solution to her problems. But not now. Now, more than ever before, she wanted to live. Live to clear Luke's name. Live for the chance of loving and being loved once again.

Her stomach churned with the residue of fear mixed with relief. She could no more control the sickness than she could the memory flashback that had caused her wreck. Kneeling there in the pasture, Deanna tossed back her head, letting the warm breeze caress her. She breathed deeply, in and out, repeatedly, until the nausea subsided.

Rising to her feet, she returned to her car, reached inside and removed her purse from the floorboard. She scrambled around inside until she found her cellular phone, then jerked it out, dialed the number for Montrose and waited.

"Montrose," he said. "Luke McClendon."

"Luke!"

"Deanna? What's wrong? You sound odd."

"I—I've had a little accident. Could you come and get me?"

"What sort of accident? Where? I thought you were over at Patsy Ruth's."

"I'm on the road about halfway between the Circle A and Montrose," Deanna said.

"What the hell are you—"

"I'll explain everything," she said. "Just come get me. Please."

"Have you had car trouble?" he asked.

"Yes, something like that."

"I'll be right there."

"Dammit, Deanna, why didn't you tell me you'd had a wreck?" He grabbed her shoulders, then quickly ran his hands over her body, checking for injuries.

"I'm all right. I was able to stop my car before it hit the tree."

"How the hell did you lose control of the car like that?" He cradled her chin in his big hand. "Did an armadillo run out in front of you?"

"No." She shook her head negatively. "I had another memory flashback and for a couple of seconds I almost lost consciousness."

"Oh, God," Luke groaned. "What are you doing on this back road? Patsy Ruth's house is in the opposite direction."

"I...uh...I didn't go to Patsy Ruth's. I went to the Circle A."

Luke cursed, his voice loud, his tone sharp. "Why did you do that? Haven't you got sense enough to know you're in danger over there? Those people may be your family, but—"

Deanna placed her hand over Luke's mouth, silencing him. He glared at her, his green eyes smoldering.

"Hush. Please. I know all the reasons I shouldn't have gone to the Circle A. But I had one very good reason for going."

Deanna eased her hand away from Luke's mouth, then tenderly caressed his cheek. "I was sure that if I could make myself go back to the stables—"

Luke gasped. "Ah, babe, you didn't."

"I had to," she said. "And I'm glad I did. I know now that my whole family—mother, Junior, Benita and Eddie—were all there that night. They all know what really happened. Every one of them knows who killed Daddy."

"Are you sure?" Luke asked.

"Yes, I'm sure. And I'm sure of something else."

He stared at her quizzically. She gripped his shoulder. "I know that Eddie is the one who tried to kill you. He as much as admitted it to me."

"I'm not surprised. Eddie has been the Atchley henchman for years, hasn't he?" A cold, angry expression crossed Luke's face.

Deanna shuddered. "What are you not telling me?"

"Your old man was the one who used that whip on me," Luke said. "But it was Eddie who helped him catch me and tie me to the tree. And it was Eddie who later dumped me in the ditch and spit on me."

"Oh, Luke."

"Junior was with them, but he just sat on his horse and watched. I had the strangest feeling that Junior almost felt sorry for me."

"Junior was afraid of Daddy. He never would have crossed him. And he wouldn't betray Mother, either."

"So, nobody's going to admit the truth, not even Junior or Benita," Luke said. "If you don't remember what happened to your father, we'll never know who killed him."

"I'm remembering more and more." She clasped his forearms. "I'm so close—so very close."

"And when you do remember, will you go to Tyler and tell him the truth, even if it means he'll have to arrest someone in your family?"

"You still doubt me, don't you?"

"Family loyalty is a powerful thing."

She wanted to tell Luke that her only loyalty was to him. That if he would let it happen, he would be her family and she his.

"Whatever happens, I intend to tell the truth—no matter who Daddy's real killer is."

Luke grabbed her arm. "Come on. Let's go. I'll call

a tow truck to get your car out of this field and bring
it back to Montrose.''

Deanna had persuaded Luke to let her tag along
while he rode out to check on the new calves. Springtime was birthing time on the ranch. They talked very
little as they covered mile after mile. But just being
with Luke was enough. Somehow she felt safe with
him, as if nothing and no one could ever harm her as
long as he was near.

The day drew to a close. Evening came to Montrose
in a warm, humid, unsettling haze. Thunder rumbled
in the distance. Lightning streaked the far horizon.
They were miles from the ranch house when the first
raindrops fell, like giant crystal balls that melted upon
impact.

''Looks like we're in for a heavy downpour,'' Luke
said.

''We sure could use the rain,'' Deanna commented,
keeping their conversation on mundane matters, as
Luke had done all afternoon.

About two miles from the ranch house, the bottom
fell out, sending a flood over the dry earth. Luke eased
the truck to a halt and killed the motor.

''I can't see two feet in front of me,'' he said. ''Best
we wait it out here. You don't need to be in another
wreck today.''

''Kizzie won't be worried, will she?''

''She'll know we've stopped somewhere until the
worst of this storm passes over.'' He glanced at
Deanna. ''It's going to get warm in here, with the windows up and the air conditioning off.''

''I'll be all right,'' she told him.

The wind howled as it whipped the rain across the

truck in heavy rivulets. Lightning flashed from the gray evening sky to the earth below, followed by explosive thunderclaps.

Luke watched Deanna, his eyes hooded and his expression questioning. Perspiration damped her hair, curling it about her face. Moisture coated her blouse, sticking it to her skin in various spots, the most obvious, across her pebble-hard nipples. She was the most beautiful woman on earth. And the sexiest. When his body tightened, he silently cursed himself for his lack of control.

Deanna leaned her head back and rested it on the cushioned leather. She wiped the sweat from her face with her fingertips.

"I love you, Luke," she said quietly, calmly, her voice a mere whisper. "I've never loved anyone else. And I haven't had another lover."

She felt the tension in his big body, saw the disbelief in his eyes and heard the sharpness of his indrawn breath.

"It's been fifteen years," he said. "I certainly haven't been celibate. Not since I came home from Huntsville. Why the hell should I believe that you have?"

"Because it's the truth."

Studying her intently, he realized she wasn't lying to him. Not about this. But why? Why would a beautiful, desirable, young woman remain celibate for fifteen years?

"Where did you go when you left Stone Creek, after my trial?" he asked. "There wasn't a day I spent in Huntsville that I didn't wonder where you were, what you were doing, who you were doing it with."

Deanna closed her eyes and sighed, absorbing

Luke's pain inside her, like a sponge soaking up water. Since the night of the barbecue, the night she had gone to Luke and asked for his help, she had known this moment would come. She had to share her tormented past with him. If anyone on earth had a right to know about her five years in a mental hospital, Luke Mc-Clendon did.

Only recently had the memories of those first horrible months at Millones returned to her. The birth of her stillborn son. The voices inside her head. The hallucinations. The tortured dreams. The drugs that numbed her senses. And the long, endless nights she had wept into her pillow, calling quietly for Luke. But Luke never came. No one came to rescue her from hell.

"I went to California," she said.

"California? Why did you go to California?"

"Mother took me there."

"I don't understand," he said. "Why did—"

Deanna opened her eyes and looked at Luke. "I suffered a complete nervous breakdown after I testified about what happened that night," she said, her voice calm and controlled. "Only in the past few weeks have I regained the memory of the months that followed your trial."

"You had a breakdown?"

"Mother didn't want anyone to know that her only daughter was crazy as a betsy bug." Deanna laughed, the sound a hollow, mirthless cry. "Dr. Penson found a private clinic in California. The place was very expensive, very exclusive and totally secluded."

Luke stared at her, stunned by her revelation. Not once had he ever considered the possibility that Deanna had been mentally ill. He lifted his arm, spread it out across the back of the seat and hesitantly touched her shoulder.

She glanced at his fingers where they rubbed a circle around the material that covered her damp shoulder. "The day the jury found you guilty of manslaughter, I was on a plane to California. I didn't know where I was or what was happening. I kept asking for you, but no one would tell me why you wouldn't come to me. Dr. Penson had given me a shot to calm me and I kept drifting in and out of sleep. Mother—Mother told me that everything was going to be all right."

Luke's body tensed, every muscle tight with rage. "You were in this mental hospital when you lost our baby?"

"Yes." Her eyes were dry; her voice was steady and unemotional, as if she were talking about someone other than herself. "I think the staff there believed it was for the best. After all, I was considered totally incompetent and… My mother had given them instructions that when the child was born, he was to be given—" Deanna's voice broke then, and she looked away, the heartache of her loss returning to her. "Even in my condition—mentally sick and spaced out on medication—I wanted my baby. Your baby."

"How long did you stay in this place?" Luke asked, inching his fingers up Deanna's shoulder.

When she turned to face him again, he clasped the back of her neck in his big hand. "I stayed four years, ten months and six days at Millones. And when I left, I was sane. I was well and stronger than I'd ever been in my life. I thought I could find you and tell you what had happened and we could rebuild our lives. But when I learned that you'd been sent to prison, I realized that I couldn't return to Stone Creek."

"During the five years I spent in Huntsville, you were in a mental hospital," Luke said, as if he had to voice the truth aloud in order to believe it. "Every damn day I spent in that place, I pictured you enjoying yourself, laughing behind my back, going on with your life as if I'd never existed."

"I had no life. Not for five years. And when I was released from Millones, I struggled to put the past behind me, to build a new life for myself. I went to college. I got a teaching position in Jackson. I bought a house and a car. I made friends. But…there were no men, not even one man. I was a wounded, imperfect woman, who had betrayed the man she loved, had lost a child and spent five years in a mental institution. Don't you see? Can't you understand that just staying sane and in control was a full-time job. I've lived the past ten years trying to stay strong, trying to become totally independent. And then several months ago, the dreams started again. And the flashbacks. And I knew that I had to come home and face what had happened the night Daddy was killed. I had to face you."

Luke tightened his hold on her neck. She waited breathlessly for his response. He just stared at her for a long, long time. And then he pulled her into his arms and held her. Neither of them said anything.

The rain continued its bombardment and the wind its merciless beating. And there in the hot, damp confinement of Luke's old truck, the hard, cold, impenetrable shield around his heart cracked. The light of truth and love seeped into the those small crevices, obliterating the dark anger and hatred that had grown so powerful inside him.

"I hated being imprisoned," Luke said, his lips against her neck. "I was a tough kid, but I didn't have the vaguest idea of what it would take to survive in Huntsville."

Deanna held him close, her hands soothing the tense muscles in his back. "I'm so sorry, Luke. I'm sorry that I was so weak that I couldn't stand up to my mother. If only I'd been stronger, I wouldn't have lost my memory and I wouldn't—"

He covered her lips with his, silencing her self-condemnation. The kiss was tender beyond anything she'd ever known. Sweet and soft and loving. She responded to his gentle assault, returning the kiss, accepting the moment for what it was. Regret. Sorrow. Longing for what could never be again. Lost youth. Lost love.

Ending the kiss, Luke breathed deeply, then rested his forehead against hers. "I've been so hard on you, babe. I punished you for crimes you never committed."

"I understood why you wanted revenge," she said. "Why you needed to hurt me. Humiliate me. I had betrayed you. I deserved your hatred and your anger."

"No, you didn't." He cupped her face in his hands. "If only I'd known that you've suffered as much— maybe more—than I have. All those years ago, I never realized how fragile you were. It never occurred to me that you'd had a nervous breakdown."

"I lost everything," she breathed the words against his lips. "You. Our baby. My family. I had nothing except those four walls surrounding me. And the pitiful looks from the nurses. And the drugs the doctors ordered to keep me calm and quiet."

Luke hugged her to him fiercely, not wanting to hear another word about her days at the mental hospital and yet knowing that eventually he would need to hear it all. She clung to him, allowing him to comfort her, to hold her close. He thought he had experienced all the pain that existed, that nothing could touch his heart, not ever again. But he'd been wrong. Learning about Deanna's imprisonment, her days of torment hurt him as nothing—not even her betrayal—ever had. If he'd been a man instead of an insecure, angry boy, he might have been able to save her. But he'd been young and headstrong and lost in his own grief.

"If I could go back and do it over again…" he murmured.

"We can never go back." Deanna lifted her head and looked deeply into his eyes. Moss green and moist. Eyes that revealed his thoughts. His innermost sorrows. "Once we…after I regain the complete memory of the night Daddy was killed and I clear your name, then we won't ever have to look back again. We'll both be free to move ahead, to have a future worth living."

"I don't think I can ever forget those years I spent in Huntsville," Luke said. "You don't really think you can forget that you spent nearly five years in a mental hospital, do you?"

"I'll never forget," she admitted. "But I can let go. I can stop holding on to the pain and the regrets. I can stop living in a world of *if onlys*. And so can you, Luke. If you can forgive me…if you can—"

"I never thought I could." He kissed her forehead, her cheeks and then her lips. "I thought I'd hate you forever, that I'd never forgive you for betraying me, but…" he hesitated briefly, then kissed her again, with tender passion. "I can forgive you. Knowing now that you suffered so terribly makes me ashamed that I… God, help us! Deanna, can you ever forgive me for the way I've treated you?"

"There's nothing to forgive." She rested her head on his shoulder and eased her arm around his waist. "I would have done anything…paid any price to save you from yourself.''

''Deanna?'' He gently stroked her cheek with his big, callused fingers.

''What?'' She looked up at him.

''Will you let me make love to you?'' he asked, his voice husky and thick. ''I want to take you back to the cottage and spend all night loving you.''

''Make love to me the way you used to,'' she told him. ''The way you did when you loved me.''

''Ah, babe.''

His lips covered hers, gently at first, his thoughts solely of her. How fragile Deanna was. How greatly she had suffered. How deeply he had wounded her with his hatred and anger. But when she responded so fervently, her tongue seeking his, her moans enticing, he deepened the kiss. The desire curling inside him like hot smoke encouraged him to act, not think, to take and give with mindless abandon. Her hands sought him, clung to him, caressed him. Impassioned to the point of madness, she gave herself over to the joy of being pleasured by the man she loved. The man who had forgiven her.

When Deanna popped open the pearl snaps on Luke's shirt and sought the heat of his body, he grabbed her fondling hands and brought them to his lips.

''We've got to stop. Now, Deanna,'' he said, his breathing labored. ''If we don't I'm going to take you here in the truck.''

''Don't stop.''

''But Deanna—''

She planted a quick kiss on his mouth. ''I don't want you to stop.''

"But I wanted this time to be really special. Back at the cottage we could—"

She kissed him again. "We can go back to the cottage later and take all night. But right now, I don't want to wait. Do you?"

"Hell, no!" The weak dam of his control burst, releasing the full force of his need.

With clumsy haste, they undressed, all the while kissing and touching and moaning. Urgent to mate again in that old sweet way that young lovers come together, Deanna and Luke allowed fifteen years to melt away like snow in the warm springtime sun. There had been no betrayal, no nervous breakdown, no manslaughter sentence. She was seventeen again and untouched by pain and sorrow. And he was twenty again, a boy in love, a boy on the verge of self-acceptance.

As their lips devoured, their bodies meshed together, perspiration coating their flesh. Luke's mouth played with her nipples, eliciting a cry of pleasure from Deanna. She bucked up, her hips rising to meet the first powerful thrust of his big body.

"Oh, Luke. Love me. Love me."

And he did. With the overwhelming need that could not be appeased with less than her complete fulfillment, Luke made love to her with feverish passion.

While Mother Nature put on a vivid show outside the truck, sending torrents of rain from the heavens and enlivening the evening with blazes of lightning and drum rolls of thunder, Deanna and Luke found heaven in each other's arms. In the hot, fervid joining of their bodies. In the pure, sweet act of forgiveness. In the tenderness of love.

Chapter 15

Deanna and Luke rushed inside the guest cottage. Drenched from the rain, they went into each other's arms, their mouths greedily seeking, their hands hungrily touching. Luke lifted her up in his arms and carried her to the bathroom, where they both stripped out of their soggy boots and soaked jeans and shirts. Luke turned on the warm water and led Deanna into the small shower. She shivered in his arms as he lowered his head and kissed her. The kiss went on and on, until they were both breathless and aroused beyond reason. And then he washed her, slowly, tenderly, caressing every inch of her body. When he completed his task, she took the soap from him and lathered his broad chest and wide shoulders, then worked her way downward. Clasping his tight buttocks in her hands, she urged him to turn into the spray to rinse away the soap. While the warm water jetted down on them, Deanna caressed him intimately, her hand circling and then pumping. Luke growled, deep and rough. He speared his fingers into her hair and held her head in place while she used her tongue to pleasure him. When she took him into her mouth, he braced his trembling body against the shower enclosure and gave himself over to her pure, selfless act of love. He unraveled completely, allowing Deanna the mastery of his body as she brought him to a powerful release. With the aftershocks of fulfillment still rippling through him, Luke led Deanna out of the shower, then began a slow, sensual seduction. He dried her damp skin, concentrating on her breasts and the apex between her thighs. She swayed, her legs rubbery, her knees weak. He towel-dried her hair and then carried her to the bed. With his body braced over hers, he tormented her nipples with his tongue and teeth until she was wild for him, and then he licked and nipped a pathway down her stomach, over and into her navel and finally down and into the secret depths of her femininity. She cried out with the earth-shattering ecstasy of the climax Luke gave her.

They drifted off into a sated sleep, their bodies damp, naked and uncovered on the bed in the Montrose guest house.

When they awoke, almost simultaneously, Luke only a couple of minutes before Deanna, they looked at each other and smiled.

"I'm hungry," Luke said as he reached out to twine a stray lock of her hair around his index finger. "How about you?"

"Starved," she said. "Want me to fix us some supper?"

"A woman after my own heart." Luke grinned.

"Always," she replied, returning his smile, but a sheen of tears misted her eyes.

He pulled her close, encompassing her in his arms. Resting his chin on her head, he hugged her fiercely. "Don't cry, babe. Please don't cry. We'll find our way through this mess, all the way to the end. We'll do it together, side by side. No matter what happens, we aren't alone anymore."

Deanna thought her heart would burst with happiness. The man who had prided himself on being a loner had opened himself up to her and admitted his loneliness. Lifting her hand to his face, she stroked his cheek. "Sometimes the loneliness was almost more than I could bear," she admitted. "No matter how busy I stayed, no matter how many people I surrounded myself with, I was always so alone."

He pressed her hand against his cheek. "I've been alone all my life. Even before my mother died. She never was there for me. Not really. And even in the midst of the McClendon clan, I always felt outside the fold. Only with you, Deanna, did I ever feel a part of someone else. And when you left my life, it was worse than it had been before I knew you. Much worse."

She hugged him fiercely. "Do you think there's any way we can get back what we lost?"

Luke eased away from her, swung his legs off the bed and stood. Looking down at her, he held out his hand. "Let's go find ourselves something to eat."

She took his hand. He lifted her from the bed to her feet.

"I'm sorry, Luke," she said. "I guess I'm asking for too much. Knowing that you don't hate me and that you've forgiven me is more than I'd ever hoped for."

"We can't ever get back what we lost," he told her. "What we had together then is gone forever."

Deanna sadly nodded agreement. "We should get

dressed. I'm afraid I don't have anything that you can wear, but—''

He grasped her chin, forcing her to face him. ''We don't need any clothes. There's no reason why we can't enjoy supper just the way we are—buck naked.''

He grinned at her and for one brief, sweet moment in time, she didn't care that the past was irretrievably lost to her, as lost as Luke's son. This precious night with Luke was a dream come true, a chance to build new memories to replace the old ones. A gift from the gods that she would cherish forever.

Even if Luke could never love her again the way he once had, it was enough that by gaining his forgiveness, she had returned Luke to the land of the living. She had retrieved his soul from the black depths of Hades.

They sat together in the tiny kitchenette, munching on potato chips and swigging on sugary colas, after they finished off ham sandwiches. Naked and completely at ease in their undressed state, Luke and Deanna shared more than a meal. They discussed the ranch and Luke's love for the land and his desire to someday return to Oklahoma and find out if there were any members of his mother's family still on the Cherokee reservation. Deanna told him about her life in Jackson, about the special boys and girls to whom she had dedicated the past six years of her life.

The distant past was not mentioned again by either of them, nor did they talk about the future. It was as if they had telepathically made a pact to hold the demons at bay for this one night. They were taking the first steps in a journey of self-discovery, of shared intimacies and pleasures that they could experience with no other. Luke was not the boy she remembered—the boy she had adored with such complete abandon. Nor was she the girl Luke had worshiped so passionately. Fifteen long, lonely, painful years had matured them both into self-sufficient, independent adults. Adults who had learned to survive alone, without the comfort of love. Scarred, flawed individuals who, more than most, needed the healing power of love and forgiveness.

They stacked the dirty dishes in the sink and, hand in hand, returned to the bedroom.

"Should you call Kizzie?" Deanna asked.

"She'll see my truck and know that we're out here," he said.

Deanna nodded.

"I could go back to the house," he told her. "But I don't want to leave you. Not tonight."

He stood beside her, the dim glow from the bedside lamp outlining his magnificent body in a yellow-white aura. Every feminine instinct within her reacted to his raw masculinity. She tugged on his hand and led him to the bed. Bringing him with her as she lay down, she invited him to stay. To share with her what he could share with no other woman. The joining not only of bodies, but of hearts and souls. Luke hadn't told her he loved her, but in her heart of hearts, Deanna believed that he did. And she held tightly to that belief when she offered herself to him, without any promises or commitments for the future.

"I want you to stay tonight," she said. *I want you to stay with me forever, my love.*

There was a gentleness in their lovemaking that had been missing in their previous joinings. A caring that went beyond the physical, as if they were trying to make love to each other's wounded souls.

Luke caressed her, his hands and fingers moving with slow, deliberate seduction. His touch was feather-light as he stroked her vulnerable neck. She writhed with pleasure as he found and paid homage to each sexually sensitive spot on her body. He ran his big fingers between her slender ones and brought her hand to his mouth. He sucked the tips of each finger, one by one. Shudders of desire rippled over her nerve endings. He licked a moist circle around one ear and then the other, all the while he moved his fingers in and out of her damp core. He spread her legs to reach her inner thighs, where he painted her flesh, using his tongue as a brush.

She reveled in his ardent attention, loving each touch, each whispered earthy phrase as he praised her beauty and described his intentions in crude, masculine detail.

The moment he entered her, she fell apart, spiraling out of control, climaxing immediately.

Luke loved that he could give her such pleasure, that he instinctively knew what she wanted and needed.

"It has never been like this with anyone else," he said, his voice a raw growl.

"I'm glad," was all she could say.

He cupped her buttocks, lifting her up so that he could delve deeply, joining them completely. Her lush body was the beginning and end of his world. Luke heard the rush of blood through his veins, the pumping of his heart and his harsh, ragged breathing. He wished this wild, uncontrollable surge toward completion could last for hours instead of minutes, but if he stayed inside her, he'd be lost and so would she.

Deanna whimpered when Luke withdrew from her. Clutching his shoulders, she tried to bring him back inside, back into the depths of her throbbing body. She gazed up into his half-closed eyes and saw the agony he could not disguise. And she understood his actions. He knew as well as she that this night would be hours out of time, hours that would end at daybreak, hours that might be all they'd ever share. He did not want the loving to end. He wanted this night to last forever. And so did she.

But they could no more hold back the dawn than they could control their passion.

She encompassed his sex with her hand and drew him back to her. "Love me now," she told him. "Don't think about tomorrow."

He thrust into her and she took him into her body, empowered by all the love and longing within her heart. They thrashed about in the bed, twisting and turning, moving together in a wild, frenzy of unbridled need. And when Luke's climax came, it washed over them both like a tidal wave, exploding inside him with maximum force and igniting her own cataclysmic release.

They lay in each other's arms, sated, totally spent, and satisfied both physically and emotionally. They had shared true loving at its best, their bodies in tune, their feelings united as surely as their bodies had been.

When Deanna began to doze off to sleep, Luke dragged her out of bed and lifted her in his arms, pulling the blanket up with her. He carried her outside, onto the porch. After draping the cotton blanket around them, he sat down on the wooden bench and placed her in his lap. The rainstorm had passed, leaving behind that fresh, sweet scent that wafted in the air, rarer by far than any expensive Parisian perfume. Overhead the night sky had cleared and the array of tiny, winking stars spread out over them like a diamond-studded black canopy.

Deanna rested her head on his shoulder and absorbed the most exhilarating contentment she had ever known. This is what life should be, she thought. Every day. Every hour. But if it were, there would be no need for heaven.

"I wish I knew the right words," Luke said. "I've never been very good at talking."

"It's all right," she told him. "You don't have to say any more. You've shown me how you feel."

"I'd like to forget the past, put it behind us and... Will you be patient with me, babe? Can you give me time to learn how to be human again?"

She cuddled in his arms, loving him and loving the way he made her feel. "I'll give you all the time you need."

He kissed her forehead, then rubbed his cheek against hers. She sighed deeply and closed her eyes.

An hour later, Luke carried a sleeping Deanna back inside the house, back to the bed they had shared. He eased her onto the soft sheet, lay down beside her and covered them both with the cotton blanket.

Luke had left her. He'd walked away and not even looked back. She turned to run to him, to chase him down and tell him that she would go with him, that even if her father killed them both, she wanted to be with him.

"Don't follow him, Dede," Rayburn Atchley warned. "If you don't want that boy dead, you'd better stay right where you are."

"But I love him, Daddy. Can't you understand

that?'' She looked pleadingly at her father. ''I'm going to have Luke's baby.''

''There's no way in hell I'll let you have that breed's baby. I'll have his seed ripped out of you, girl!''

''No, Daddy. No, you won't. I won't let you!''

Rayburn Atchley moved closer and closer, backing her up against the fence. He loomed over her, big and furious and dangerous. Until recently, she had never feared her father. But she feared him now. He lifted his hand to strike her.

''Don't, Daddy! Don't hit her!'' Junior called out in a loud but trembling voice.

Rayburn snapped his head around and glared at his son. ''You stay out of this, boy!''

''No, Daddy, I can't. I didn't lift a hand to stop you from beating Luke McClendon nearly to death, but I can't just stand here and watch you beat my sister.''

''Yeah, you and what army's going to stop me? Tell me that, mama's boy. You haven't got the balls to stop me and we both know it.''

''Don't do it, Daddy.'' Junior took a tentative step forward, out of the darkness. Benita moved like a shadow to stand at his side.

''Your sister whored around with that young bastard and got herself pregnant with his baby. But I'm not going to have a child of his come into this family. I'll beat it out of her.''

Deanna trembled, her fear a living, breathing reality, growing inside her as surely as the child she carried.

Rayburn balled his big hand into a fist, drew back and rammed it into Deanna's stomach. Doubling over, she cried out in pain, then slumped to the ground. Her father grabbed her shoulder, lifted her to her feet and drew back his fist again.

Junior shot toward his father, bombarding him with his stocky, young body. He tried to pull Rayburn away from Deanna. Like a raging bull, the big man turned on his son and used his hard fist to knock the boy into the dirt. Benita ran crying to Junior, dropping to her knees to cradle his head.

"Stay down there, if you know what's good for you," Rayburn said. *"You're a weakling, boy. You're no match for me."* Rayburn sneered, then let his gaze rest on his son's girlfriend. *"Isn't that right, Benita? Tell my son that he's not half the man in the sack that his old man is."*

Grinning broadly, Rayburn turned back around to Deanna, who clung to the fence. "Either you agree to an abortion or I'll beat that heathen's baby out of you right here and now."

"Please, Daddy…" Tears streamed down Deanna's face. Pain sliced through her body.

"Leave her alone, you son of a bitch!" Junior said.

When Rayburn turned sideways to answer his son's threat, Deanna gasped when she saw the pitchfork in Junior's hand.

Rayburn laughed. "Put that down, boy. If Luke McClendon didn't have the guts to use that thing on me, then you sure as hell don't."

"You think I don't know what kind of man you really are." Junior glared at his father. *"I know. I've always known. Mama hates you and so do I. And now Deanna does, too."*

Benita tugged on Junior's arm. "Please, Junior, you know I love only you. You know what he did to me."

Junior shoved Benita away from him. "You raped her. You couldn't keep your hands off her because you knew she was mine. You knew that I loved her."

"Put that pitchfork down, son. Don't make a bigger fool of yourself than you already have." Rayburn moved toward Junior, confident in his power over the boy. *"If your little Mexican piece told you that I raped her, she lied. She wanted me all right. Wanted me bad. Didn't you, honey?"*

Junior's eyes brightened, his cheeks flushed. His hands tightened around the handle of the pitchfork.

As if in slow motion, Deanna watched helplessly as her brother rammed the prongs of the pitchfork into their father's chest, shoving him to the ground and pinning him there. Rayburn stared up at his son in total shock and disbelief for one brief second and then gasped his final breath.

Deanna heard someone screaming and at first thought that she herself was making the dreadful noise. But she quickly realized that Benita was screaming hysterically. Within minutes, or so it seemed, Eddie and Phyllis came running to the stables. And while Deanna stood by helplessly, her mother and the ranch foreman plotted to save Junior by framing Luke McClendon for Rayburn Atchley's death.

Deanna shot straight up in bed, sweat dripping from her naked body. Luke awoke instantly and realized she was crying silently. He gripped her trembling shoulders gently, turned her and drew her into his arms.

"Another dream?" he asked.

She couldn't speak, but nodded affirmatively.

"Was it a bad one?"

She nodded again.

"Can you tell me about it?"

She took a deep breath, then said in quivering voice, "Junior."

"What?"

"Junior killed Daddy," she said.

He tensed when he heard her declaration. "Are you sure? Maybe you just dreamed that Junior killed your father, but in reality—"

"No," she said. "No. It wasn't just a dream. I remember now. I remember everything."

"Tell me. Start at the beginning and tell me what happened that night after I left."

He held her within the safety of his arms, protecting her as much as he could from the painful truth. She spoke slowly, calmly, at first and then, before she ended the recollection of the most traumatic night of her life, Deanna cried. Tears of regret. Tears of remorse. And tears of relief.

"Your brother was defending you," Luke said. "Any court of law could have been convinced that he did what he had to do to keep your father from hurting you, from destroying the child inside you."

"Junior didn't want to go along with Mother and Eddie's scheme to frame you. He kept begging them to let him tell the truth." Deanna clung to Luke as heart-cleansing tears streamed down her face. "But before the sheriff arrived, he gave in and allowed Mother to have her way. He was just a kid, the way we were. And like me, he didn't have the backbone to stand up against Mother."

"What are you going to do?" Luke asked, turning her in his arms, so that she faced him.

"What am I... Oh, God, Luke, I was so sure that Mother or Eddie killed Daddy. I had no idea that Junior had plunged that pitchfork into Daddy. That he was trying to protect me. And—and trying to avenge what Daddy did to Benita."

Luke released her and eased out of bed. Deanna

looked up into his shadowed face, into his hooded eyes, and felt his withdrawal. Once again she had to choose between her family and Luke. This time it was a choice between a brother who had killed to protect her and the man she loved, the man who had spent five years in prison for a crime he didn't commit.

"Luke?"

"No one ever has to know," he said. "The truth doesn't have to go any further than this room. Junior's your brother. You can't—"

"I can't lie anymore." She slid to the edge of the bed. "Not to myself. I know the truth now and, if you'll go with me, I'll face Junior and my mother and tell them that I remember everything."

She held out her hand to him, silently pleading for his understanding. He hesitated momentarily, then took her hand in his and lifted her up and into his arms.

"I'll go with you," he said, as he buried his face in the soft fall of honey-brown hair draped over her shoulder.

Chapter 16

"I don't think you and Deanna should go over to the Circle A and confront her family alone," Kizzie said. "You should call Tyler and have him go with y'all."

"I thought I explained why I didn't want to involve Tyler at this point." Luke placed his hand on Kizzie's shoulder. "I don't know how Deanna's going to handle this situation. Once she has a chance to talk to Junior, all her sisterly instincts will kick in and she might not be able to go through with turning him in to the law."

"That girl loves you, son." Kizzie patted Luke's hand where it lay on her shoulder. "She came back to Texas to regain her memory and she's done that. Now, all she needs to do to fulfill her mission is clear your name. Unless she reveals the true killer's identity, she can't do that."

"I'm not sure that I want my name cleared bad enough to see Deanna destroyed by having to turn against her own brother." Luke released his hold on

Kizzie's shoulder, walked out on the back porch and lifted his Stetson from the hat rack. Glancing back, he said, "I don't want to risk her having another break-down. She's suffered enough."

"I wish we'd known just what that child went through all those years ago." Kizzie stood in the open kitchen doorway. "To think that during the five years you spent in Huntsville, she was in a mental hospital."

"She's a strong woman now," Luke said. "But there's still a part of her that's very fragile. And she always loved Junior. It's going to kill her if she has to—"

"You're right." Kizzie shook her head sadly. "But don't tell me that you and Deanna will have any kind of future together if she chooses her brother's best interests over yours."

"I don't know," he admitted. "Selfishly, I want the truth to come out. The whole truth. And yes, I want Deanna to love me enough to stand against her family. Even stand against the brother she loves."

"Won't y'all sit down," Phyllis Atchley, model-perfect in her navy slacks and white silk blouse, invited. "I must admit that when you called, Deanna, and asked to meet with the whole family, I was surprised." Phyllis glanced at Luke, who stood rigidly at Deanna's side. "And I'm even more surprised to see Luke McClendon with you."

"Where's Eddie and Junior and Benita?" Deanna asked, making no move to sit down in her mother's elegant living room.

"They'll be here shortly," Phyllis said. "Perhaps you could tell me the meaning of this urgent meeting today? I'm at a total loss for why you would bring Luke into a private family gathering.''

"Luke is with me because what I have to tell my family involves him, too. After all, he's the one you and Eddie framed for Daddy's murder. He's the one who spent five years in prison for a crime he didn't commit. And he's the one whose name I intend to clear. Today!''

"You must be having another breakdown,'' Phyllis said softly, fixing her daughter with a pleading look. "You're delusional if you think anyone framed Luke for Rayburn's murder.''

"Cut the act, Mother! I remember. I remember everything.''

All natural color drained from Phyllis's face.

"What do you think you remember, DeDe?'' Eddie Nunley asked from where he stood outside in the entrance foyer.

Deanna's body jerked, reacting to the ranch foreman's sudden appearance. Looking over her shoulder, she gasped when she saw the rifle Eddie held.

Luke glanced back at Eddie, noting the rifle. So, this was going to be an armed confrontation, he thought. He had suspected as much and that's why he had come prepared. Hidden inside his jacket pocket was the Firestar 9 mm pistol Grant had left at the house several years ago. He wasn't fool enough to come into enemy territory unarmed.

"I remember everything about the night Daddy died,'' Deanna said. "Every detail. Everything that was said and done. I know who really killed my father.''

"And just who do you think killed our daddy?'' Junior Atchley wheeled into the living room, his wife at his side.

Deanna looked at her paralyzed brother—her weak, helpless brother, whom she had always loved. Her brother, who had stood up against their father, defending her and avenging Benita.

"You did, Junior," she said, her voice strong and sure.

"No, my Junior did nothing," Benita cried out, her hands gripping Junior's shoulders. "Why do you lie about your own brother? A man so kind and good and…" Benita burst into tears.

Junior leaned his head to one side and rubbed her left hand with his cheek. "Hush up, sugar. Don't fret. We knew it would come to this sooner or later, once Sister came home to the Circle A."

"I say your memories are false," Phyllis said. "No jury in the world would believe you. A former mental patient. I'm telling you that a smart lawyer could tear you apart on the witness stand and you know it."

"No, Mother, I don't know anything of the sort." Deanna looked past her mother, her gaze resting on her brother. "But it doesn't matter one way or the other, because I'm not planning to testify against Junior."

Luke's body tensed. His nerves rioted. Eddie Nunley eased the rifle he held down to his side. Benita wiped the tears from her face. Phyllis took a deep breath and smiled hesitantly.

"Now, you've come to your senses, gal." Eddie walked into the living room and moved quickly to Phyllis's side. "See, what'd I tell you. Our DeDe would never betray her family. She stood by us once, she'll do it again."

"Is that true?" Phyllis asked. "If you have no intention of telling the sheriff that Junior killed Rayburn, then why is this family meeting in front of Luke McClendon?''

Deanna ignored her mother completely as she walked across the room, knelt in front of her brother and took his hands into hers. ''I know why you did it.'' Her words were a soft, understanding whisper. ''I know what Daddy did to Benita. And I realize that Daddy might have killed me—that he surely would have killed my baby—if you hadn't stopped him.''

''I hated that sorry son of a bitch,'' Junior said in a quiet, controlled voice. ''He made my life a living hell. When I found out that he had raped Benita, I wanted to kill him then. But...he was right. I didn't have the guts to kill him. Not until that night. Not until I saw him brutalizing you. He'd never laid a hand on you until he found out about you and Luke, and I was glad you'd never known his fury the way Mother and I had. But I could tell he meant to beat you until you lost that baby, even if it meant killing you in the process.''

''I know.'' Heavy tears accumulated in Deanna's eyes. ''Thank you for saving my life.'' She embraced her brother.

Junior wrapped his arms around his sister and hugged her fiercely. ''You want me to confess, don't you, Sister? That's why you came here today. You want to give me a chance to turn myself in.''

''I'll be there with you through it all,'' Deanna promised. ''I'll explain what happened, that your actions probably saved my life.''

''No!'' Phyllis yelled, then said in a calmer voice, ''No. Your brother will not confess to anything. I won't allow it! Do you hear me? For pity's sake, Deanna, look at him. He's paralyzed!''

Junior lifted his head and sighed. ''Give it up,

Mother. It's past time I did the right thing, don't you think?''

"Please, darling, don't say any more," Phyllis said. "We'll make Deanna see reason. She's your sister. She won't—she can't betray you."

Eddie lifted his rifle, using it as a threat. "Your mother and I did what we had to do to protect Junior. And to protect you from Luke McClendon." Eddie glowered at Luke as his hands tightened on the rifle.

"You shot Luke, didn't you?" Deanna moved slowly toward Eddie. "You tried to kill him, after slaughtering the cattle and setting fire to the pasture-land didn't run me away from Montrose." Deanna focused her gaze on her mother. "And you're the one who gave the orders."

"No, Sister, you can't believe that Mother ordered Eddie to kill Luke!" Junior's face turned scarlet. His nervous glance jumped back and forth between Eddie and Phyllis. "My God, you did it on your own, didn't you, Eddie? Wasn't it enough that we sent him to prison, that we destroyed Deanna's life?"

"Eddie, you didn't…you wouldn't have," Phyllis stammered. "Letting Luke go to prison to save Junior and get him away from Deanna was one thing, but to kill him… Please tell me—"

"You didn't know what Eddie was doing, did you?" Deanna stared at her mother as if seeing her for the first time.

Eddie aimed his rifle at Luke. Instinctively Deanna stepped in front of Luke, trying to protect him with her own body.

"I did what had to be done." Eddie spoke directly to Phyllis. "All your pleas to Deanna weren't having any effect on her. I couldn't let her stay here and re-

member everything, could I? We framed an innocent
man for murder to protect Junior. We couldn't be sure
of Deanna's loyalty this time. We could all wind up in
jail if she tells what really happened."

Phyllis turned to Deanna, held out a trembling hand
and said, "What are you going to do? Are you going
to tell the authorities that your brother killed his own
father? If you do, it won't change anything for Luke
or for you. Nothing can undo what's been done."

"She ain't going to turn Junior in," Eddie said.
"There ain't no need to try to clear the name of a dead
man."

Phyllis gasped. Deanna stood her ground in front of
Luke, her gaze riveted to Eddie's face.

"So, you're going to kill me?" Luke asked.

"Yep," Eddie said. "You didn't give me no choice.
Deanna came home to us. Disturbed and frantic. Luke,
you didn't want us to help her. You tried to make her
leave with you against her will. When I tried to stop
you, you shot at me, so I had no choice but to shoot
you first."

"But Luke doesn't have a gun," Deanna said.

"You've got a gun, haven't you, McClendon?"
Eddie grinned. "A man like you wouldn't be stupid
enough to come over to the Circle A unarmed."

"You can't get away with murdering Luke,"
Deanna said. "Kizzie knows that Luke and I came here
together and she knows why."

"Kizzie's knowing about your delusional ramblings
doesn't alter the fact that you're having another nervous breakdown or that Luke's influence over you
forced you to confront us with your lies." Eddie told
Deanna. "When we—your family—tried to help you,

Luke became violent. He pulled a gun on me and...
Well, you see how this has to end.''

''No! No, you're not going to do this!'' Junior
wheeled across the room, Benita rushing behind him.
''I can't stand by and see you—''

''Shut up!'' Eddie narrowed his gaze on Junior.
''I'm trying to protect you. Protect this family. And
once and for all, we'll free ourselves from the curse of
Luke McClendon.''

Luke moved Deanna aside. And when she tried to
shield him again, he shoved her toward Junior. In that
instant—when all eyes were on Deanna spinning away
from Luke—Luke drew the Firestar from his jacket and
rushed Eddie Nunley. Momentarily caught off guard,
Eddie reacted a split-second too slowly and the rifle
shot he got off whizzed past Luke and embedded the
bullet in the wall.

Deanna flopped down, her backside hitting the floor.
When she realized what was happening, she jumped to
her feet in time to see Luke barrel into Eddie, knocking
the man's rifle out of his hand. But during the ensuing
struggle, Luke also lost his gun. The pistol hit the floor
and slid across the polished hardwood.

Phyllis dashed toward the gun. Deanna dove onto
the floor, reaching for the 9 mm. Mother and daughter
collided. Phyllis snatched the gun up into her hand.

''Stop! Do you hear me, Eddie! Stop this insanity!''
Phyllis held the gun in both hands and aimed it at the
two struggling men.''

Luke landed one final blow to Eddie Nunley's jaw,
knocking him to the floor. Eddie stared up at Phyllis,
his bloody mouth curving into a smile.

''Shoot him!'' Eddie ordered. ''Kill the son of a
bitch!''

"No." Phyllis dropped the 9 mm to the floor, then crumpled onto her knees. "No more of this. Do you hear me?"

Eddie dove forward, his arm extended, as he reached for the weapon. Luke jumped him just as he grasped the gun. The two men rose to their feet in a struggle— Eddie trying to aim the gun barrel into Luke's belly and Luke trying to take the weapon away from his opponent.

The sound of a gun firing—once, then once again— echoed in Deanna's ears. Spinning around, she stared helplessly as Luke fell backwards. Eddie fell forward, landing on top of him.

"Luke!" Deanna screamed.

Luke shoved Eddie Nunley's body off his. "I—I'm all right."

Kneeling over Eddie's body, Phyllis felt for a pulse. "He's still alive. We must call for an ambulance."

While Benita dialed 911, a car screeched to a halt in front of the Atchley home. Within seconds, the front door flew open and Tyler McClendon stood in the foyer.

"What the hell happened here?" he asked. "Dammit, Deanna, I told you to wait until I got here before you and Luke confronted your family."

"What?" Luke asked, puzzled by his stepbrother's statement.

"Deanna called me this morning and told me that she remembered everything and that she wanted me to meet you and her here at the Circle A. She seemed certain that her brother would have something to tell me."

"Well, I'll be damned!" Luke said.

Deanna stood over her mother, who had sat down

on the floor and lifted Eddie's head onto her lap. She stroked his cheek and brushed a strand of hair out of his eyes.

Phyllis moaned. "Deanna."

"Yes, Mother?"

"I'm so very, very sorry," Phyllis said. "I did what I thought was right for both you and Junior. I never meant—"

"Oh, Mother!" Tears poured down Deanna's cheeks.

Luke hovered behind Deanna, wanting desperately to pull her away and enfold her in his arms.

Junior Atchley wheeled over to Tyler. "You'll be arresting Eddie if he lives. He's the one who slaughtered Montrose cattle, set fire to Montrose range and tried to kill Luke."

"Then he's still alive?" Tyler asked.

"Just barely," Deanna said.

"Poor Eddie," Junior said. "He thought he was protecting Mother and me." Junior looked up at Deanna. "I'm sorry, Sister. God, I'm so very sorry. But I'm going to make it right, if I can. I promise you that."

Benita fell to her knees and wrapped her arms around her husband.

Eddie Nunley died on the way to the hospital. Phyllis Atchley buried him in the family cemetery on the Circle A.

Two weeks later, after he had confessed to killing his father, Junior Atchley was sentenced to prison. But due to the circumstances, Junior's physical condition, and the plea for mercy by Deanna and Luke, the judge gave Junior the minimum sentence.

Phyllis Atchley was sentenced to probation and two

years of community service, which seemed appropriate punishment for a woman whose social standing had once meant everything to her.

Luke helped Deanna pack, but when she headed for her car, he kept walking—straight toward the main house.

"Where are you taking my luggage?" she asked.

"Up to the house," he said, not slowing his gait. "To my room. Where else would I take my future wife's luggage?"

"What?" She ran after him, catching him just as he stepped onto the back porch. "What did you say?"

He dropped the luggage, turned and smiled. "I don't want you to leave. I don't want you to go back to Jackson. I want you to stay here on Montrose." He knelt down on one knee, took her hand in his and said, "Deanna, will you marry me?"

Not once in the weeks following the deadly confrontation at the Circle A had Luke mentioned the future. He had stood by her, protecting her, supporting her and caring for her. He had even encouraged her to accept the plea from Phyllis for a second chance at being a real family. But she hadn't dared hope that when everything was settled Luke would ask her to marry him.

He hadn't told her that he loved her.

"Luke, I don't know what to say."

"Say, yes."

"But...are you sure?"

"I've never been surer of anything in my life. We've lost fifteen years that we should have spent together," he told her. "Let's not waste the rest of our lives."

She tugged on Luke's hand, urging him to stand. He

rose from his kneeling position, brought her hands to his lips and kissed them.

"I know it may be too soon after everything that's happened," he said. "But maybe we could plan a fall wedding or a winter one, if you need more time. I'm sure you can find a teaching job here, if you're willing to give up your position in Jackson."

"A fall wedding would be wonderful, and I'm willing to give up my job in Jackson, but..." But do you love me? she wanted to shout. "Why do you want to marry me?"

"Why do I want to marry you? Why do you think?" He drew her into his arms.

"I need the words, Luke. I have to hear you say them."

He swung her up into his arms. "Because I love you, Deanna. I love you more than anything in this world."

"Then yes, I'll marry you," she said, throwing her arms around his neck. "I love you, too, you know. I'll love you forever...and then some."

Epilogue

"Where are you taking me?" Deanna asked, as Luke tightened the blindfold around her eyes. "And why can't I see where we're going?"

"Because I want your anniversary present to be a surprise," he told her as he lifted her onto Cherokee's back, then mounted the horse and settled behind her into the saddle. "Now, stop fussing."

Deanna allowed Luke to have his way, knowing that she, too, had a surprise to share for their first anniversary. *Their first anniversary.* Sometimes she could hardly believe that she'd been Luke's wife for an entire year. Three hundred and sixty-five days of happiness.

It didn't take her long to realize that Cherokee was taking them up into the hills. With each passing moment, the excitement built within her. What sort of gift could Luke have waiting for her? A picnic in a secluded glade perhaps?

Luke brought Cherokee to a halt, dismounted and then lifted Deanna into his arms.

"You can take off your blindfold now, Mrs. McClendon," he said.

She smiled, loving it when he called her Mrs. McClendon. Her stomach quivered with anticipation. She reached up and jerked away the scarf that covered her eyes, and her smile was instantly replaced by an expression of astonishment.

"Luke," she breathed his name aloud.

"Do you like it, babe?"

She stared in wonderment at the cabin that had been erected on the site where *their* old cabin had stood. A cool autumn breeze ruffled the treetops and stirred the dry leaves lying on the ground. She could hardly believe what she saw, but there it was—a small log cabin, new and fresh and shining like gold in the afternoon sunlight.

"When? How? Why?" she murmured the questions in rapid succession.

Luke carried her up the stone walkway and onto the porch. He kicked open the front door and carried his wife over the threshold and into the cabin he had spent months secretly building for her.

"Do you like it?" he asked, as he eased her down on the sofa in front of the fireplace.

She gazed at the roaring fire, then glanced around the room filled with rustic furniture. In the corner by the double windows, an old iron bed awaited. The pristine white sheets had been turned down. The feather pillows had been fluffed.

"I love it," she said. "But...oh, Luke." She held open her arms to him.

He went down on his knees before her, then allowed

her to take him into her embrace. "I wanted our special place back," he said. "I was the one who destroyed it and I needed to be the one who rebuilt it."

With his arms draped around her hips and his head resting in her lap, she caressed him tenderly. "A new cabin to replace the old. A new and better life to replace the unhappy, lonely lives we lived. Sweet, new memories to cherish."

"I love you," he said. "You know that don't you? You know that I regret—"

She covered his lips with her fingers. "No regrets. We've put them in the past with all the bad memories. You've forgiven me. I've forgiven you. And here in our special place, in a cabin you built to show me how much you love me, is the perfect place and the perfect moment for me to give my anniversary gift to you."

"You have something to give me?" he asked. "It must be tiny if you have it with you." He lifted his head from her lap and ran his hands over the front pockets of her jeans, then when he found nothing, he lifted her hips and checked the back pockets.

She giggled, then grabbed his wandering hands and placed them over her stomach. "Right now my gift is very tiny. But it's going to grow bigger and bigger. And when it's grown to about seven or eight pounds, I'll give it to you."

Luke stared at her, a look of total awe on his face. "Are you saying what I think you're saying?"

"Yes. I'm pregnant," she said. "Probably not much more than a month. I took the test yesterday morning."

"Deanna…"

"I'm going to have your baby, Luke."

He ran his hands lovingly over her still flat belly,

then he laid his head against the spot where his child was nestled inside Deanna. He kissed her stomach.

Deanna took his face in her hands and lifted it. Tears glistened in Luke's moss-green eyes. Tears of happiness. And tears of grief for a little boy who would have been fifteen years old now.

"It's all right, you know," she told him. "I think our little boy will be a guardian angel for his little brother or sister. Nothing is going to happen to this baby. He or she is protected by heaven. I know it in my soul."

Luke lifted her up and into his arms, then carried her across the room to the bed. They undressed each other slowly, savoring the deliriously sweet moments that led them from earth to paradise. From love to ecstasy. From the sorrows of the past to the joys of the future.

* * * * *

Escape to a place where a kiss is still a kiss...
Feel the breathless connection...
Fall in love as though it were
the very first time...
Experience the power of love!

Come to where favorite authors——such as
Diana Palmer, Stella Bagwell,
Marie Ferrarella *and many more——*
deliver heart-warming romance and genuine
emotion, time after time after time....

Silhouette Romance——
stories straight from the heart!

Silhouette®
Where love comes alive™

Where love comes alive™

From first love to forever, these love stories are for today's woman with traditional values.

A highly passionate, emotionally powerful and always provocative read.

SPECIAL EDITION™

Emotional, compelling stories that capture the intensity of living, loving and creating a family in today's world.

INTIMATE MOMENTS™

A roller-coaster read that delivers romantic thrills in a world of suspense, adventure and more.